FOR My DAUGHTE
    Love Always, Dad.

    Didos. Dug du h

FLOAT ME THROUGH THE DEEP
by
F. Jos. Diaz de Leon

EDITED
by
Kathryn T. Guidero

This is a work of fiction. Any similarity between names And characters in this book and any real persons, living or dead, is entirely coincidental.

SECOND EDITION

Published by Tribes Thirteen Publishing
1201 Quing-ah Ln., Lone Pine, CA 93545-1063

ISBN-10 1479271934
ISBN-13 978-1-479-27193-1
Library of Congress No: 2012944001

INTRODUCTION

Titanic: Float Me Through The Deep, is a fictionalized story set in 1915. It recounts the journey of Inar Katerpar, an aging Inuit, who has spent his entire life on Baffin Island. Unable to hunt and provide for his village, he feels it is time to join his loved ones in a journey to the Sky World. On a chosen day, his family and friends are there to see him swept away on an ice floe. The traveler takes only a few days of food and water, just enough supply to see him through the journey.

As he lives out what are supposed to be his last days, the journey becomes arduous. His supplies begin to dwindle, along with his traditional beliefs, and Inar finds that to die is not so easy. His survival instincts kick in, and as the large slab of floe ice continues to melt, he is flipped onto an iceberg by a Killer Whale. Realizing the iceberg is to become a main source of temporary survival, Inar builds an igloo. As the days wear on, the sea provides him with food, and pools of iceberg water quench his thirst.

One night, a thunderous roar is heard, and blinding lights shine brightly into his eyes. Inar climbs to the tip of the iceberg and begins his death song. Suddenly, the iceberg begins to tremble, then shake, causing him to tumble downwards, knocking him unconscious. Inar awakens on the deck of the RMS Titanic in the hands of crew members, who take him into custody as a stowaway. In the critical minutes that follow, no one knows, the moment Inar hit the deck, the Titanic began to sink. After the fateful sinking, he is found floating on the wreckage debris and is rescued.

In New York, Inar is held captive on Ellis Island. Jane Reynolds, an Immigration Attorney, comes to his aid, and this is where the real story begins.

PREFACE

In conducting the research needed to tie the book together, it was fascinating to read the actual 1912 U.S. Senate Hearing transcripts, regarding the Titanic tragedy. The investigative hearing was headed by Senator Smith, who at times, seemed to be overly tactful. It was hard to keep in mind while reading the transcripts, that the printed matter were proceedings of a hearing - not a trial. As the research continued for over a year, it became clear that all the information needed to write a fictionalized story was contained in the hearing transcripts. Photos were needed, but for personal effect only, photos were not intended to be published as part of the book. Newspaper articles were used to fill in parts of the novel that could have been written as fiction. This sort of reporting fit right in with the writing, as news print was often sensationalized and blown into conspiracy theory, even back then.

In the end, all emotions suffered while developing the story, left an empty feeling that came to be ever present throughout the project. In writing the novel, it was very hard not to add a lengthly legal process that took the owners of the Titanic to trial. The legal process would have taken the reader away from the main character. Inar Katerpar was to remain the eyes of the tragedy, harboring no ulterior motives. The need to depict the aging Inuit in his homeland environment, was a very important aspect in telling the story. Inar's plight was woven into the Titanic tragedy to bring out some of the unanswered questions that still haunt the tragic event. The main character was used as a fresh look back into the past, and he became that voice. The language spoken was not understood, but once placed into translation, the subject matter beckoned to be revisited. It was Senator Smith's intention to bring out the truth, and have the general public translate the Senate Hearing, in order to find out the truth for ourselves, so it could be put to rest.

Inar turned out be an excellent vehicle, he could tell of his experience without bias. The story required that type of vehicle to bring out the dynamics of the aftermath. There are questions which still remain to be answered in that sad and mysterious event. The sinking appeared to be caused by negligence, if not outright intent.

CHAPTER ONE
Huntfield, Turner and Barnes

Under a cloud covered sky, a morning fog bank can be seen below, slowly rolling into the streets of New York City. It is early spring on the eastern seaboard, the driving snow has ceased, but some of the wintery frost lingers. As always winter is stubborn and unwilling to give way to Mother Nature's warmer months. As the day progresses, the sun will come out with teasing warm rays of sunlight, but the city's inhabitants will continue to bundle up in winter clothing, not willing to be fooled by a few rays of sunshine.

As usual, the city is bustling with morning activity. It is a work day, and thousands of office employees, service workers, and employers are making their way into workspaces. A deep, sonic blur of a ship's fog horn reverberates through the high rise structures of the modern city. To most New Yorkers, the sound is specific, it is a constant reminder to all, that seafaring ships have sailed into the Hudson River, safely arriving from crossing the treacherous North Atlantic.

It is April 17, 1915, on this day three years before, the RMS Titanic was to arrive at the White Star Ocean Line Pier, number 59, at 5:00 in the morning. The pier had been prepared for her grand arrival. Employees had placed flags, banners and patriotic draping throughout the landing. It was to be a crowning moment for Titanic in the completion of her maiden voyage.

A 10:00 A.M. celebration was planned, and at that exact time a band would strike up "Alexander's Ragtime Band." The press was to report the voyage party as jubilant, with hundreds of pounds of confetti showering down from Titanic's upper decks. The passengers were to be seen lining her deck rails, waving and throwing confetti to the thousands below. The crew would be displaying their sea worthy disciplines, lowering the gang plank, mooring the giant ship to the dock for all to see. The feeling of excitement and anticipation would be depicted as triumphant, with passengers being greeted by awaiting friends and relatives. Likewise, after loading passengers for her return voyage to England, Titanic's disembarking was to be just as dramatic.It was a vision being conjured around world. The tragedy still lingers, echoing deep longings for the great ship to somehow reappear out of the misty ocean waters. The Titanic did not arrive in the early morning hours of April 17, 1912. Instead, it was late into the evening on April 18th, through a drizzling rain, that throngs of onlookers, friends, and relatives waited for the arrival of a rescue ship bearing the 705 survivors of the ill fated Titanic.

The RMS Carpathia, a Cunard Line passenger and cargo ship, arrived in New York Harbor on Tuesday, at 9:25 p.m., with Titanic's lifeboats on deck. The crew had readied the life boats to be lowered down, as they slowly passed the White Star pier. On command, they were ordered to lower the lifeboats, cutting them away one at a time. The small boats drifted until a harbor tug pulled them along side and towed them to the dock. The Carpathia then continued to steam through sheets of pouring rain to arrive at Cunard Pier 54. As the survivor passengers disembarked, many who witnessed it, would look back on that day. Deeming it harsh to rid the last remaining parts of the great ship, to be cut away in such an unceremonious manner.

It is now three years after the Titanic disaster. The last of the insurance claims against Titanic's owners are being processed. The Oceanic Navigation

Steamship Company, a major stockholder of the RMS Titanic, is being represented by the law firm of Huntfield, Turner, and Barnes. The firm is one of New York's most prestigious insurance law firms, and touts its success with its lavish law offices in Manhattan. On the twenty-third floor of the Park Avenue Building in Manhattan, a team of insurance attorneys have assembled for a meeting on the continuing mitigation of insurance claims. The claims against Titanic's owners, Oceanic have been ongoing since April 15, 1912, and the last of 1200 claims have been filed. The law firm can finally see the end of the tunnel.

Inside a spacious conference room, the firms' attorneys have gathered in a conference room. On both sides of a long table, a row of attorneys stand at almost military stance. Randall Huntfield, president of the firm, nods his head in approval at the troupe and their appearance. Dressed much like their boss, an unwritten rule maintained by the executive officer to encourage style as well as professionalism. The style of the day called for Edwardian Eaton brand trousers, checked single-breasted waistcoat, with vest, dangling gold watch chain, and highly polished shoes. Cold weather coats taken at the door were mainly thick, knee length frock coats and hats of choice.

All eyes are focused on Thomas J. Huntfield, a prominent attorney in his younger days, had founded the firm and nurtured the business until it became full bloom. Born March 4, 1847, Huntfield's birthday falls on the day Abraham Lincoln was inaugurated as the 16th President of the United States. It was Lincoln's early years as a lawyer that inspired Huntfield to become an attorney. His leathery white skin and gruff voice were unavoidable traits that led to imitations among the more daring firm attorneys. A stroke has left him with a speech impediment and wheel chair bound.

Looking down the conference table is Executive Officer, Joseph Hillcrest, the firm's ramrod. He is feared by the attorneys for his diligent management of the firm. Nephew to Huntfield, he is next in line to head the firm and will stop at nothing to achieve that goal. In his late 40's, Hillcrest prides himself on his physical appearance. He is intelligent, handsome, and well mannered, but at times can carry himself like a gangster to whom cunning had come as second nature.

Without a word, President Huntfield motions for them to be seated with a gesture of a long bony finger. The rustling of new clothing and sliding chairs fill the room as they take their seats. Hillcrest stands, he tugs at his single breasted waistcoat and adjusts his wing collar and bow tie. A calm comes over him before addressing the members of the firm.

"Gentlemen, today, the Law Offices of Huntfield, Turner and Barnes are two months away from of closing all claims and settlements against Oceanic Steamship Navigation Company and White Star. You may pat yourselves on the back for jobs well done, but the victory celebration is a merit yet to be achieved. The remaining claims will be dealt with on a different level that will require time and energy from every one of you. With application of strict and correct procedure, these cases can be closed in a matter of months, without question," says Hillcrest. He stands, leaves his seat, and slowly begins to pace the conference room.

"Our settlement schedule, it seems, is at the mercy of legislators and senators who deem it necessary to drum up votes instead of looking out for their more contributive constituents. Today, a deposit to the U.S. District Court in the amount of $119,000, was paid. This will guarantee the bond that will allow us to complete the settlement cases," says Hillcrest. "It's simply an outrage," says an attorney under his breath. "Do you wish to add to my presentation Attorney Scott?" Hillcrest asks, in an annoyed tone. The young attorney becomes acquiescent then stands to defend his behavior.

"Please forgive my intrusive behavior. I did not mean to interrupt sir. It's just that, I feel it's outright blackmail. Without the firm's generous contributions, that scoundrel of a politician would still be pushing pencils along side his Pages on Capitol Hill. He is merely a creature of the government, openly defecating onto the hand that paved his way to success. I feel HT&B will be around long after his time in office is up," Scott explains.

"It is a fair hypothesis Mr. Scott," says Hillcrest. "Nonetheless, he is still clerk of the United States District Court. It's how the rules of the game are played gentlemen, and I intend to play it by their rules, for now," adds Hillcrest. "Yes, sir." Attorney Scott replies as he takes his seat.

The other attorneys at the conference table, take the interruption in stride. Occasional subtle maneuvers are expected from Hillcrest, bestowed as a privilege by the firm's staff of lawyers. Although planned, the ploy is always harmless, and without repercussion. Hillcrest often uses his favored attorneys to implicate matters of which he will not dignify.

Lindell Scott, an ambitious 27 year-old attorney has been taken under wing. A highly competitive staff have accepted their place on the company ladder, but are ever vigilant of chance to advance. Scott is known as 'Mr. Diligent' by his colleagues, and for good reason. With his wire rimmed eye glasses, impeccable hair, and always-in-style wardrobe, he has set the bar for every junior attorney at the firm.

"Have there been any further claims in from the Third Class survivors?" Sr. Vice President, Charles Barnes asks. "I cannot imagine the poor wretches wanting more than $1,000 for their trouble," he adds.

"Therein lies the problem. To prove worth towards any personal injury, in loss of life or property, the billing hours will be thousand more than they had when they disembarked from their homelands," replies Barnes.

"Now, what to do about attorney Harrison Bennett. It is my understanding that this individual is an Injury Attorney, with no previous achievements other than slip and fall law suits," Huntfield says as the attorneys shuffle through their folders, not familiar with the so-called ambulance chaser.

"I did a workup on the background of Harrison Witmer Bennett, born March 30, 1868, to Joshua T. Bennett, and Martha Osborn Bennett, both of Watertown, New York...," continues Scott.

The background research continues for another fifteen minutes, and is thorough to the point of how many cavities he had on his last dental visit. No part of his life had escaped violation where his privacy is concerned, even his medical records were compromised.

"Bennett is a successful trial lawyer, mostly representing the poor on a pro bono basis. At one time in his career, he had been considered to join the defense team with Clarence Darrow. Known as the sophisticated 'Country Lawyer' to most who were aware of his legalese. Darrow offered Bennett a position in the high profile, MacNamara trial of 1911," continues Scott.

"A year earlier in 1910, Bennett and Reynolds became acquainted at a political rally. Both were dedicated to getting Franklin D. Roosevelt elected to the New York Senate. They became associates in July of 1912, three months after the Titanic disaster. Theresa Jane Reynolds, or "Jane" as she prefers to be called, began her career in law as an Immigration Attorney. Her major influence is, Clara Foltz, Criminal Attorney. Her involvement with Bennett is strictly on a professional level and is non-relative to Bennett's ulterior motives regarding the Titanic insurance claims. Otherwise, Miss Reynolds background check yielded very little.

"It is a fair assumption to expect Bennett's interests lay in a more complicated approach to the claims against Oceanic. It will be in our best interest to keep this in mind, and consider an agenda that will put into place a significant information and intelligence gathering strategy," concludes Scott.

"Thank you for that in-depth report, Attorney Scott. I am of the persuasion to humor this claim. The claimant, Inar Katerpar, will be most fortunate to receive any amount from Oceanic," says Hillcrest.

"Which of the attorneys have we assigned for today's deposition with Bennett's client?" Turner asks.

Before the question can be answered, the conference room doors burst open. Attention turns toward the disturbance, a silence comes over the group of attorneys. Corporate President, Blake Ramsi stomps toward the conference table, he drops a daily newspaper down with a slap, breaking the silence. Poking a finger into the newspaper headline, which reads: "WHITE STAR RULED RESPONSIBLE UNDER BRITISH LAW"

"This is what one-third of our depository is being squandered on; claimants that have been accepted to receive damages for simply witnessing the event. With this sort of blanket award, anyone will be able to file a claim against Oceanic. Do you realize that every person that booked passage on Titanic for the return crossing, can now file a claim for failure to provide a service as advertised?" Ramsi shouts.

"Please Blake, calm down. We can handle the matter, give the firm a little time," pleads Turner. "You have had enough time. Settle with whatever means it takes. The Titanic claim ledger must be cleared," demands Ramsi.

"We have stayed the course Mr. Ramsi, nothing has changed, and the court ruling changes nothing. True, the ruling may have claimants sitting back and waiting for an offer from H.T & B., but in the end they will all receive the amount set by the firm, and no more," says Huntfield. Ramsi holds the copy of the New York Times for all to see. Peering over the newspaper, Ramsi's behavior begins to make some of the attorneys uncomfortable. The room remains silent as he continues the villainous glare, his eyes grow more intense and equally beady. The attorneys startle when Hillcrest clears his throat, in an intentional manner.

"Blake, maybe we should continue this discussion in my office; it'll be more private," says Hillcrest. "The simple fact is, our limitation of liability will be dropped into the hands of the United States Federal District Court system. As I see it, not a one of you had the least bit of foresight to see this coming. Where is this much touted political clout this firm is supposed to possess?" Ramsi asks.

"I beg your pardon, but, we've devoted nothing but hard work towards this case," says a board member. "I feel that in this case, if loyalty would have been applied, it would have placed us in the position we so desire, that as victims instead of defendants," says Ramsi. "We are all aware what is at stake here Mr. Ramsi. I think the record will show that you have brought these issues and they are valid concerns. We have acknowledged your disagreement, and will work to resolve these issues," says Barnes poignantly.

"All well said and done. Again, read the headlines. What escapes the Board is that;

this is just one New York City newsprint, the reporters are going to have a field day with this," says Ramsi.

"You have brought these questions to the Board and they have been recorded. The Board agrees entirely, and you may be interested to know, a cable went out to Britain before the ruling was handed down. The message contained specific language as directed, instructions to our solicitors. It is our opinion that a withdraw of all filings be brought, and claims against White Star and Oceanic will be dropped by default. Through the firms' diligence in these matters, the greater part of claims have been closed. Fortunately, some of those claims were beyond our means of jurisdiction. It should be acknowledged, Mr. Ramsi, that we as a firm did mitigate the losses substantially, as you will find in the final report. The District Court of the United States, leaned in our favor and agreed on this matter. The Firm negotiated $16,804,112 in claims settlements," says Huntfield.

"If I may, as lead attorney, I would like to have it noted that Huntfield, Turner and Barnes succeeded in scaling down the amount of claims from 17 million, the original sum, to 2.5 million, with the most current amount coming in at $664,000. To this date, the largest individual claim is at $50,000, which is hardly a giveaway Mr. Ramsi. I feel that we here at the Firm have gone far beyond the normal sense of legalese considering the enormity of the case," says Scott.

"There is the looming possibility that more claims may be filed against Oceanic and White Star. We at the Firm are preparing briefs for motions that will suppress any charge of willful neglect or conspiracy on part of our clients. There are other concerns that have not reached the point of action. We have tested, with every extenuating line of defense, three separate scenarios. The findings proved not substantial enough to continue with a defense line. It will be an ongoing and daunting task to keep these implications from the press but, nonetheless we will succeed in doing so," explains Turner.

The depositions and hearing testimony's of the survivors can be extremely damning to our defense should any claims go to trial. The time and expense involved in building a defense arising from transcripts of the U.S. Senate Hearings alone is staggering," adds Huntfield, with folded arms and a convicting stare. Ramsi fails to intimidate any of the law firm's Board.

"Within the three years since the sinking, mounting suspicion and rumors of an intentional sinking has taken a toll on the mental state of many White Star investors. The firm realizes this deep concern, but investors will continue to rage about legal expenses and insurance deductions. After all, they are investors not attorneys," says Hillcrest.

"At this point in the legal proceedings, HT&B have realized that if just one claim makes it to trial, the truth will come out about the horrific tragedy. Come on gentlemen, the truth is out. There were mistakes made, but that's all they were mistakes. A premeditated plot to destroy hundreds of lives is not in the equation. We are all survivors of this tragic accident. I say that because, if not for a matter of luck, it wouldn't have been possible for the Liner company to stay above board. HT&B accomplishments are shining with victory and we will continue to do so," A board member adds. "Are we nearing a close on this matter?" Ramsi asks. "Yes, we are Blake. We are confident the completion of the claims process will be ready for review and be forwarded to the District Court. We have notified the court that our intentions will be brought within sixty days. As you well know Mr. Ramsi, this is not the end, but may be the beginning," says Turner.

"I will expect a full claims report in the corporate office within the week," says Ramsi. All eyes follow Ramsi as he stalks out of the conference room. The room fills with relief. Hillcrest continues: "As I was saying, on the matter of Mr. Bennett and his client, a Mr. Inar Katerpar.

CHAPTER TWO
Ellis Island

On the street below the law offices of H.T.& the day has begun for thousands of office workers. The early morning fog has yet to burn off, as workers file into modern brick buildings.

Nestled between two buildings in Manhattan, is a small cafe. The "Gateway Cafe" is situated in the shadows of surrounding multistory buildings. A mom and pop business, with a long history of being a favorite of New Yorkers. Just down from New York City Hall, its customers range from judges, to janitors.

Outside the restaurant, a forlorn face can be seen staring out through a foggy plate glass window. Theresa Jane Reynolds sits alone at a table, her far away eyes tell that she is preoccupied. The days forthcoming events have her pondering an outcome.

"I should have some friends," she thinks to herself. "If I had friends, we would be here at this table, discussing my aspirations to succeed in the legal world, my career choices from Hollywood actress to courtroom diva. They would tell me how smartly I dress, and how much they wished they could be me," she twirls her hair. "If I had friends," she says, thinking aloud.

Really though, it's not that Jane can't make friends. To Jane, it is simply a matter of priority, survive a career, or have friends. It is demanding just living in New York City. So, to her the order of principles have already niched out her choices," she continues in thought. A new frustration surfaces when she realizes that her nit-picking is a telltale sign that she is in a defensive mode to hide her butterflies.

Jane, has spent a restless night mentally roll playing her position as lead attorney in a deposition that is scheduled for today. She pats her wavy hair into place, wondering if the 'Gibson Girl' hair style will be proper for the proceeding. Maybe she should have styled it in a more casual fashion. Has she dressed appropriately for the deposition? A small voice inside tells her: Hurry home, throw open her closet doors, and search for something better. Jane takes a long draw off a cigarette and slowly exhales while she studies her bright red fingernails. "Geeze. It's just a deposition, not the trial of the century," she says in a hushed voice.

In the year of 1915 and earlier, the field of law is one of which few women ventured into. But, as an Immigrant Attorney, Jane's reputation has gained her notoriety in the lower courts. While other women in their careers chose to move-on in the field of law, Jane chose to continue her practice in immigration. Helping those who could not defend themselves in a court of law mattered. Her ambition pushed her towards opportunities that many of her colleagues envied, but nothing was more gratifying than helping immigrants win a chance at a new life of freedom, and a chance to work towards prosperity.

In her practice of seven years, she has not come across a more intriguing client, an Inuit native, Inar Katerpar. Even though she has been representing him for almost a year, he remains a mystery to her. Inar is always quiet, forgiving and trusting, but never knowing what he is thinking makes it a difficult situation. In his elderly wise ways and knowing eyes, tells her he may know what she is thinking.

Today she will introduce Inar to her associate attorney, Harrison Bennett. A waitress arrives at her table. Jane turns to see a waitress looking down into her smiling brown eyes. A cup of tea is placed in front of her. "I can see by your handsome business outfit that you must be a lawyer, or a secretary of one," says the waitress in jest. "Lawyer," replies Jane drearily.

"Well, to tell you the truth, that's the way I dressed when I was a secretary. You know, being right down the street from City Hall, I get a ton of lawyers in here everyday. I've never seen a lady lawyer," says the waitress.

"Is it that obvious? I mean, I've been beating myself up all morning, thinking I may have over dressed. Do I look intimidating?" I'm supposed to look intimidating," says Jane.

"More of a Pickford-ish intimidating," says the waitress as Jane strikes a pose. "Yeah, that's it, Mary Pickford, playing a roll of an intimidating lawyer," says the waitress.

"Big tip for you girl," says Jane, tapping her long manicured fingernails on her briefcase.

"No joke, some mornings I wake up and I wish I were just a waitress, like my mom," says Jane.

"I'm Lorna, and I am glad to see a gal who is willing to stay in the trenches and fight for womankind."

Jane kindly smiles at the waitress, who is polishing the fork and knife from Jane's table. "Will you be having breakfast this morning, dear?" Asks the waitress.

"I don't have much of an appetite this morning, but when my partner gets here he might have a bite," says Jane. Her attention turns toward her associate walking up to her table.

Harrison Bennett has arrived for the breakfast meeting. "Good morning ladies," he says, and takes a seat at Jane's table. He smiles at the waitress as he seats himself across from Jane.

"I feel like breakfast, how about you Jane?" Harrison asks. "No, but feel free, I don't mind," says Jane. "The usual?" The waitress asks. She receives a thumbs up.

"Is that rouge on your cheeks" Because if it is, you don't need it. That bright red lipstick kinda steals the whole effect," says Harrison, matter-of-factly. Jane raises a mean brow, then takes a powder case from her purse.

"I had a feeling it was a bit much, and thank you for that somewhat obtuse observation," says Jane as she wipes the make-up from her cheeks.

"Listen, this deposition is no different from any other, they ask questions until we start stammering and our eyes cross. I know these guys, big words and meaningless banter, just don't nod-off during the proceeding. Also, if I start to snore, give me a swift kick," jokes Harrison.

"That's easy for you to say, I'm still earning my wings," says Jane with frustration.

"Now, if it goes the way I think it will, we will come away from the deposition with a settlement agreement. Remember this, the moment we walk into the deposition room, we have the upper hand. They know it and I know it. We will be among the first to file suit in the Titanic tragedy. Even so, usually it's those who are first to file, are the first to win a judgment.

"We haven't given them any indication that we desire settlement. It's driving them nuts, they'll treat us like royalty," proclaims Harrison with confidence. The waitress arrives at the table and places a breakfast plate in front of Harrison, his usual bacon and eggs, sour dough toast.

Harrison is 47 years of age, he has a full head of hair, and it is prematurely graying. He is a bit overweight for his 6' 1" frame and paunch says it all about his eating habits. Harrison drinks, smokes, and is not above a bar brawl every now and then. Harrison has been practicing law for twenty-two years. His practice is a successful one, for one reason; he is an exceptional trial lawyer.

The law firm representing Oceanic are aware of Bennett's talent as an attorney. The court room is his field of battle, and his battle tactics are strategic and when charged with drama, he is powerfully effective. Harrison fancies himself after his colleague Clarence Darrow. Just as Darrow, many of Bennett's cases are pro bono. Just as Darrow, he finds that representing poor and taking their up causes, often lead to a predicament worthy of further challenge.

After fifteen years of practice, the Bennett law office, to say the least, does not reflect the sophistication of other successful practices. The law office office has always been a two room flat, and at times serves as a second home, but it is how he prefers it. The location of his law office is within walking distance of the New York City Courthouse, and it is now considered to be prime real estate, but in his view, the Gateway Cafe, is the prime location.

In his profession, Harrison has become a loner, only because of the high profile cases he is known to take on. In most of most cases there is always an exception, and to him, this one case was truly exceptional. From the moment he considered the circumstances stemming from the claim of Jane's client, he was sure it was a case he wanted to take on. Harrison's decision to accept Jane's invitation to become her associate, gave the case clout, under a cloud of meritless claims. To be on a case as Harrison Bennett's First-associate was something she would have ever guessed would happen..

"Well, What do you know about that," Harrison says behind the pages of the New York Tribune. He turns the paper towards Jane.

"TITANIC OFFICIALS HEAD FOR THE STAND"

Harrison puts the paper aside. "It'll be three years tomorrow that she went down," he says. Harrison senses a distance between he and Jane. "Are you in there?" He asks.

"Honest to God Harrison, I don't know what's going on with me, but I should feel all giddy about finally getting to move into this deposition. Instead, I'm nervous as a Christmas goose," she says.

"Well, to tell you the truth, I'm a little uneasy about the outcome too. I figured White Star dare not place our client on their list of deponents, not after that last conference," replies Harrison. "No kidding. I'll never forget the look on their faces when we entered the conference room. I thought a creature from outerspace followed us in," laughs Jane.

"Scott nearly jumped out of his chair," laughs Harrison.

"Serves them right for not doing their homework. I mean, if you know what an Eskimo looks like clad in traditional clothing, you would know that an Inuit, wouldn't be far from it," says Jane. The association between Jane and Harrison is an odd pairing, with Harrison being a polished trial criminal lawyer and Jane being an immigration attorney. They have brought a lawsuit of negligence against White Star. The claim 'against' is for damages that were a result of personal bodily injury and mental distress caused the RMS Titanic and its owners. Their client Inar Katerpar, a native Inuit, was found at the wreck location floating on top of wooden debris set afloat by the sinking ship. He was rescued by the Steamship Carpathia on the morning of April 15th, according to ship records.

At the Ellis Island Facility, immigration officials could not figure how Katerpar became a rescued survivor of the Titanic. They could only assume he was a stowaway, aboard when the wreck occurred. As a matter of procedure, stowaway's had been deported by the Immigration Service before, but in Inar's case, deportation was a problem. Without proper identification and port of origin, they could not deport him.

The traditional parka and trousers of seal skins and fur, gave them a hint that he may be from the territory of Alaska. Nonetheless, it was the protective outerwear that prevented him from freezing in the icy waters of the North Atlantic. One official believed that Inar must have come from the Baffin Islands, or somewhere in that part of the world, but the suggestion was ignored.

Having no way to identify him, the powers-that-be, placed Inar in an isolated cell. After a few weeks being treated as a stowaway prisoner, immigrant officials decided to place him in quarantine until the situation could be resolved. Enter Jane Reynolds, Immigrant Attorney, who is able to speak five languages. Unfortunately, she does not know one word of the Inuit language.

Eventually his freedom was won when Miss Reynolds requested the help of an acquaintance. The situation was a unique one, mainly because deportation was not possible. Inar was listed as a survivor of the Titanic and granted a 'temporary resident' until his port of embarkation and could be determined.

Tanaya Navaran, a 25 year old Inuit native, and a kitchen worker at the immigration facility at Ellis Island, recognized Jane. It was while she was visiting clients at the facility.

"A few years before, I had applied for a position as a legal secretary," says Tanaya.

"A few years back? Yeah!" Jane says, not really sure.

"At your office, a few years back?" Tanaya asks with a blank look.

A light goes on over Jane's head, and after some conversation, Jane discovers that Inar is of Inuit origins. Tanaya offered her assistance as a translator, since she too is of an Inuit tribe, but in a different part of the Baffin. Jane then recalled the job interview when she asked Tanaya about her background.

In the background history of Tanaya's interview, Jane was told by that she was placed in an Indian school at the age of seven. After she graduated, the Indian School Employment Placement Program sent her to work at the Ellis Island Facility. For Tanaya working as a kitchen aid did not suit her ambitions, so she then applied for secretarial position at Jane's law office.

Upon hearing of the tragedy on April 15, Tanaya was left in shock by the event, as was everyone else. The haunting visions of the passengers, screaming and hollering for help in the freezing North Atlantic, became the cause of sleepless nights. Her living quarters on Ellis Island was a picture setting for every ship that entered or departed New York Harbor. The "Torch View" was her reason for living on the Island instead of the mainland. From her bedroom window she had a perfect view of Liberty Island and the Statue of Liberty. Except for images of the Titanic printed on front pages of newspapers, she would never get to see the great ship steaming into New York Harbor as she did the sister ship, the Olympic.

On that day, seeing the colossal ship, cutting through the waves, was the most fantastic site ever. Now, with the Titanic at the bottom of the sea, that moment will never return. Thursday morning April 18, the kitchen staff was alerted by immigration officials of the planned arrival of the Third Class passenger survivors. A small contingent of kitchen staff was to be on standby to serve hot meals to the immigrant survivors. Tanaya was among those required to work that night.

Any news of the arrival of Carpathia was monitored by whatever means possible. In this instance, it was by a ferry crew delivering supplies to the island. The Ellis Island Ferry crew received news of the rescue ship's arrival and the news spread quickly among the staff on the island. The arrival was broadcast by a wireless radio station on top of Wannamakers Department Store at Broadway and Tenth Street. The broadcast announced that Carpathia was due to arrive at approximately 7:30 p.m. in New York Harbor. Tanaya decided to trudge through pouring rain and gusty winds, to wait on east Ellis Island dock.

At 7:00 p.m., not long after reaching the dock, she saw the Carpathia steaming towards the harbor. There were numerous other vessels encircling her, acting as an escort. Other workers had joined Tanaya, and watched in silence as the Carpathia passed. An entourage of smaller vessels steamed along side, seemingly to protect her survivor passengers from further harm. Deeply moved, she and the others wept quietly, their tears awash with rain. As they huddled tightly together, a comfort is felt among them, the feeling of sorrow is shared. Slowly, the small group made their back to the Ellis Island Arrival Center to greet the Third Class passenger survivors.

It was 10:30 p.m. when the Ellis Island ferry made its way through choppy waters, to steam its way up to the westside landing dock. Immigration Officials and the staff, were waiting to receive the new arrivals. The plan was to lead them to the Arrivals Hall. As they stood in the drizzling rain, The officials became puzzled at the fact there was no one aboard the ferry except the captain and crew. They became equally confused when a lone immigrant stepped onto the landing dock.

A fog horn sounds in the distance, then the surrounding area fades to silence. Only a sporadic sound of rain splashing off the umbrella tops can be heard. An Immigration officer goes to question the ferry captain about the lack of passengers. Walking towards the gang plank, he passes Inar, who is standing next to his journey bundles on the landing. The officer comes face to face with the captain.

"What's the meaning of this?" Where are the passenger survivors?" He asks the captain.

"Immigration officers at the Cunard Pier put this man on my boat, they told me he was a stowaway rescued from the Titanic wreck site. As far as I know, the Third

Class survivors went on their separate ways, with the consent of Immigration. They instructed me to deliver him to Ellis Island. Now, as you can see, I'm here, he's here, and now he's all yours to deal with," says the ferry boat captain. The ferry is running late, so without saying another word, the captain turns, walks up the gang plank, and onto his boat. The crew prepares to shove off, and soon after, the boat's steam engines thrust, and the ferry heads into the choppy waters of the Hudson River.

In an awkward moment, Inar continues to stand, facing the group of staff and workers. The traditional clothing he is wearing, prompts Tanaya to intervene and help the bewildered Inuit. In her native language, she asks him his name. When Inar replies in a familiar dialect, she smiles and locks arms with him and walks him past the staff and into the main hall. Tanaya continues to talk with him as they climb the steps, she does her best to make him feel at ease.

It was not her intention to lead him into the facility to prepare him for what was to happen next. After all he had been through, Inar was placed into custody by Immigration officials and taken to holding cell. Tanaya felt bad for him, her protest

39.

went unheeded as Ellis Island security led him away.

Throughout his stay on the Island, Tanaya continued to help Inar in anyway she could, so she visited him everyday, learning more about his plight. The meeting between Tanaya and Jane opened the door to acquiring help for Inar. Information was shared which was needed for Jane to intervene on behalf of Inar. As the process wore on, Jane began to make headway, with Tanaya's help. Together, Jane and Tanaya helped the immigration officials determine a course to process Inar as an immigrant. It was a matter of time before Tanaya would become a court appointed interpreter for Inar. Born on Baffin Island and educated in a New York Indian School, she is of the Inuit clan of the Fox. Tanaya is 22 years old, statuesque and beautiful. Her long dark hair is never without a native adornment, and she has almond eyes that most Hollywood stars would die for.

Her years at the Thomas Indian School taught her the English language, but she still retained the ability to speak her native tongue. A friendship was struck when she realized Inar looked much like her grand father, who passed away some years before in their village on Baffin Island

CHAPTER THREE
Katerpar, Reynolds, and Bennett

Inside the Gateway Cafe, Harrison is seated with Jane. He looks at his watch.

"You did make it clear to both of them that they were required to attend the deposition?" He asks.

"Katerpar wasn't thrilled about it. It's a good thing the interpreter understood, and coaxed him into it, by telling him about the Otis Elevators," says Jane. "Ah...the first elevator ride, good carrot," says Harrison.

"And by-the-way, the interpreters name is Tan-a-ya, not Tanya," she says. "While we're on the subject, is there any reason I should not be wondering why our client has not grasped the idea of learning a little bit of English? I mean, he doesn't speak a word, but I get the feeling he knows what we are saying," says Harrison.

"It's his decision. Learning a new language is like learning a whole new way of life, it comes with the territory. Besides, it's the Judge's orders. No translator, no lawsuit," says Jane.

"I had the privilege of reading some of the court transcripts from the Senate Hearing, you wouldn't believe how

Senator Smith came off in the court room," says Harrison as a fork load of scrambled eggs are put into his mouth. "The Lighttoller deposition. This guy was definitely hiding something. On top of it, he made Senator Smith look like some sort of river bank lawyer. Some of the deposition is unbelievable," says Harrison. "Really?" Jane says. The actual deposition, how did that come about?" Jane asks, as she turns her full attention to what he says next. "Sworn to secrecy, but I told my cousin I wouldn't mention his name if it got out," says Harrison.

"Got it." Jane says. "Do you remember when we had that heated discussion about the cause of Titanic's sinking?" Harrison asks. "Heated discussion? That was a full on spit-in-your-eye, get down in the dirt, argument. Yes, you implied that something was fishy about the whole thing," says Jane, feigning exasperation. "A pun only you could come up with, Harrison," she adds. "Insurance?" Harrison mocks. "You know darn well that's what it was...you insisted the iceberg was just a matter of convenience, used as a deodorant to hide the fact that Titanic was a doomed vessel. When I challenged your choice of words, you explained that the tragedy was caused by a series of events perpetrated within in a premeditated scheme to sink the ship," says Jane, deadpan. "Precisely Watson," says Harrison with a bad English accent.

"Wait a minute." Jane says. "You're not thinking to bring that conspiracy theory into the deposition, are you?" Jane asks with a small voice. Harrison does not answer, holding up a finger that points to his mouth - full of food. "This is not happening, tell me you won't," pleads Jane. "Well, I have no control, or influence on the questions the Oceanic attorneys will ask, but then, that's the beauty of a deposition. Only one, possibly two of the one thousand questions asked may open that one particular door," he replies. Jane sits back and eyes Harrison for a few moments, fondling the handle on her tea cup. Jane then adds, curiously.

"The court transcripts are pretty interesting, huh?" She asks. "Most interesting." Harrison says. "At times the Senator's questions were weak, but somewhat to the point. Maybe it's the way I read into the document, but to me it seemed that he invariably circled back to one main question, the insurance.

"He strongly suggested that their confidence level placed in the ship was unreliable. Which to me meant that he was questioning Titanic's sea worthiness," he says. Harrison's understanding of the transcripts has Jane confused.

"I'm not making the connection. The Titanic struck an iceberg, she didn't sink because of mechanical failure. Surely you're not saying the maiden-voyage was marked?" Jane asks in a hushed voice. Harrison places his finger to his lips, signaling a hush.

"You're going to feneggle your case into the hearing! Oh someone help me. I'm going to trial with a cuckoo bird," cries Jane, placing the back of her hand to her forehead.

"Seriously Jane, hear me out on this. We're not going to trial. Mark my words, they will settle," says Harrison, he can see that she has become distracted.

"Don't look now, but here comes your secretary, and it doesn't look like she's bearing good news," says Jane.

Martha Mills, Harrison's secretary, has hurried from the office to deliver an important message.

"Oceanic's office called, the deposition schedule of deponents include our client," Martha says with anticipation. Harrison drops his fork and grabs a napkin. Without saying another word Martha places an envelope on the table and nudges it toward

Harrison, then stands back attentively. Jane watches as Harrison opens the envelope.

"Counter suit," he says as the document floats down onto the table.

"So what, we expected a counter suit, why the long face?" Jane asks. Martha pats Harrison on the shoulder.

"We made a bet. If Huntfield, Turner and Barnes did not counter file before today's deposition, I would forego this year's raise until next year, and guess what?" Martha asks.

"Pull all the necessary files. Prepare for their deposition and take the rest of the day off, lucky dog," says Harrison. Martha gives a little hop, and with a girl-like squeal, clasps her hands and looks up as if giving thanks.

"Oh Well, I gave it a shot, she was going to get the raise anyway. I was counting on a settlement conference, looks like a few more months," says Harrison.

"On a lesser note, I called the facility on Ellis Island. The interpreter isn't on the Island," says Martha. Jane looks to her associate, who is waiting for an explanation.

"That having been said, I think we should try to find our client and our interpreter," says Jane. She rises from the table as

Harrison reaches into his coat pocket for his wallet.

"What in the world?" Harrison hears Jane say. He turns in the booth to see the interpreter, Tanaya walking up to their table. "There's one of them, where's the other one?" Harrison ask. "Oh lord, that is the other one," says Jane. As Tanaya nears their table, they see she is with an older gentleman. They are astonished at the pinstripe vested suit, with cane and top hat.

"I thought the inauguration was two years ago," says Harrison under his breath as he rises from the booth. "Tanaya, this is Mr. Bennett, Harry this is our client, Mr. Inar Katerpar."

"Well, Mr. Katerpar, I'm so glad you could make it today," says Harrison. Inar politely corrects the pronunciation; "Kha-ter-par," he says with a gracious smile. Jane looks to an equally shocked Harrison Bennett.

"EE-yes, Mr. Kka-ter-par," Harrison says with an emphasis on pronunciation. Jane looks at Tanaya, who is enjoying their reaction to the little surprise.

"Can I speak with you in private, Tanaya?" Jane excuses herself. Harrison cordially offers Inar a seat. "What's this all about?" Jane asks in a hushed voice. "This was all Uncle's idea. I couldn't talk him out of it. He explained that wearing the suit makes him look like Arrluk, The Killer Whale, now they both wear the same colors," says Tanaya.

"Whatever that means, my goodness, and his hair, he had it cut," says Jane. "Yes, all his idea." Tanaya replies. Over Tanaya's shoulder, Jane can see Harrison looking at his watch. It is her cue to gather everyone for the short walk to City Hall. "Okay, we had better get going." Jane says. Harrison helps Inar up out of the booth. Tanaya explains to him what will be expected of him for the rest of the day.

"Let him know that we'll be talking to men who will want to know who he is, and how you got to be in the big water," says Harrison. "Big water? All of a sudden you're talking like Hiawatha," Jane mocks. "Just let him know they will want him to...oh, never-mind," says Harrison in a dispirited voice.

"I've explained every aspect of the deposition. He replied that it's no different than back home. Everyone wants to know everyone else's business," says Tanaya. "Satisfied?" Jane asks.

Stepping out into the chilly morning air, Jane confides in Tanaya while the men walk ahead, Inar using a cane to stroll along side of Harrison. Not used to walking in anything but mukluks, he tries his best to walk dignified as possible. Harrison can see that Inar is without an overcoat. He begins to bring up the subject, but then realizes an important fact. Inar's home in the cold north cannot be compared to the mild spring weather in New York.

"It must have cost you a fortune," Jane comments as they make their way to the city hall. "Not me, remember the job placement at the Indian School? Well, pay day was yesterday, and he was paid all of his back wages," explains Tanaya.

"I began to worry that you would not make it here on time. I remembered, me being the big dummy that I am, I forgot to put the appointment time in the message," says Jane. "Thank the cab driver, he must have set a record. What time is the deposition?" Tanaya asks. "In exactly ten minutes," says Tanaya. "It was good to see that you and Harrison were surprised when we walked into the cafe," says Tanaya.

"Shocked is a better word," says Jane. "Good. I can tell Uncle he'll be happy, he can sneak up on white people," says Tanaya

"Uncle Inar, when did that happen?" Jane asks. "All us Inuits call our elders uncle, auntie, grandpa or grandma," she says.

"Not to be unappreciative, but Inar looks like a grandpa to me," says Jane. "I'm working on that." Tanaya replies. "The cane; just a bit too much," she adds. "His idea," says Tanaya melodically.

CHAPTER FOUR
Mr. Peanut And The Boat Whale

Harrison's legal team arrives at City Hall just before the morning rush has increased. At a crosswalk, they join others who are waiting for a break in the traffic. Standing looking up, Inar beholds the stately elegance of the enormous structure of city hall. Turning to Tanaya, he speaks to her in their native tongue, and she smiles with understanding. "He said this structure is almost as big as the iceberg that the boat hit," Tanaya explains. Without hesitation, Harrison and Jane fumble inside their coat pockets for a pad and pencil. They take a look at the building again, this time with a different understanding.

As they cross the boulevard, Jane locks her arm into Tanaya's and pulls her close. "Ever see a curious dog when it cocks its head to one side? Wait until you see their stuffy faces when we walk into the conference room," says Jane. "That's going to be the best part of my day," replies Tanaya.

At the main entrance of City Hall, Harrison holds open the heavy brass door as they file into a highly active ground floor. "What floor is this deposition going to take place?" Tanaya asks, in a concerned voice. "The fifth floor." Harrison says, as they arrive at the elevator doors. They then come to a realization, all three looking at Inar's smiling face. He has no idea what an elevator ride feels like. The others silently agree. The level of distraction has to be kept a minimal level. They understand it would be better to wait another day for the elevator ride.

"Is everybody ready for five flights of stairs?" Jane asks as she hands her briefcase to Inar. "I'm ready if you are," says a reluctant Tanaya.

On each floor of City Hall, there is a bench for tired and weary step climbers. The legal team can be heard trudging up the last flight of stairs. At the last step on the fifth floor, Inar stands in waiting, the others are still struggling up the last set of steps. Exerted, all three take a seat on the resting bench. "Was it my imagination?" I could swear those steps were getting steeper with every flight," says Harrison.

"No, it wasn't your imagination, I thought the fifth floor was going to be a ladder climb," says Jane breathlessly. "Uncle asked me why these people want to know about some old Inuit man. They should want to know about Arrluk. He thinks that is a better story," says Tanaya in translation.

"That would be an excellent question to ask White Star attorneys. Unfortunately, it is they who will be asking the questions," says Harrison. "Yes, and speaking of questions, we have a minute and a half to get to the deposition," says Jane.

Inside the deposition room, six attorneys and one board officer are waiting. At the rear of the room is a coffee urn, with four of the attorneys gathered around the law firm's Junior Vice President, Brandon McCullough. The door opens, and Harrison, Jane, Tanaya and Inar file in. They find their seats at the conference table and stand facing the lawyers at the rear of the room. At first, it seems like a gunfight is about to breakout. A heartbeat of clarity brings a deafening silence. The exact effect that Harrison predicted.

After everyone is seated, an introduction of White Star and Oceanic attorneys are given for the record. "Is everything all set Miss Williams?" Hillcrest asks the stenographer, who is entering the commencement information.

"I trust your client will be here soon, Mr. Bennett, we have a significant amount of deposition to cover today," says McCullough.

"I assure you, Mr. Katerpar will not delay this deposition in any way," says Harrison.

"Is the court reporter prepared to begin recording?" Harrison asks. With a nod she begins recording the commencement of the deposition.

"Gentleman, for the record, I am Harrison Theodore Bennett, Attorney, I am licensed to practice law in New York State. In the seat next to mine is my client, Inar Katerpar, pronounced Kha-ter-pah, with a silent ' r '," advises Harrison.

"Excuse me, I don't mean to interrupt but, this is not your client. We sent an office memo to Bennett Law Office this morning with the schedule of deponents. This is not one of them," says McCullough, adamantly.

"Let the record show that Oceanic and White Star are declining to continue with the deposition that they requested through filing. In doing so, my client is being denied his right to a due process," says Harrison. Inar becomes aware of the dispute by the tone of voices. A cold wolf-like stare becomes a distraction at the table. One of the attorneys whispers to McCullough.

"I beg to differ," says attorney Jones. "We want proof. Attorney Bennett will do well by having his client produce some valid identification at once," barks Jones. Tanaya translates the demand to Inar.

"Mr. Katerpar says he can only show you his birth mark, on the left cheek of his buttocks, if that's what you want to see."

"This is preposterous, your client does not have proper identification" I should call security and have this impostor escorted from the building. We will have him arrested for fraud!" McCullough threatens.

"Let the record show that Oceanic representatives are badgering my client, purposely, causing my client to suffer further emotional distress. You are shameless sir, my client is a survivor of the Titanic tragedy," says Harrison calmly.

Another attorney approaches McCullough to confirm the warning. He takes another look at Inar, then starts to shuffle though a stack of documents. Attorney Scott slips him a document. McCullough clears his throat.

"I have here a document acquired from Ellis Island dated April 29, 1912, in which a medical examination was performed on Inar Katerpar, and this document reads; a six inch laceration requiring twenty-three stitches and dressing," reads McCullough.

"May I see the document?" Harrison asks as he reads the medical examination report. "This document seems to be authentic, I have no reason to doubt its content," says Harrison.

"I'm confused, who is deposing my client? White Star attorneys or their law firm board members?" Harrison asks.

"It is my duty as a board member to safeguard the Firm's interest in this matter, I will not allow HT&B attorneys to depose this man if there's doubt of your client's presence." McCullough says.

"Gentlemen I believe you've had the pleasure of meeting Miss Tanaya Navaran, the court appointed interpreter. Let the record show that our client shall be instructed to show the wound described in the medical examination report."

Tanaya turns to Inar and directs him to show the attorneys the scar left from his injury. Inar nods, stands, and unbuckles his pants to show his birthmark. Tanaya stops him and repeats the request. She helps him slip off his suit jacket, then his vest.

Inar then pulls up his shirt, revealing a six inch scar. Oceanic attorneys all walk over to witness that Inar has revealed the scar. "Let the record show Bennett's client, the deponent, is present and has been accounted for," Hillcrest says dejectedly.

"Shall we move on?" Harrison asks.

"The time is 9:45 a.m., Tuesday, April fifteen, nineteen hundred and fifteen. We are addressing the matter of the Oceanic Navigation Steamship Company and the White Star Ocean Liner Company, owners of the RMS Titanic. The deponent, Mr. Inar Katerpar, is represented by attorneys Harrison Bennett and Miss Theresa Jane Reynolds. Under court order they have been instructed to provide the services of Miss Tanaya Navaran as interpreter. Attorney Scott, I believe you are up." Hillcrest advises.

"Mr. Katerpar, are you a citizen of the United States?" Scott asks.

"He answers, no," says Tanaya.

"What nationality are you, or to be more exact, where do you come from?"

"He answers; 'From the village of Kalaiapac, in the land of Inuksukt, a place your people call Baffin,'" translates Tanaya.

"Were you a stowaway on the ship Titanic on the morning of April 14, 1912?" Scott asks. Tanaya has difficulty translating "stowaway" and settles on a free ride.

"He denies riding for free," says Tanaya.

"How did you get on the steamship Titanic?" Scott asks.

"Mr. Katerpar answers; a whale made from an iron boat, hit his iceberg," translates Tanaya, fighting back a smile.

"Made out of a whale?" Are we to take that answer as the transatlantic ocean liner, Titanic?" Scott asks. "Yes, that is his answer," Tanaya answers.

"Within the same answer, you stated 'your' iceberg. How did you come to own this iceberg, Mr. Katerpar?" Scott asks, which at that point Harrison interjects.

"In the United States and in countries all over the world, possession is ninety-percent of the law. My client was the only person on the iceberg at the time of the collision. Also, I might add that; under International Law: Nations such as the United States, do not have the jurisdiction or authority to regulate the activities of foreign vessels operating outside their territorial sea and exclusive economic zones. There are no international laws that stipulate whether a person can claim the ownership of an iceberg...thus, it was his iceberg," explains Harrison.

"Well, that being the case, Mr. Katerpar, do you own more than one iceberg?" Scott asks. "That's not a relevant question, my client is being deposed on his account of one iceberg, the one struck by the Titanic. If through a matter of discovery, it is found that the said ship hit more than one iceberg, as you are suggesting, then we will be more than happy to revisit the question," admonishes Harrison, glancing towards the ceiling.

"It is a question, and it was asked by an attorney. In the interest of our clients, we feel the question should be answered. Please, answer the question Mr. Katerpar." Huntfield says. Tanaya conveys the question, and Inar roars with laughter.

"He said, that if he were as rich as you, he would have one iceberg for each of his wives." Tanaya says, stifling a laugh.

"You asked for it." Jane says in an inaudible tone. "No, he does not own another iceberg," translates Tanaya.

A note is handed to Scott by one of his colleagues. After a quick glance, attorney Scott continues with the deposition. "How was it that you were on the iceberg?" Who put you there?" Scott asks. "Arrluk put me there," Inar says through translation.

"This Arrluk, is it Mr. or Mrs.?" Scott asks. "His answer is: 'Arrluk the Killer whale, put me on the Iceberg,' translates Tanaya. Attorney Scott is not prepared for the response. The line of questioning has been derailed by Inar's answers. Frustrated, Scott decides to hand the deposition to another of the attorney team. "All right, I'm done here. Anyone...?" Attorney Scott calls on J.J. Jones.

"J.J. you're up...have a go at it, old chap?" asks Scott. Jeremiah Jones announces his name for the record, allowing Jones to begin his line of questioning.

"Allegedly, Mr. Katerpar, you claim that you were aboard the Titanic at the time of the sinking. How exactly, did you find yourself on the Titanic? We know there was a collision, but how exactly did you end up on the ship?" As Tanaya continues to relate the question. Inar becomes confused at first, he then explains how the collision occurred.

A sadness comes over Inar as he takes himself back. His arms raise up and he continues to explain what took place on what was calculated to be April 11, 1912.

CHAPTER FIVE
Inar And The Killer Whale

The sun was out that day and the ice was very slippery because it was melting. I could hear the ocean waves crashing against the iceberg below me. I've heard the sound before, but not as loud. I could tell it was a big iceberg.

"It was on that day I decided to survive. I am Inuit, my heart tells me when to die, we as a people cannot deny the will to survive. I was going to live on top of that iceberg until it was my time, but on that day, a strong wind had pushed the iceberg further down the ice corridor, toward warmer waters. I knew it would not be long before the iceberg rolled and took me with it.

"When Inuit leaders get old, and the winter food storage is lean, it is hard to watch the children cry from hunger. It is an old man's way to decide if he will want to hear them again next season. When it was decided to go on my journey, I chose, not the others. If you believe like my people do, sometimes the ice flow can be a gentle way of taking. We fall to sleep, and when we awake, the last moments of peace in this world are that of the ice flow. The start place of birthright. Inuits believe that it is an honor to give your own life, so that others should live. In the beginning of my Sky World journey, it was my desire to lay down and accept death. After a while, I did not feel death was upon me.

"I have felt the weight of a White Bear as he lay on top of me, breathing his last breath. I know when death is upon me. It was then, my journey became a challenge and my will grew stronger as the days passed. My death did not come. I felt deprived, then I felt that I was not worthy, then I got angry, very angry.

"I drifted on the sea for as long as I could, then one day, my Death Song came to me. I looked upon the supply bundles my relatives and friends gave to me upon departing from my homeland. Those supplies were for me to use in my after life, now they were used in this world. Seeing all my belongings, there are many adornments, beads and carved bone for me to wear when arriving in the Sky World. Everything was laid out in order of necessity. My ice cleats made of walrus tusks, these were the first to be used in my quest to survive. I climbed and walked that big iceberg, and found a flat part. The flat part was wide, and there was still some snow pack.

"My whale bone hand saw and knife were pulled from one of my supply bundle. The intended use was to build an ice shelter, an Igloo. I exhausted nearly all of my food supply, but I am a good fisher man and my food was yet to be caught," says Inar, through translation. Tanaya has discontinued the translation, as Inar pauses searching his memory. The room is silent. At once, attorney Jones stands and seizes the moment.

"Now, let me understand, you were placed on the iceberg to die?" Jones asks.

"Mr. Katerpar answered; 'In the beginning I would accept death when it came,' says Tanaya.

"The fact is, you were on the iceberg, your iceberg, with full intention of taking your own life; to commit suicide?" He asks.

At this point Jane interjects. "There's a difference in taking ones' life, and accepting death when it comes," says Jane.

"Really? Then please, explain to me the difference, because in this country, it is against the law to take your own life, or do something with the intent to cause your own death, is that not right?" Jones asks.

"I'm sure, if you were to drink three quarts of whiskey a day, every day, and you knew it could kill you, does the law deem that action as an attempted suicide?" Jane asks.

"No. Because you would wake up in the morning and tell yourself that you will never do it again and live a long and happy life afterward. My client's actions were not a case of attempted suicide. Nor do my client's actions stem from an act of desperation, or from mental illness," recites Jane.

"I have to express an objection. Miss Reynolds may have been many things in her career..." Jones begins. Harrison stands to interrupt.

"Enough of that attorney Jones, try conduct yourself in a more professional manner," admonishes Harrison.

"Now today, in this undertaking of deposition, Miss Reynolds is definitely not a psychiatrist," continues Jones.

"If I may reiterate. My client did not indicate or express any intention of 'self-harm' and, as he has stated...a grandfather seeing a grandchild go hungry...You can argue if my client can be held under the law, for an act of conscience. The truth is, my client made a conscious decision, based upon the survival of his tribe, and that, is an act of heroism. No different from a soldier throwing himself upon a small bomb to save his brothers-in-arms.

Furthermore, the act of sacrifice stems from a centuries old account, reasoned in churches everyday through out the world," argues Jane.

"In any event, you decided to live. What happened in the midnight hours of April 14, 1912?" The question is not understood. Tanaya repeats the question, but Inar begins the account of the first night he completed his igloo on top of the iceberg, through the translation of Tanaya.

"The sun was touching the ocean, and that bit of dying light gave me a chance to see where the Igloo needed to be patched. There was still snow pack in the crevices I could use for this. As the sun sank further, I lit a fire inside with the last of the seal fat. I had not made a shelter from blue ice before. It looked good, I went out a little ways to look. I could see the fire made my igloo shine like a blue star. "That evening while lying inside my ice shelter, I heard a faint cry of distress. I recognized it, it was a distinctive cry of the seal, calling to others for help. It's deep throaty sounds told me it was the seal. I determined it was 'Oogrooq' the Old Seal.

It was hurt, and in a natural way I wanted to help. I feel a kinship with this animal. The Inuit people had hunted the animal for centuries, while honoring its gift of life. It gave to the people, in turn we sing songs about the seal, we pray for its return each season." Tanaya's translation is stopped.

Attorney Scott attempts to interrupt the translation. "Need we present the question again, Mr. Katerpar?" Scott says. The question is rendered ineffective by Board member McCullough, who pulls Scott close. "Somewhere along the line of this deposition there may be some information we can use against his case. Let him ramble on," advises McCullough. Scott reluctantly agrees then sits back into his seat. "I'm sorry for the interruption. Please, carry on," says Scott.

Tanaya pauses for a moment, long enough to complete a stink-eye in Scott's direction, she then asks Inar to continue. "Okay, then I strapped the walrus bone ice cleats onto my mukluks and tied them tight. There was still enough sunlight to see my way down the iceberg, and it sounded to me that the cry was at least fifty steps from the shelter. I made my way towards the sound of the seal. When I was closer I could see the fin of a shark, circling very close to the iceberg. I trudged nearer and could see that it was a Oogrooq, and it was female. She was floundering on a shelf part of the iceberg, and she was caught up in a fishnet. There was blood, because it was pulled tight around her neck. I halted my advance, I did not want her to flee back into the sea to the circling shark. I was standing still, she looked up, and at that moment I saw her spirit. She was looking back at me, I could tell she saw my spirit as well. I then approached slowly, and I kept my eyes locked on the shark.

"The cry of distress ceased and she began to call to me in greeting. The seal lay her chin on the ice, allowing me to kneel beside her. I could see the shark now angry, they don't like to give up their prey. That shark wanted its meal, and let me know about it. He came so close, his splash rained down onto Oogrooq and me, she leaned into me like a child asking for protection.

"In a low growling voice, I spoke to the shark. 'You go away from here, or I will cut off your fin. It was an ineffective and hollow threat, but nonetheless, a threat," Tanaya conveyed.

"Oogrooq, the old seal lay still while I gently cut the tight net from her neck. As the last binding was cut, I could hear her lungs fill with air, she began to breath. The escape had left her exhausted and weak, she was unwilling to fight any more.

"I had not been so close to a seal that was not being hunted by the Inuit. I took off my hand mitten and began to stroke her head, humming the Inuit farewell song. The song lasted until the sun sank below the horizon, taking Oogrooq into its fold. I pulled the remaining fish net out of the water, and began trudging back to the igloo, with the seal in tow…"

"Miss..Navaran ran, is it? I am going against some well grounded advice offered by my esteemed colleague. I have to ask that you kindly explain to Mr. Katerpar that the story of the old seal is an interesting one. The only thing is, it has nothing to do with being placed on the Titanic. Please Miss Navaran, explain that he must be deposed on his account of April 14, leading into April 15, 1912 - the time of collision?" Attorney Jones asks adamantly.

In translation, Tanaya conveys Inar's words. "I would like for you to know, the seal had nothing to do with the 'boat whale' but she saved my life. I had not eaten in three days. If the old seal had not come to me, I may have died the very night of the of the collision. I would not be here speaking with you if not for the seal," conveys Tanaya.

"Very Well, Mr. Katerpar, we'll come back to that question. Incidentally, back to your allegation of being on the iceberg. How long were you on this iceberg?" Jones asks. Tanaya hesitates for a few seconds. The question is a difficult one, so she must ask it in a way Inar can process the translation. Inar can see that everyone expects an answer.

"Mr. Katerpar, we find it only fair to inform you that the Oceanic attorneys have figured the ice floe calculations in preparation for this deposition. We have acquired the latest scientific data pertaining to the ice floe in the Grand Banks of Newfoundland corridor," says Jones. "The research gathered involved scientific studies that began in early spring and lasted until August. Oceanic calculations were based upon the speed, and the distance an iceberg can travel. How much time in distance, Mr. Katerpar, did it take 'your iceberg' to travel the distance to where the collision took place?" Jones asks. After the translation, Tanaya can see that Inar is having trouble finding an answer.

"The Newfoundland Sea, Baffin Island and the Norwegian Sea are the main parts of the world that glaciers calf icebergs. White Star attorneys have gathered scientific data based on studies by oceanographers and mathematician scholars of the day, and have come-up with formulas that establish approximate equations.

"One fact is that an iceberg does not stay intact. Changing weather can cause its demise by breaking apart into smaller bergs.

It is highly unlikely that an iceberg can take on boarders, that is, not without some sort of natural caused eviction," suggests Jones. "I suggest you ask Mr. Katerpar about that bit of theoretical information," says Harrison.

"Mr. Katerpar - allegedly, while you were living on said iceberg, was there any event that occurred that would have made your living accommodations unlivable?" Jones asks.

"Mr. Katerpar answers this way: 'I had to build two separate igloos because the iceberg broke apart three different times.'" Tanaya translates.

"Oh come now, Mr. Katerpar. You claim that you survived three violent catastrophic events without a scratch?" Jones rebukes.

"There is no need for intimidation. Since my client was on the iceberg as it traveled, I'm sure he can come up with his own calculation that could provide better information for this Hearing. There are many variables that complicate the matter," says Harrison as he opens a folder.

"An Iceberg's size can range anywhere from 150 feet high and 90 feet in approximate length or width. Yet, icebergs such as these are considered to be small. Caught in a moderate wind, icebergs can clip along at 15 to 20 miles-per-hour. Also, since the mass of an iceberg is underwater, it is constantly in motion, pushed along by the ocean current. Unless attorney Jones can produce a farmers almanac, showing the weather on those exact days and nights, his calculations would not be admissible."

Tanaya has explained the question to Inar. He nods his head in agreement and again attempts to answer the question. "By counting the nights and the movements of the moon, I am able to say 60 days. My first night on the iceberg was the night of the new moon. When the lunar cycle completed and a new moon was due, the moon became new the night after the sinking. I remember this, because it was a time to make the experience into a song. Through song is the way my people keep their history. When the day turned to night it was his calling to make a song," discloses Tanaya.

"Let the record show that we too have done some calculations based upon our client's word. He has indicated that he was on the iceberg at the time of the collision. Using that date and time, we can count backward and account for every day our client was on the said iceberg. We have prepared charts and graphs, although not ready for display at this hearing, they will be readily available for a trial, where we fully intend to put them on display. These exhibits will show that Mr. Katerpar was the soul occupant of the iceberg for one month and twenty-nine days. He was adrift at sea on April 15 for the better part of that day, a total of 60 days.

"Further, let the record show that not only was he the sole occupant on the iceberg, the iceberg provided my client with food, water, and shelter. If not for said iceberg, my client would have possibly drowned at sea, been eaten by sharks or succumbed to dehydration. Under oath, he has been deposed and he has answered every question that he was required to answer. If there are no further questions, I suggest we break for lunch." Harrison suggests.

"Yes, a lunch break will be fine. As for answering all the questions required, well I'm sure Oceanic attorneys have much more than that," says Hillcrest. Harrison and Jane start to gather their documents. As Harrison places the papers into his briefcase, Hillcrest calls him over.

"I have been to many depositions throughout my tenure Harrison, but never one quite so interesting. Tell me what you want Harrison. I'll take it to the board, and see what they think. What do you say?"

"Oh come on Joe, the party's just begun. I can remember when you would relentlessly depose someone for at least three or four days," says Harrison. "We are prepared to settle for fifty-thousand today. We can have the papers drawn up in an hour." Hillcrest says with raised eyebrows.

"You know, to tell you the truth, my associate and I really haven't discussed a settlement. I feel the story of the Titanic tragedy is a fantastic one. Our research alone reads like a best seller. I think we're going to need a little more time to prepare for trial," says Harrison without eye contact.

"Don't be a fool Harrison!" Hillcrest shouts with restraint. No jury panel in the world will award your client anything but a plug nickel. Be sensible man, take the fifty-thousand, Harrison," pleads Hillcrest in a more subtle tone.

"It was a horrific tragedy Joe. Don't rub salt in the wound by throwing dollars at the memory of Titanic and the souls that perished with her."

"You're a jackass! We are going to bury you, the whole world is going to know what a gold digger you really are. This deposition has ended," shouts Hillcrest angrily.

CHAPTER SIX
The Claims Game

At the "Gateway Cafe" a quiet celebration is underway. Inar's gang is ordering a victory meal. A toast is raised to what they have concluded as a small triumph, but still a victory. "Here's to the future of iceberg zoning laws," announces Jane.

"The sole occupant. How do I come up with such a genius legalese lexicon?" Jane says sarcastically. Tanaya is quietly translating to Inar what is being said.

"Uncle says that if it ever happens again, he will name the iceberg. Its name will be The Harrison Bennett," says Tanaya.

"Tanaya, please tell the story of Inar seeing the Statue of Liberty for the very first time?" Jane asks. Tanaya turns to Inar and asks if she could tell the others about the story of the frozen woman that he conveyed a few days before. He agrees.

"As Uncle explained in translation; he stayed on deck of the boat that had rescued him. As it was cutting its way towards the city lights, there was fog and a light rain, like a mist. He said he was watching the lights of the big bright city. He said the lights were shining through the fog he was looking upon like many fires. All of a sudden he heard a big, deep sound that shook him to his bones. To me, I interpreted this as Carpathia's fog horn," says Tanaya.

"Uncle said he dropped down to one knee, and reached for his whale spear, but it wasn't there. Then the fog cleared for just a little bit, and through it, the biggest woman he ever saw was standing in a light. He thought she was frozen. When she made that noise again, he climbed into a hanging-boat and stayed there until the ship pulled up to the dock. He said, 'those men kept calling for me to come out, but he was afraid that big woman might make that terribly rude noise again.' Tanaya laughs. Inar smiles passively, as he has no idea why they are laughing.

Several city blocks from the Gateway Cafe stands a 30-story ceramic brick office building. Inside the Manhattan corporate office of T.J. Huntfield, Corporate President, of H.T.& B., a secretive meeting is taking place. Standing before a large antique office desk, Joseph Hillcrest, Executive Officer for H.T.&B., is delivering a briefing on the Bennett and Reynolds deposition.

"The time set for filing claims with the Commissioner of the Federal District

Court will expire in 7 days. From what we hear from our sources, the Commissioner has an armful of claims filed against Oceanic; twenty-five more claims were filed today," says Hillcrest as he takes a seat. "Why has this become complicated? The firm's strategy hasn't changed. We make an offer and they accept, the settlements have been moving along as expected," says Huntfield.

"I agree wholeheartedly. Until this news today, we figured we were at an end. If the Federal District Court finds there is cause to extend the claims period, we will have to reevaluate our position on final claims amount," says Hillcrest. "It is my understanding, there is only a handful of families that are holding out, hoping a Judge will find in their favor and make decision on their claims. I expect that armful of claims are damages for the deaths caused by the disaster," says Huntfield.

"Yes, Mr. Huntfield, that is correct, and it is fortunate for us that these families are parties to the limitation of damage. Proceedings were initiated early in the limitation time limit to maximize claims options by HT&B on behalf of client. Right now, there are lawyers from all over the Northeast and eastern seaboard filing claims. The Federal Court is leaning toward whether they have the right to bring suit against Oceanic in any court they choose as U.S. law provides. Claims against Oceanic must be filed within the interior boundaries of the United States, at any time within the twelve month statute of limitations placed on the Titanic sinking," says Hillcrest.

"The firm's strategy in going into opposing the limitations extension apparently was not effective. Is there another strategy for the appeal of settlement?" Huntfield asks.

"It was decided those claimants who have not filed will hold out for a maximum amount, and granted there will be plenty of time for those death claims to be filed against Oceanic. Our hands are tied, thanks to the honorable Senator. The extended time now stands at April 22, 1915, of which after that date, no claims for damages can be received. We feel that our efforts to block the extension proved very effective. During the year it was debated, the number of prospective claimants dropped by 15 percent. Regardless of what Ramsi thinks of our handling of the settlements, we have emerged successfully," replies Hillcrest.

"Tell me, what have you in store for the Bennett client?" Huntfield asks. "This case has been set aside separately from the other claims, and it is being handled on a priority basis. There is a certainty that the Katerpar claim will sink under its own preposterous demands. Our strategy is to flood the jury with expert testimony. We have called upon these experts and they range from meteorologists, mathematicians and oceanographers who will disprove any evidence presented by Bennett and Reynolds," explains Hillcrest.

"A wise decision, Harrison Bennett is one of the finest trial attorneys that Harvard has produced. A word to the wise; make sure the team you assemble can work all the angles.

"If you corner Bennett, he will fight dirty. If you fight back, he will use it against you. Don't waste our time with empty threats, he will sense fear and move on us like a fat cat," says Huntfield. "Thank you for the advice sir, but I don't quite see how he could possibly fight a case with a client who was clearly stowed away at the time of the sinking," explains Hillcrest.

"As I was saying, do not assume to know what Bennett's strategy is going to be. If he has not accepted a settlement, you can bet your bottom dollar, his intention is to take White Star to court. It would behoove you to try your best to keep this case from going to trial," advises Huntfield.

"What, if any indication, has he given as basis for landing Oceanic in court?" Huntfield asks.

"I believe, as others on the team, that he is leaning towards negligence of the Titanic crew and its commander," says Hillcrest.

"I would also prepare a defense for conspiracy to commit insurance fraud. Cover all the angles, Joseph."

"His client is claiming the Titanic caused his injury by negligently striking the iceberg, of which his client was aboard at the time of collision," says Hillcrest. He smiles as Huntfield laughs hardily.

"That's the kind of laugh we hope to be coming from a jury box," says Hillcrest. "I am confident my team of attorney's are looking forward to the court challenge," he adds.

"Joseph, Joseph. I wasn't laughing with you. Don't get me wrong, but I just spent the better part of twenty minutes giving you pearls as a form of advice. If you think Bennett will not seize an opportunity to entertain a jury, you're wrong. He will get past the laughter, he expects it. The jury will be granted a little latitude by the judge, and Bennett will take an admonishment at the expense of his case. In the end, it will be our law firm that will suffer the humiliation. Stay on top of this case, Joseph," advises Huntfield. The double-doors are pulled open, and Huntfield turns to Joseph Hillcrest.

"What ever I may think of the legal team you have assembled, Joseph, let me assure you, I have confidence that we will prevail in all aspects of the claims process, that is to include Harrison Bennett's case, trial or not. A good evening to you all," says Huntfield as he leaves.

Later, in the evening, after the celebration at the cafe, instructions were given to Jane by Harrison.

"I have a small window of opportunity to build our case further. Inar's account of April 15th must be concrete. Keep digging, the old guy has a memory of a steel trap, push deeper. I'll be back later tonight." Harrison says as they part company.

Harrison has traveled to Long Island to meet covertly with an accomplice that he had contacted earlier in the day. He is toting a leather document bag in which he has $1,000. A bulge protrudes from his jacket where he carries a concealed weapon.

Arriving at his destination at Long Island Grand Central Station, Harrison makes his way through the crowded transfer station to the designated meeting place. He walks towards the loading platform and past a sign that reads Inter-Borough Rapid Transit Company. A man with a cigarette hanging from his mouth steps out from behind a cement column. Harrison can see that he has a brown leather briefcase in his hand, which he slowly places onto the cement platform.

"Can I trouble you for a light?" Harrison asks the man. As Harrison leans forward to draw off a flame from cupped hands, a brusque voice is heard. "I have what you want, but I need you to know the procurement expenses were steep, so the price isn't what we agreed on," says the man.

"Guarantee its worth, and the expenses will be covered in full," says Harrison in a low confident voice. "Have you ever been disappointed with my work? Let's go with the amount we agreed on, plus a bonus in the way of a cashiers check, and the briefcase is yours," the man says. Harrison agrees with a nod and the exchange is made.

Outside the train station, Harrison has hailed down a taxi. Once inside, he begins to go examine the contents of the briefcase. As he thumbs through a ream of documents the information brings a smile to his face. Harrison lets go with an exuberant but silent victory shout. The documents are placed back into the briefcase and tucked tightly under his arm. Later, after arriving at his apartment, Harrison wastes no time reading through the documents, acquired earlier at the train station. A cover page is the first of the documents pulled from the briefcase, it reads:

U.S. SENATE INQUIRY

"All right, that's what I'm talking about," says Harrison as he begins to read aloud.

"U.S. Senator William Alden Smith, who had sailed with Captain Smith in 1906, and had a chance to meet the man, wanted to know why, under Smith's command, the Titanic went down. On Tuesday morning, the 16TH of April 1912, he sat down and began typing out a draft. The following morning, word had been received showing that there were no other survivors of the disaster, apart from those on board the Carpathia. The true scope of the disaster was now known to all.

"On April 17Th, one day before the Carpathia was to sail into the Port of New York Harbor, the U.S. Senate convened for an emergency session. The floor was turned over to Senator Smith, who asked for passage of his resolution which authorized the Committee on Commerce to investigate the RMS Titanic disaster.

"Senator Smith's resolution called for a hearing. The surviving passengers, rescue ship personnel and personnel aboard any ship within the vicinity of rescue were to be subpoenaed. With very little opposition, the resolution was carried. Smith was appointed by the Commerce Committee as Chairman. A Senate subcommittee was also appointed to investigate the disaster, with Nelson Klute as the Chair.

"Senator Smith and Klute went to work immediately, selecting a panel of Senators for the inquiry. At the end of the day they had selected an equal number of Republicans and Democrats," reads Harrison.

Back at Jane's apartment, she is at a work desk in her living room. Tanaya and Inar are talking quietly by the coffee table. Jane's dog 'Hurley', a Pomeranian breed, is snuggled into Inar's lap. The phone rings. "Harrison, what a surprise. I was just going through some case files and I was thinking about today...now?" Well, if it's that important, sure why not...but I have to drop Tanaya off at the dock before the last ferry trip to the Island. I will be there with Inar, he may have to stay the night at your apartment. Is it okay with you?" Jane asks.

A few hours later at Harrison's apartment, the entry buzzer interrupts his reading. Jane's voice comes over the intercom. Harrison buzzes her in.

There is a knock at the door. "It's open," says Harrison. Jane walks into the apartment followed by Inar and Tanaya. Jane, stop abruptly when she sees Harrison sitting in the middle of his living room floor surrounded by documents.

"I thought you put a cap on the hours of research. That definitely looks like research to me," says Jane.

"It's not research yet, right now it's just me; slack-jawed and bushy tailed," says Harrison jokingly. He looks up to see Inar, he is wearing his seal skin parka complete with hood.

"What happened to Mr. Peanut?" Harrison asks with a smile. "When he gets homesick, he feels better in traditional clothing," says Tanaya.

"Well-then, come on in, thank you for coming over on such short notice. Make yourselves at home, there is coffee on the stove, pastry on the table. The liquor cabinet is right over there. If I were you

Jane, I'd pour some courage into a glass and brace yourself," says Harrison.

"Oh no, I don't like the sound of that," she says as she leans over to pick up a few pages. Harrison pours two drinks and watches Jane's reaction when she realizes that she is reading court transcripts, and they are not of their deposition taken that morning. "You've got to be kidding me. These are the court transcripts into the investigation of the Titanic," Jane says, holding the documents with a limp wrist. 'No,' I'm not, and yes they are! Welcome to the world of law and order, put on your lawyer hat because we are going to trial," says an excited Harrison. Jane walks over and falls onto the sofa as Tanaya tries to explain the situation to Inar. Jane hands Harrison a whiskey glass and clinks his glass in a silent toast.

"I received an anonymous call a few days back, offering the full court transcripts of the Senate Hearing. For a small fee that is. Naturally I was skeptical, until the voice on the other end offered specific information of which I had prior knowledge of being in the actual transcripts." Harrison hands one page of transcript to Jane. He does not take his eyes off her as she reads the document.

"Even though the 'Titanic Disaster Report' was released by the 62nd Congress in 1912, it did not contain the entire court transcript of the hearings," says Harrison as Jane continues to read into the document. "This would be absolutely unbelievable. If not for the fact it was said under oath, these statements are blatantly incriminating. It's more than negligence, it's conspiracy to commit mass homicide," says Jane with sadness in her voice.

"Jane, I want you to know that I had absolutely no idea how this simple injury claim would take such a turn. When you contacted me in the months after the sinking, my motive was to help you with Inar's case. Now, it's he who is in the position to help me. I want this case in court, because the truth has to be known that there was a premeditated scheme to sink the Titanic. If not for the hundreds that died, they may have gotten away with it. As it stands now, it looks like they're succeeding. We're going to see to it that they don't," says Harrison solemnly. Jane looks past Harrison, she sees Inar sitting in the kitchen, quietly talking with Tanaya.

"So, where is all this taking us Harry? I can only play dumb for so long before I have to ask. How do you plan to get this into a criminal court?" Jane asks.

"I can't tell you that, because frankly I don't know. This is what I do know; there is a mountain of evidence that screams to be uncovered. If I dig around long enough, something will pop up, or someone will come forward and open the whole can of worms. There is just no way I can justify not going into this with both guns blazing," he says.

"The only reason you remain on the Katerpar insurance case is, why?" Jane asks in a confused tone. "Other than feeling very grateful for the discovery material, inadvertent as it was, I have to say, you are fearless. I respect that. There is no way I could jump ship and let you walk into that court room alone.

"Then, there is no time to waste, it's going to be a long night, I hope Inar is up to it. We're going to need all the ammunition we can get. Isn't that right Harry?" Jane asks as she and Tanaya silently agree with a confident glance.

"I'll put on some more coffee, we'll use the kitchen, let's go get them gang," cheers Harrison.

As the hours pass further into the night, the kitchen table becomes cluttered with coffee cups, whiskey glasses, transcripts, and ash trays. Harrison continues to read into the Senate Hearing transcripts. Jane is taking notes on Inar's account of the sea disaster. Opening a folder, she places several 5" X 7" photo's in front of Inar.

"Ask him if he can recall any of these men," she says to Tanaya. Inar studies the photos and eagerly nods as he points to one particular photo.

"Uncle says, while the ship was sinking, he found himself near the top of the ship; the boat deck. He said that this man," says Tanaya, pointing to a photo. "Was a leader, Uncle remembers him because to him, he looked like a walrus, a white walrus," explains Tanaya as she pulls a photo from the spread. "This is a photo of Captain Smith," says Jane, stunned.

Tanaya continues the translation. "This man," says Tanaya handing another photo to Jane, who takes it and studies it momentarily. "This is Titanic's Second Officer, Lightoller," says Jane.

"Uncle says that man, Lightoller, pushed him away and hollered at him, he would not let him near a small boat. He also said it was the last small boat," says Tanaya.

"My guess is that small 'boat means' lifeboat. Who are the others? Ask him that," says Harrison, joining in on the exchange. Tanaya translates as she points to Ramsi. "He says, when everybody was getting into the lifeboats, this man," says

Tanaya, holding a photo of Ramsi. "He was just standing on that roof watching everything," she translates. Harrison takes the photo and flips it over to read the information on the back.

"He goes on to say, and these are his words," says Tanaya. 'Then, I thought in sadness. These people, they are all going to die. Why is this man pretending he is not going to die in that freezing water? The cold ocean water kept rising onto the ship, so I went up to the roof with the rest of them. Up there, those men were struggling with a flat boat, trying to get it off of the roof. Then the ship, it bobbed in the front, and a big wave of sea water washed onto the roof. Everyone ran to a higher part of the ship, there were many, many people all over, the women were screaming and the children were crying. I was getting pushed around. I fell down and almost rolled off the roof into the water," recalls Inar.

Harrison places a photo of First Officer Murdock on the table. "Did he see this man?" he asks Tanaya. "That man," says Inar pointing to Murdock. 'Was on the side of the ship that hit the iceberg. He was undoing some ropes, but I did not see him after the boat dipped in the front. I was not on the roof for very long. The lights went out, the women and children began to scream again. I felt bad for everyone, but I realized it was their death not mine, and I should respect that. Death will come upon me, but not at this time," says Tanaya in narration.

"Everything Inar has described is in line with what has been brought out in the news articles on the survivors.

We have yet to read the Senate Hearing transcripts to verify his account," says Harrison.

"I am concerned. If Inar was handcuffed, and stowed below in the hull of the ship, how could he be on the Boat Deck with Ramsi, Smith and Lightoller? It's one of the first questions the defense will ask," says Jane.

Tanaya begins to translate, Inar nods his head in agreement. Inar now understands that his account of the sinking must begin when he was taken into custody on the Titanic.

CHAPTER SEVEN
A Look Back Through The Tears

On the night of April 14, 1912, Inar was blinded by a brilliant light in the cold darkness of the North Atlantic. With closed eyes, Inar hears a ringing bell. The sound of a bell is a sign, he begins his death chant to the timing of the ringing bell and its pitch. Inar goes into a trance like state of mind, concentrating on the prayer chant that will transport him to the Sky World. The collision is imminent, the engines have been ordered to full stop, and the Titanic is completely quiet as she cuts through the water.

A slight trembling causes Inar to open his eyes for a moment, and in that moment, he sees a cluster of lights. The iceberg shutters and dips downward. The collision causes Inar to tumble downwards and onto the deck of the Titanic.

The fall has left him injured and unconscious. A few minutes had passed before he is sighted by two Second Class passengers who are star gazing on the Port side of the Boat deck. The frightened woman screams when she sees a body, sprawled on the deck of the Forward well.

The commotion alerts two sea men, Earnest Arter and William Brice, patrolling the Promenade Deck. Both crew members scurry up the stair well to investigate the disturbance. Leaning over the forward deck railing, the passengers are pointing downward. One of the seamen reports to the bridge to dispatch crewmen to investigate.

Upon arrival on the Forward Well, the crewmen see what looks to be a small bear curled up on the deck. Not wanting to touch the body, one of the crewmen pushes Inar onto his back, with a push of his heel. A flashlight is shined on Inar's face, and his eyes slowly flicker, then open. He can hear faint sounds of people talking in a strange language. There is a nudge in his side which prompts him to his feet. As he rolls on his back he becomes aware that he has been injured. Reaching into his parka, he places his hand just below his rib cage. He puts his hand in front of his face and sees that it is covered with blood.

The Titanic's crew members can see that Inar is injured, but it is not a matter they are concerned with. The crew members have already determined that he is a stowaway, and he is apprehended. Inar is pulled away from the well-deck and taken to the Bridge of the Titanic. Sea men Arter and Brice haven't a clue that the ship has struck an iceberg, and in just under three hours, the majestic Titanic will be at the bottom of the Atlantic.

On the Bridge Deck, where ship is steered and controlled, First Officer, William Murdock, is in command of the Titanic. The incident has forced Murdock to summon Captain Smith to the Bridge. A short time before, Murdock had relieved Second Officer Charles Lighttoller. While conducting the change of command briefing, the night's activities are passed to Murdock. Lightoller fails to give Murdock the wireless messages concerning icebergs near by. Instead, he merely mentions there are ice fields straight ahead in Titanic's course.

Earlier, during Lighttoller's bridge watch, six wireless messages were received in the Marconi Room - all were warnings of icebergs dead ahead of Titanic. Some of the messages also contained information of Titanic's set course, which was congested with ice floes. After the change of command, Lightoller retires to the officers quarters, situated directly behind the Bridge. The entire ship is now in Murdock's hands.

One hour and forty minutes into Murdock's watch, the Titanic strikes the iceberg. The Bridge slowly builds with activity as Inar lay on the deck. Damage reports are being received over the Bridge intercom. The engine room is reporting water flooding upward through the hull flooring. The coal compartments are reporting flooding as well. Crew members are fleeing topside, and officers are reporting to the Bridge awaiting orders. Written messages are handed to Murdock from the Marconi Room, and he begins dispatch of orders to ships officers.

Arriving on the Bridge Deck are sea men Arter and Brice. They have taken Inar onto the Bridge and over to First Officer Murdock. Amidst the escalating activity, Murdock turns slightly to address the two sea men. A second look has him staring, he is taken aback by Inar's appearance. Murdock looks Inar up and down, his seal skin parka and mukluks still glistening with speckles and ice chips from the iceberg. "Explain to me, what is going on here," insists Murdock.

"Sir! We found this man on the forward well-deck. I think he is a stowaway," shouts Arter over the din of activity.

"On the forward well? What in bloody blazes is a stowaway doing on the deck of the forward well?" Murdock asks.

"We don't rightly know sir, he was found by a few Third Class passengers," explains Brice.

"What do you want from me? Can't you see I'm in the middle of a bloody crises?" shouts Murdock. "Yes, sir. We need orders to take custody of this prisoner, with full arrest powers, sir," says Brice. Murdock rolls his eyes. "That you have, now put him in cuffs and take him below to the Orlop!" Murdock orders. Inar is pulled out of the congested Bridge, and they continue to the Orlop Deck at the bottom of the hull. Only a few meters away from the Bridge, they come across more crew members and officers. Orders are being requested from the crew and ship's engineers. The officers begin shouting out emergency status commands.

Captain Smith arrives on the bridge, just as Third Officer Pittman pushes his way in. Pittman informs Murdock and Smith in a grave voice.

"The ship has struck an iceberg!" Pittman proclaims in a restrained shout. A large quantity of ice has tumbled down onto the forward decks and I ordered its removal over the side, sir," reports Pittman. "Very well, assemble your crew and ready them to uncover the lifeboats. Captain Smith shall take command of the Bridge," says Murdock.

Second Officer Lightoller steps out of the officers quarters wearing only his pajamas. Standing at the Bridge Deck railing, Lightoller surveys the surrounding area on the starboard side of the ship. Looking towards the bridge he sees Murdock and Captain Smith standing inside the bridge amidst other officers.

Even though Lightoller had knowledge of iceberg warnings, he somehow felt that there is no call for him to be on deck. With nothing to be concerned about, Lightoller returns to his berth. From the corner of his eye he sees Inar being escorted down the stairwell.

"What have you there?" Lightoller hollers. The two sea men pull Inar to a halt. Brice looks at Inar, then turns to Lightoller. "A stowaway sir, we found him on the forward well-deck amidst the ice, sir?" says Arter.

"Ice you say?" Lightoller asks. "Yes, sir. Apparently we scraped along side an iceberg," the crew member says. Lightoller falls silent, and slowly turns to go back into his sleeping quarters. The two sea men continue to the Orlop with their prisoner.

Descending the decks they pass the ship's Infirmary. "Do you think it would have made more sense to take the prisoner to quarantine at the ship's infirmary?" Arter asks. "If Mr. Murdock wanted him in quarantine quarters, he would have instructed us to do so, but I see your point, there are bars over the port windows in the Infirmary," says Brice.

"Where do you suppose we should put him?" Arter asks. "My guess would be near the stern of the Orlop. There are still some empty store rooms there, being that First Class wasn't full booked," says Brice.

Tanaya continues the narration of Inar's account. "We kept going down into that big boat, down towards the bottom. The man that hobbled my wrists, he did it wrong. I could move my arms just a little bit and pull my wrists out, but they did not know, so we just kept walking.

"It was a big boat, the deeper we went, the hotter it got for me. We just kept walking until we ran across some men that looked more hotter than I. They had sweat and fire soot all over their skin and clothes," Inar says through translation.

Jane hands Harrison a page out of the Senate Hearing transcripts. "This is an account of the steam engine room Engineer and other personnel as they fled from the bottom compartments of the ship," says Harrison as he begins to read the transcript aloud;

"We were scrambling towards topside, still wondering why the bloody engines were still powered at near full speed. We came upon two of the ship's sea men with an Eskimo! I hollered to them, what're doing down here? You fools! The ship is taking on water, she's flooding out!" Harrison reads. He then glances over to Jane.

"Well, you can't get any plainer than that. The two sea men were Arter and Brice." Jane says as she takes down notes. Tanaya continues narrating Inar's account.

"Those men seemed angry, they shouted something at us. Then I got pulled away again. I don't know why, but those two kept pulling me faster and faster," says Tanaya.

Jane interjects. "Why didn't they just follow the fleeing men to the upper decks?" Jane asks.

"Orders are orders." Harrison replies. "That must've been it, because according to Uncle's account, he didn't know what was happening, but he knew they were all in danger," says Tanaya. Harrison pulls out a diagram of Titanic's Orlop Deck and spreads it on the table.

"This deck diagram shows that they were nearing the mail room when they ran into the steam engineer. The sea men come upon the rapidly rising sea water, which would put them right about here," says Harrison as he points to the diagram.

"Arter locates a ship's intercom and makes contact with the Bridge, but before the he can get two words out, their orders are shouted out through the intercom. 'Get topside at once!' Unable to complete their detail, they hastily find a storage room.

"This is as good as any brig," says Arter. "We can't do this, the ship's compartments are flooding! This man will surely drown," says Brice. As he begins to unlock the door.

"This man is a prisoner, a stowaway, we have been charged with his custody. Our orders are to have him jailed, this storage room is now a brig," says Arter. Brice looks Inar in the eyes as he pulls the key out of the door lock. Arter turns a light switch and Inar is pushed inside. The door is slammed shut, and a key slides under the door. The two sea men begin running up the corridor towards the stair well," reads Jane from a transcript.

"Those two men, they shoved me into a room. Then I could hear the pounding of their feet when they ran away from me. I thought, maybe I should followed them, but I didn't like those two men. I decided to stay away from them and try to get out of that place, I tried the door and it wasn't even locked," he adds smiling to himself.

"So I peeked outside, and they were gone. It made me glad, I was tired of them dragging me around. After I pulled the handcuff off the other hand I stayed there in that room. There was something wrong with that light above me, it kept going off and on," he says.

Inar is sitting on a stack of boxes, wondering what he should do next. Looking around his confined quarters, he can see stacks of fish. After surviving on seal meat for weeks, his hunger showed through his stomach. While staring at a gallon can of fish, a deep growl dominated his flight instincts.

"I reached for the can. It had a salmon on it, but to me it looked like a small whale," says Inar in recollection. "'I had this knife that was from my grandfather. In prayer my thoughts of thanks were offered. I pulled out my knife and stabbed the fish until its juices came out. It was good a fish." Inar says in translation.

"The angle of the ship kept going tilting. It was now at a point that those canned fish were reaching the edge of the shelf. Then all at once, all those cans of salmon tumbled down onto the floor. Water began to flow under the door. It was time for me to get out of that room. I took a can of fish, and slowly pulled the door open. There was no great pressure on the other side so I opened it wide. Only a weak ebb of sea water flowed in. I left as fast as I could.

"I began to make my way up towards the top of the boat. There was this man, he had white clothes on, he came running down the stairs and ran right into me. He jumped up and started yelling at me. Those people sure get angry over nothing," says Tanaya through Inar's translation.

"In the transcripts, there are a few lines where a steward named McMurry, testified that there was an Eskimo wandering around in the Second Class State Room corridor," says Jane.

"You can't be here, this is the Second Class Deck. Get back to Steerage wait until you are called," reads Jane.

Tanaya picks up the translation again; "There were a few men with hand tools, they are trying to open a metal plate in the floor. For whatever reason, they did not succeed and walked further towards the upside of the ship. There were others, pounding on doors and hollering something, and they had things that looked like white goose bags piled into their arms," relates Inar. "Life preservers," adds Tanaya.

"That's very interesting. I ran across a part of the transcripts that depicts an incident where Senator Smith was told of crew members opening hatches in the floor of the Titanic before she went down. Here read this account and decide for yourself," says Harrison handing Jane a some pages.

Jane begins to read from the Senate Hearing transcripts as stated by a First Class passenger named Mr. George Harder.

Senator SMITH:

What occurred Sunday night between the hours of 11 and 12 o'clock?

Mr. HARDER:

About a quarter to 11 I went down to my stateroom with Mrs. Harder and retired for the night; and at 20 minutes to 12 we were not asleep yet, and I heard this thump. It was not a loud thump; just a dull thump. Then I could feel the boat quiver and could feel a sort of rumbling, scraping noise along the side of the boat. When I went to the porthole I saw this iceberg go by. The porthole was closed. The iceberg was, I should say, about 50 to 100 feet away. I should say it was about as high as the top deck of the boat. I just got a glimpse of it, and it is hard to tell how high it was.

Senator SMITH:

What did you do then?

Mr. HARDER:

I thought we would go up on deck to see what had happened; what damage had been done. So we dressed fully and went up on deck, and there we saw quite a number of people talking; and nobody seemed to think anything serious had happened. There were such remarks as 'Oh, it will only be a few hours before we will be on the way again.' I walked around the deck two or three times, when I noticed that the boat was listing quite a good deal on the starboard side; so Mrs. Harder and myself thought we would go inside and see if there was any news. We went in there and talked to a few people, and all of them seemed of the opinion that it was nothing serious.

Senator SMITH:

Who were these people with whom you talked? Do you know?

Mr. HARDER:

I do not know. I do not know the names.

Senator SMITH:

Were Mr. and Mrs. Bishop there?

Mr. HARDER:
Yes. I saw Mr. and Mrs. Bishop, and I saw Colonel and Mrs. Astor, and they all seemed to be of the opinion that there was no danger. A little while after that an officer appeared at the foot of the stairs, and he announced that everybody should go to their staterooms and put on their lifebelts.

Senator SMITH:
How long was that after the collision?

Mr. HARDER:
That, I think, was a little after 12 - about 12 o'clock; that is, roughly. So, we immediately went down to our stateroom and took our lifebelts and coats and started up the stairs and went to the top deck. There, we saw the crew manning the lifeboats; getting them ready; swinging them out. So we waited around there, and we were finally told "Go over this way; go over this way." So we followed and went over toward the first lifeboat, where Mr. and Mrs. Bishop were. That boat was filled, and so they told us to move on to the next one.

Senator SMITH:
On which side?

Mr. HARDER:
The starboard side.

Senator SMITH:
So that the first boat was filled.
Mr. HARDER:
Yes. Somebody told us to move down toward the second one. We got to the second one, and we were told to go right in there. I have been told that Ismay took hold of my wife's arm, I do not know him, but I have been told that he did and pushed her right in. Then I followed.
Senator SMITH:
How far did you have to step from the side of the ship into the lifeboat?
Mr. HARDER:
I should say it was about a foot and a half. Anyway, you had to jump. When I jumped in there, one foot went in between the oars, and I got in there and could not move until somebody pulled me over. I forgot to say that when I went down into my stateroom in order to get the lifebelts, when we came out of the stateroom with the lifebelts I noticed about four or five men on this deck, and one of them had one of those T-handled wrenches, used to turn some kind of a nut or bolt, and two or three of the other men had wrenches with them, Stilson wrenches, or something like that. I did not take any particular notice, but I did notice this one man trying to turn this thing in the

floor. There was a brass plate or something there.

Senator SMITH:

Was it marked "W. T."?

Mr. HARDER:

Yes; it was marked, "W. T.," and I do not know whether it was a "D" after that or something else. A few days before that, however, I noticed that brass plate, and, naturally, seeing the initials, "W. T.," I thought it meant watertight doors, or compartments.

Senator SMITH:

Was it in the floor?

Mr. HARDER:

Yes.

Senator SMITH:

On what deck?

Mr. HARDER:

On E deck. It was on the starboard side of the boat, in the alleyway. I think this brass plate was situated between the stairs and the elevators. The stairs were right in front of the elevators, and right in between there, I think, was this brass plate. We heard one of these men with the wrenches say: 'Well, it's no use. This one won't work. Let's try another one.' They did not seem to be nervous at all; so I thought at the time there was no danger; that they were just doing that for the sake of precaution.

Senator SMITH:

Did any of those men state, in your hearing, the importance of being able to turn that bolt or not?

Mr. HARDER:

No, sir; they did not.

Senator SMITH:

Did you gather from what you saw that it was connected directly with the watertight compartments?

Mr. HARDER:

Yes, sir, I thought it was. I related the incident to Mr. Bishop after the accident.

Senator SMITH:

How large was this plate?

Mr. HARDER:

The plate was, I should say, about ten inches or a foot wide. It was about circular. I do not remember anything else about it, except that it had the initials, "W. T. C." or "W. T. D." or something like that. I know it had the initials "W. T." and something else."

Harrison takes the documents as Jane hands them back. "I don't understand. Why would they be opening the water tight hatches?" Jane asks.

"I'm thinking that they were trying to open escape hatches for passengers and crew men who may've been trapped below," says Harrison.

Meanwhile, all officers have reported to their stations, and stewards are frantically combing First and Second Class cabins for passengers. Terrified women and children are screaming as they make their way to the lifeboats. The chaos becomes greater as Inar nears the upper decks.

"I could tell by the sounds that things were getting worse and the people were thinking of the freezing water, and I could see in their eyes, their will to survive was becoming weaker. I kept climbing, fighting the people, trying to stay on my feet. Then, I felt the cold of the open air, when I reached the top, then somebody knocked me down. There were people running in all directions, trying to get into small boats," relates Inar.

On the streets below, a siren from a New York City Police car breaks Inar's account of the sinking. Jane and Harrison sit motionless in their seats, waiting for Inar to continue telling Tanaya what he experienced in the early morning hours of April 15, 1912. Just as Inar resumes his experience, the door buzzer sounds.

"Hooray for food and drink, it's intermission time folks," says Harrison as he goes to buzz in a delivery boy. Inar begins to perspire and stands to take off his parka. Jane watches with interest as he lays the parka over the chair.

"May I?" She asks as she points to his parka. Inar nods "yes" and the parka is lifted off the chair, she it drops to the floor.

"Jeez, it must weigh at least fifteen pounds." Jane says. "It's made from seal, and it's why Uncle survived the freezing waters of the Atlantic," says Tanaya. Jane applies both hands as she lifts the heavy parka from the floor.

"The story is absolutely fascinating and equally as frightening. Reading about it in the papers is one thing, but hearing it first hand - damned scary." Jane explains. Harrison opens his apartment door to pay for the delivery.

"Orlop. What is that, I've never heard such a word, Uncle could not explain it, but he said that's what the sea men called it," says Tanaya.

"The word is pronounced or-lap. It is Middle English from Dutch, pronounced over-loop. It's the lowest deck of a wooden sailing ship with three or more decks. That's the way Webster described it in his book." Harrison says as he walks into the kitchen with a large bag of Chinese food. "Thank you for that, now I can sleep tonight." Jane says feigning relief.

"For our friend Inar, I have a surprise - Prawns! Bet you've never had these before." Harrison hands Inar the container and watches as he takes his first bite of prawn. A smile comes over his face as he takes another bite.

A photo of the Titanic captain falls out of a folder and onto the floor. Inar reaches down to pick up the photo and as he does, he begins to explain something in his native tongue. Tanaya places her chop sticks down neatly on the table, and asks him to repeat what he had just said.

"Uncle just explained something that I think you should know." Tanaya says as she takes a photo from a pile of Titanic's officers and crew. Uncle says this man also stopped him from getting into a small boat," says Tanaya.

"Captain Smith, by all accounts, remained on the bridge to the very end," offers Jane.

"Hold on, lets hear what Inar has to say. He just identified a photo of the captain, who's to say it wasn't the last anyone saw of the man," says Harrison. Tanaya continues the conversation with Inar. "The boat was a smaller one, not the same size as white boats or lifeboats; he says this one was as black as the sea," translates Tanaya.

Harrison spoons another portion of chow mien into his mouth, and explains that Smith returned to the bridge just before she sank. Had Smith been at one of the davits waiting to board a life boat, someone would have seen him and it would have been reported," says Harrison.

"What if Inar was the last to see the captain alive?" Jane challenges.

Tanaya continues the conversation with Inar, and he begins to explain assertively using his hands to emphasize his point. In translation, Tanaya begins.

"On the night the big boat sank, I was pushed away from a skin boat..."

"Collapsible boat." Tanaya interjects.

"...by this man." Inar says, pointing to Second Officer Lightoller.

"Then this man, pushed me away too." He adds.

"That being Captain Smith." Tanaya says.

"This, same man, right there! Climbed into the small boat that was black, not white," Tanaya translates further. At this point, Harrison and Jane put their chopsticks down.

Looking at each other, they turn to Inar just as he happily devours the remainder of prawns. Both spring to their feet and hurry towards the coffee table where the deposition documents are sorted. Harrison shuffles through the documents then divides the ream in-half.

"Here, I've got it right here." Harrison says, as he begins to read the court transcript.

"...after several attempts to communicate with other ships, the nearest to Titanic was a vessel that was all but blacked out. This vessel was recorded as being an "unknown" ship, and she failed to respond, after numerous attempts." Harrison reads.

"Harrison, Uncle would like to know if you are going to eat the rest of your chow mien?" Tanaya asks.

"If this turns out to be what we think it is, he'll be able to book a cruise to China and eat all the chow mien he wants. Help yourself Inar...I've seemed to have lost my appetite over this little inadvertent discovery," says Harrison.

"I may not eat for a week. Now, listen to this; as recorded from witness testimony of Fourth Officer Boxall; 'From the bridge, the lights of a ship could be seen off the starboard side, she was approximately 10 to 15 miles away. The ship was not responding to our wireless messages, nor was she responding to the distress rockets being launched every fifteen minutes. Quartermaster George Thomas Rowe and myself attempted to signal the ship with a

Morse Lamp, but the ship never appeared to respond," reads Jane from the court transcripts.

"If we count the 'unknown' vessel, that's three ships within the vicinity of the Titanic as she sank. Considering ice fields, and other ice bergs. How long do you think it would take to travel ten to fifteen miles at sea?" Jane asks.

"Court records show that at twenty nautical knots...half an hour, forty-five minutes at the most. A ship as big as Titanic, traveling in calm waters at 21 knots, can cover 600 to 700 meters in one minute." Harrison replies.

"Tell me, how long can the average human being last in freezing waters before succumbing to hypothermia?" Jane asks in disgust.

"Every minute was crucial to the survival of the passengers. As I recall, there had been a considerable amount of speculation about this 'unknown' ship. Without taking on a single person from the wreck, the ship sailed off without returning to the wreck site," says Harrison.

"I read in another part of the hearing transcripts, that there were public inquiries into independent statements given by Captain Moore of the S.S. Mount Temple and Captain Arthur Rostron of the S.S.

Carpathia. Both captains stated that they had sighted the lights of a vessel close by the sinking. They prayed this ship would reach the Titanic in time to take on her passengers, or aid in a rescue," says Harrison.

CHAPTER EIGHT
The Black Boat

The problem is, in a court of law, there has to be a degree of certainty. In their testimonies, both were certain they sighted the same vessel, and both identified the lights to be that of a sailing vessel. Both Rostron and Moore also gave testimony that, later when daylight came on the morning of April 15, they saw a Steamer within the vicinity which they identified as having two masts and one funnel. It is very clear that the S.S. Californian had four masts." Jane offers.

"Ask Inar what happened after the 'black boat' left the sinking 'boat whale' - where did it go?" Harrison asks. Tanaya places her hand on Inar's arm as the last of the chow mien is eaten. Inar reaches for a bottle of beer and takes a long draw of the sudsy brew. Ahhh, he expresses, as he puts the bottle down. A loud burp then follows, and Inar gives a hearty laugh.

"He says that he can remember lights," says Tanaya. "There were lights from the night sky, like many days passing before me," says Inar through translation.

"My guess it was Titanic's flares." Tanaya offers. "It was after that, the small black boat rowed away, in a direction that was going against the drift of the ice field. It went out of sight, about the same time it takes to empty a full, white bear skin bladder."

"A full bear bladder," says Harrison scratching his head in frustration. "Would that be a live bear or one taken from a dead bear?" Harrison asks.

"Dead bear, Socrates. My guess it would be about the size of a large leather Bota Bag, or a primeval wine bag," Jane offers.

"Got it. Put a Bohemian Bota Bag on the list of lab test materials, jheese, can't wait to hear the judge's ruling on this objection," says Harrison.

"Definitely one for the books," says Jane, as she places several documents on the table directly in front to Harrison.

"Believe it or not, what Inar just said fits right in with the transcripts, see for yourself." Jane says.

The Boxhall Testimonial is read by Harrison aloud; "At 12:45 a.m., quartermaster George Arthur Rowe and myself began to fire rockets from an angled rail attached to Titanic's bridge. Rowe continued to do so until the rockets ran out around 1:25, and while Rowe was thus engaged, I continued to scan the horizon. It was around 1:30 a.m. when I spotted what appeared to be a Steamer in the distance, I immediately directed Rowe to try contacting the vessel by way of a Morse lamp. Strange as it was, the Steamer continued on its way and we were unsuccessful at the attempt. It was at that one point I sought reassurance from the Captain and asked if he felt the situation was really serious, Smith replied that the ship would sink within an hour."

"If I read that part of the Testimonial correctly, Senator Fletcher asked Boxhall outright, if he saw a Steamer that night about the time after the collision. Boxall answered,

'yes'," indicates Harrison. "Ask Inar if he had seen another big boat on the night of the sinking."

Inar begins to convey his story, slowly at first, then shortly into the account, he becomes excited and starts telling the story with hand motions.

"At first I saw two lights on top of a high pole, like a lodge pole, it was part of that boat. When it came closer, I could see that the boat had lights shining from its side, but not the flow of the current side."

"If I'm not mistaken, he means the starboard side." Harrison says as he settles back on the couch in deep thought.

"Okay everyone, listen-up. Tomorrow night we are all going down to the dock. There, we will watch for ships on the horizon. Inar, will then continue to reach into his miraculous memory, to show us just how far this mystery ship was away from the Titanic." Harrison says, in a studious manner.

"The transcripts read that this ship was at least five miles away and heading right towards the Titanic...and it was a clear night." Jane points out. Okay, if it's foggy, we'll go to Plan B," replies Harrison.

"That be the one following Plan A?" Jane asks, as she stares through Harrison. "There is no plan B, is there...?"

"Oh, ye of little faith. Plan B entails perching ourselves on the East dock of Ellis Island and wait for incoming ships to pass. We have to get an idea of the distance in the line-of-sight of a ship, any ship. It's circumstantial, but worth a try," says Harrison. He pulls a few more notes from several piles of documents scattered over the coffee table.

"Boxhall stated that he had been firing off rockets before he saw the mystery ships side lights. He also stated that he and another ship's officer continued to fire the distress rockets. They did so, until the oncoming ship was so close, he could see the lights on her starboard side," explains Harrison. "I saw the side lights with my naked eye," reads Jane from the Boxhall account.

"What an outrageous act of cowardliness! This was stated to a British Board of Inquiry, and the statement was allowed. Incredible," says Jane, adamantly.

"The research I had been doing, early in the investigation, had to do with Captain Smith's track record as a ship's commander. I concluded that as a commander, he was worthy upon the high sea, but was known for taking risks. There could have been a remote possibility that the sinking could have been insurance related," she adds.

"What was it that made you change your mind?" Harrison asks with a small barb. Was it your research that led you to the glaring fact that White Star attorneys were withholding evidence? How about Captain Smith's last voyage? They could not produce any documentation that could prove retirement plans were in order for Smith. If that were not a case in point, then how about this; if there is retirement, they had not designated who was going to take over his command of Titanic," says Harrison.

Jane withholds any comment, knowing he is right. Instead, she expresses herself with an inaudible. "Butt hole," she says.

"I heard that," says Harrison, too engrossed in the research, to give a decent comeback.

"What I meant to say was; but hold your horses. Here is what I came up with," she says, as she hands another page of research over to Harrison. "Notes," Harrison begins to read aloud. He glances up to see Jane recline into a comfortable position. A confident expression gives Harrison a clue that her research effort is solid.

"This account was taken by Senator Smith on day thirteen. John Robinson Binns was employed by White Star as a qualified Marconi radio operator. Mr. Binns was supposed to be on the Titanic on that fateful night, but Ismay ordered him to the Olympic. Nonetheless, he gave valuable testimony on the construction of both ships. Apparently, the Titanic and the Olympic were required to have double hulls. To win a subsidy from the British Government, the ship was to be commissioned as a mail carrier, hence R.M.S. Titanic, or Royal Mail Steamer Titanic. The Royal Mail system is Britain's equivalent to the U.S. Postal system, and it was the British Board of Trade that ordered the double hull to be mandatory," reads Harrison from Jane's research notes. He then goes on to read the Binns Hearing testimony.

Senator SMITH:
"Have you observed any part of the construction of the Olympic, on which you served, which was followed in the construction of her sister ship, the Titanic, which you think would be of interest to the committee?"

Mr. BINNS:
"The Olympic has what is known as two expansion joints. These joints are composed in this way: The ship is split completely through the deck and also through the sides of the ship to a point above the waterline; the split is then joined over by a curved piece of steel, which is riveted to each side of the severed part of the ship, The idea of this joint is to reduce the excessive vibrations caused by the high speed of the ship. In my opinion this is an element of weakness and tends to detract from its structural strength. This I observed on the Olympic; and the Titanic was built in the same way. The same feature was followed in the Titanic, which vessel I observed before her launching and the

launching of which I also witnessed in Belfast.

"I have observed steamship construction, and am quite familiar with the plans of the Olympic and the Titanic. Also, those of the Mauretania and the Lusitania of the Cunard Line.

"From the plans of the Olympic and the Titanic the vessel has been built to meet every possible accident, except for a glancing blow of an iceberg, such as the Titanic received. The ship has a certain number of watertight compartments. Moreover a double bottom; but according to the plans the sides of the ship are just a single "shell under the waterline, and in the event of a glancing blow extending from one end of the ship to the other the watertight compartments would be rendered absolutely useless, owing to the fact that there is no side protection.

"In the plans of the Mauretania and Lusitania, these vessels are shown to have double cellular sides as well as a double cellular bottom. Also, on the inside of the inner plating of the cellular sides are the coal bunkers, which can also be turned into watertight compartments. If there is a glancing blow ripping up the side of one of these vessels, the ship would still remain afloat, owing to the presence of the inner shell of the vessel's cellular sides. In the event of both the outer and inner plates of the vessel's double cellular side being pierced, an extra protection is afforded by the coal bunkers, which could be temporarily turned into watertight compartments. This is a very strong point in ship construction, and no vessel should in the future be allowed to be built without this double protection, which, in my opinion, makes a ship really unsinkable.

"As nearly as I can remember, this double cellular side construction which I have described was a condition precedent to the granting of a subsidy by the British Government to these ships," Binns testifies, he is then excused as a witness.

Harrison closes the folder. "I keep wondering why Senator Smith didn't pursue that bit of astounding testimony," say Jane.

"It's not what it seems. You have to remember, this is a hearing, not a trial. Senator Smith simply obtained the information through testimony. It was up to the public to put it together. Three years have passed and nothing has been brought into a court of law," explains Harrison.

Jane hands Harrison another folder, marked 'Boiler Explosion/Mystery Ship' and encourages him to read further. Daniel

Buckley, a Third Class passenger who claimed to have had a ship's fire stoker state to him; that it wasn't an iceberg that sank the ship, but an over stoked boiler. Buckley also gave his account on day thirteen. "More ammunition," says Jane

Senator SMITH.

"Mr. Buckley, where do you live?"

Mr. BUCKLEY.

"855 Trent Avenue, Bronx."

Senator SMITH.

"How old are you?"

Mr. BUCKLEY.

"Twenty-one years old."

Senator SMITH.

"Where did you get aboard the Titanic?"

Mr. BUCKLEY.

"At Queenstown."

Senator SMITH.

"Had you been living in Ireland?"

Mr. BUCKLEY.

"Yes; I lived in King Williamstown, Town Court. I wanted to come over here to make some money. I came in the Titanic because she was a new steamer. This night of the wreck I was sleeping in my room on the Titanic, in the steerage. There were three other boys from the same place sleeping in the same room with me.

"I heard some terrible noise and I jumped out on the floor, and the first thing I knew my feet were getting wet; the water was just coming in slightly. I told the other fellows to get up, that there was something wrong and, that the water was coming in. They only laughed at me. One of them says: 'Get back into bed. You are not in Ireland now.'

"I got on my clothes as quick as I could, and the three other fellows got out. The room was very small, so I got out, to give them room to dress themselves.

"Two sailors came along, and they were shouting: 'All up on deck! Unless you want to get drowned.'

"When I heard this, I went for the deck as quick as I could. When I got up on the deck I saw everyone having those lifebelts on only myself; so I got sorry, and said I would go back again where I was sleeping and get one of those life preservers; because there was one there for each person.

"I went back again, and just as I was going down the last flight of stairs the water was up four steps, and dashing up. I did not go back into the room, because I could not.

When I went back toward the room the water was coming up three steps up the stairs, or four steps; so I did not go any farther. I got back on the deck again, and just as I got back there, I was looking around to see if I could get any of those lifebelts, and I met a First Class passenger, and he had two. He gave me one, and fixed it on me.

"Then the lifeboats were preparing. There were five lifeboats sent out. I was in the sixth. I was holding the ropes all the time, helping to let down the five lifeboats that went down first, as well as I could.

"When the sixth lifeboat was prepared, there was a big crowd of men standing on the deck. They all jumped in. So I said I would take my chance with them.

Senator SMITH.

"Who were they?

Mr. BUCKLEY.

"Passengers and sailors and fire stokers mixed. There were no ladies there at the same time. When they jumped, I said I would go too. I went into the boat. Then two officers came along and said all the men could come out. And they brought a lot of steerage passengers with them; and they were mixed, every way, ladies and gentlemen. And they said all the men could get out and let the ladies in. But six men were left in the boat. I think they were firemen and sailors.

"I was crying. There was a woman in the boat, and she had thrown her shawl over me, and she told me to stay in there. I believe she was Mrs. Astor. Then they did not see me, and the boat was lowered down into the water, and we rowed away out from the steamer. Buckley was in lifeboat number 13 while Mrs. Astor was in boat number 4.

"The men that were in the boat at first fought, and would not get out, but the officers drew their revolvers, and fired shots over our heads, and then the men got out. When the boat was ready, we were lowered down into the water and rowed away out from the steamer. We were only about 15 minutes out when she sank."
Senator SMITH.
"What else happened?"
Mr. BUCKLEY.
"One of the firemen that was working on the Titanic told me, when I got on board the Carpathia and he was speaking to me, that he did not think it was any iceberg; that it was only that they wanted to make a record, and they ran too much steam and the boilers bursted. That is what he said.

"We sighted the lights of the big steamer, the Carpathia. All the women got into a terrible commotion and jumped around. They were hallooing and the sailors were trying to keep them sitting down, and they would not do it. They were standing up all the time.

"When we got into the Carpathia we were treated very good. We got all kinds of refreshments," relates Buckley. The witness is then excused by Senator Smith.

"A boiler explosion could explain the 'hollow thump' Mr. Harder testified to hearing about the same time the Titanic struck the iceberg," says Harrison.

"If that's the case, then the boiler would have exploded causing ship to take on water, before the helms man turned into the iceberg," says Jane.

A guttural rumbling draws their attention, at the far end of the couch, Inar lays in a deep sleep, Inar has begun to snore loudly. Trying to carry on with the work at hand, but the relentless snoring causes them to surrender to the unearthly sounds coming from Inar.

"Okay. Sounds like our star witness has caught the Chow Mien Express. Tanaya, are you all right with your sleeping arrangements at Jane's apartment tonight" Tanaya nods yes, as she and Jane gather their things and reorganize the folders of documents.

"One last thing on Captain Smith that is noteworthy. The big question is; why was Smith chosen over Captain Bertram Hays, who was promoted to Commodore for maneuvering the Olympic into position that saved her from sinking. Also more competent, was a Captain Bartlett who was commended for the brilliant evacuation of Britannic. All three liners are of the White Star Ocean Liner Company." Jane says stopping at the door.

"Hot-diggity-dog, a partner that's not afraid to admit she was wrong," Harrison says.

The comment stops Jane at the door. "I may not always be right, but I'm never wrong." She says with a smile. "Didn't you know? Wrong has been redefined in Webster's Dictionary. Wrong is when someone orders a transatlantic passenger ocean liner into a shipping lane clogged with icebergs at full speed. That is wrong," adds Jane.

"Touche. You can add my sentiments to that growing list." Harrison says as she closes the door. Harrison goes to the couch where Inar has fallen asleep. Not wanting to wake him, Harrison lifts his legs onto the couch and pulls his mukluks off of Inar's feet. A knitted afghan is then laid onto his chest.

In the solitude of his bedroom, Harrison continues his research into the evidence that Jane had generated. Reading silently into the research, Jane's last statement concerning Smith's appointed charge of the Titanic's voyage, begins to haunt him. A newspaper story is pulled from the folder.

SMITH'S VESSEL STRIKES WAR SHIP

17 April 1914   Washington Times

If the twentieth century retained a belief in the power of malignant spirits and the human passions of natural forces, the termination of the career of Captain E. J. Smith, of the Titanic, would afford a stunning example of the jealous power of Neptune. For this captain, after a clear record of forty-three years on the high seas, was the victim of a series of accidents that amounted in seriousness to the final annihilation of Captain Smith and his vessel.

Last September, as captain of the Olympic, the Titanic's sister ship, Captain Smith underwent the ordeal of an inquiry after his vessel crashed into the British cruiser Hawke. He was retained in the service. In February the Olympic struck what is supposed to have been a submerged wreck, and lost a propeller blade. The vessel was docked at great expense for repairs. Leaving Southampton last week, as captain of the largest vessel in the world, Captain Smith's ship narrowly averted crashing into the New York an American Ocean Steamer. Three times within eight months had this officer, with a previous record of nearly half a century, met with mishap that crippled the ships under his command. The fatal collision between the Titanic and an iceberg was the last chapter in Captain Smith's career was written.

It is a mystery how Captain Smith twice avoided the decree that mandated a surrender of his command, and the vessel under his command at the time of the sea borne accident. The action of the surrender of command was demanded by the ship's owners. Lloyds Marine Insurance Group, one of White Star insurers, required accident and incident reports of all its ships covered under their umbrella. Questions concerning Titanic's owners and their suspicious appointments to command the great ship, was hit upon lightly in the hearings.

Why did the insurance companies pay out for hull damage and cargo policies, if the ship's commander exhibited obvious culpability? Why didn't the insurance companies investigate Captain Smith and his appointment by Titanic's owners? Had an investigation been brought, findings would have indicated that Captain Smith, on a certain level, could not guarantee a safe Atlantic passage for the Titanic and her passengers. Investors were scrambling for cover. Under controlled informational release, Captain Smith's career was deemed excellent. It was known by White Star and Titanic investors, the history of Smith's accidents. The owners continued to retain Smith in its ranks as an officer, sea worthy, and competent.

The Olympic, also a White Star vessel, fell victim to Smith's bad luck. An oversight that will plague the owners of White Star, as long as the Titanic will be remembered. This intentional over sight will prove to be a willful violation of regulated international high sea protocol.

This protocol had been rigorously maintained by the British Merchant Marine ships, as was then by that of any other nation. The rule has been almost invariable among steamship companies to dispense with the services of officers in command of vessels that met with disaster. One reason for this regulated protocol, is at the insistence of the insurance companies. It is known among experienced and qualified sea captains, that none in their ranks would have been appointed to command another vessel, or any vessel. Under a veiled account, the night of April 14-15, 1912, it was reported that Captain Smith went down with the Titanic. Had Smith survived, his career would have been exposed in a series of legal proceedings. There would have no escape from the Rumors and questions surrounding the wreck.

The Oceanic Steam Navigation Company, another of Titanic's owners, attempted to limit its liability in the United States. The case was brought in a United States District Court in June 1913. Key to the case was the amount of money to be paid out in claim settlements. Oceanic began to seek out survivors as witnesses in their case. To prove criminal negligence, an effort would be brought by Oceanic to provide compelling evidence. Hoping that someone in First Class, had overheard J. Bruce Ismay order Smith to set a transatlantic record. This evidence would show, the loss of the Titanic was caused indirectly by the Smith, in risking life and property on a full-speed course to New York. The evidence brought by Oceanic was at best circumstantial, with survivors not willing to lean towards questioning that involved the term 'make a record' pertaining to Titanic's speed.

Bruce Ismay, was President of International Mercantile Marine Company.

The loss of the Titanic drastically effected its owners and boards under them, was not voted to remain as a director of the White Star Ocean Liner Company, and he was refused his position as president by the board of International Mercantile Marine Company. Even though his board seat had been dismissed, he was allowed to remain a director of the IMMC. Captain Smith, had he survived the Titanic, would have suffered the same fate as his cohort Ismay.

An ineffective investigation of the Titanic sinking was carried out by Lloyd's of London. This prominent British insurance group, was called upon by the court to present files specific to White Star holdings. In their guarded depositions, they check the records of marine officers, so when a man is put in command of a vessel his whole career can be immediately inspected. Whether this 'grand old man of the sea' was at fault for the disaster of the Titanic, depended in a great measure on the degree of vigilance used by his officers and crew.

When it comes to sea born accidents, White Star has been amongst the most uncompromising of the British liner companies. Case in point, as is evidenced in the fate of Captain Inman Sealby, who commanded the SS Republic on January

23, 1909 when she sank in a collision with the SS Florida. The other ship involved in the accident was a vessel out of the Lloyd Italiano Transoceanic Steamship Line. The accident left the Florida with massive damage to her bow. The design of the ship's construction, prevented her from sinking.

The damaged ship limped back to New York, and to dry dock. No blame was placed on Captain Sealby for faulty navigation of the Republic. Captain Sealby had been at sea for all his career. The history of his command over numerous ships was unimpaired. Nevertheless, White Star dismissed Sealby. Captain Smith began his sea career in 1869, when he gained an apprenticeship on board the Senator Weber, an American built clipper ship. The Senator Weber was bought by A. Gibson & Co., of Liverpool. In 1876, Smith achieved a commission as fourth officer of the square rigger Lizzie Fennel. In 1880, Smith was appointed to a fourth officer position in White Star's old steamship, Celtic. This ship, was subsequently sold to the Thingvalla Company, and later renamed the America. Afterwards, he attained the rank of captain in 1887. The promotion to captain opened the door, and access to another ship command. The owners of the Republic, requested his command. After his tour on the Republic, commission to other ships were placed in line. The owners of the old Baltic, gladly accepted him for a command position. Next he was placed in command of the freight SS Cufic, and then the Runic. Afterward he went to the old Adriatic.

It was in 1892 that the White Star bestowed its first great honor on Captain Smith, when it made him commander of its largest steamship, SS Majestic. Since that time he has commanded each large steamship of White Star on her initial trip. When he was put in command of the Titanic, it was reported that he would retire after he had conducted her across the Atlantic and back. Instead, White Star officials, afterward, announced he would have charge of the Titanic until the company built a larger and finer Steamer. Captain Smith was said to have had the utmost confidence in the safety of the ocean giants. In 1907, when he came to New York in command of the Adriatic, on her maiden trip, he said: "Shipbuilding is such a perfect art nowadays that absolute disaster, involving the passengers, is inconceivable. Whatever happens, there will be time enough before the vessel sinks to save the life of every person on board. I will go a bit further. I will say that I cannot imagine any condition that would cause the vessel to flounder. Modern shipbuilding has gone beyond that. The love of the ocean that took me to sea as a boy has never left me. In a way, a certain amount of wonder never leaves me, especially as I observe from the bridge, a vessel plunging up and down in the trough of the seas, fighting her way through and over great waves, tumbling, and yet keeping on her keel, I wonder how she does it, how she can keep afloat in such seas, and how she can go on and on, safe to port. There is wild grandeur, too, that appeals to me in the sea. A man never outgrows that. The iceberg is marked with no cross on the chart. The wise and seasoned mariner can evade rocks and reefs, and can pick his way through fogs and storms, but the iceberg brings disaster in spite of all precautions." Smith related.

After having finished the article, Harrison places it back into the folder. He sits back into his couch and takes a deep breath. Harrison begins to wonder.

"Charged with supreme authority, Smith was responsible for the safe navigation of the ship. It was his under his command that the performance in proficiency of his crew and officers made it possible for the passengers to have a safe and enjoyable crossing. The abandonment of the Titanic was a disaster in itself. Lifeboats not filled to capacity, and the officers performing their duties in an obstinate manner." Harrison is perplexed in reading that in the final minutes of the sinking, Captain Smith did not have control of his officers.

"Where was he when the life boats began to be lowered? Without adequate commands, Titanic's officers interpreted 'women and children first' to be captain's orders of 'women and children, exclusively.' If that was the intended order, why did 53 children and 109 women perish in the tragedy?" Harrison thinks to himself.

"Where was the captain all this time? Was he standing inside of the Bridge, contemplating suicide, or waiting for his mystery boat to show up?" He thinks aloud.

Deep down inside, Harrison feels the argument will not make any sense to a jury. "Unless there is cause to believe that Smith was given charge of the Titanic for one reason, and one reason only...to sink her," Harrison adds in thought.

Harrison takes another news article from the folder, and begins to read into the clipping. The article is about the RMS

Olympic and her maiden voyage to New York. Months before the Titanic tragedy, Ramsi's quotes were published in an interview by a New York Times reporter which pointed out that Captain Smith chatted to the reporters assembled, he was in excellent spirits. "If he had any reservations about talking to the Press, he must have put them aside," read the article.

"What did she cost?" One news reporter asked, to which he replied: "Eight to nine million dollars, with furniture, fittings and such, totaled about 10 million." Ramsi replied, without hesitation.

Another reporter asked: "How much was the Olympic insured" Another asked: "Records

show that White Star carried a $500,000.00 risk, the remainder covered by the underwriters." Ramsi replied.

"How much did it cost to run the ship for one voyage?" A reporter asks. "$175,000.00, approximately, and She had done all that was expected and behaved splendidly, will she ever dock on Tuesday?"

"No," Smith said emphatically. "And there will be no attempt to bring Olympic in on Tuesday, she was built for a Wednesday trip and her run, this first voyage, has demonstrated that she will fulfill all expectations of the builders." Mr. Ramsi said. Harrison rubs his tired eyes. The 'transcript' folder slips down by his side and in no time at all, he is sound asleep.

CHAPTER NINE
Girls Night Out - The Mystery Ship

The cold night air rushes into the drafty cab of Jane's vehicle as she drives down Broadway towards her apartment. Tanaya is completely unaware that Jane plans to take her to a lounge in the Soho District of Manhattan.

"This is a swell car, I hope to have something like this one day." Tanaya says.

"It's an E.M.F." Jane says. "What's that?" Tanaya asks. "Everett, Metzger, and Flanders - the company that makes these cars. Mine is a 1912, the very last year they were made, and she looks classy with the top down, a real breezer," says Jane.

"Hey, it's only 10 o'clock. I know a little piano bar a few blocks away. What do you say we drop in for a drink?" Jane asks. "Sounds good to me, but aren't you forgetting something? Tanaya asks. Jane looks herself over.

"I forgot my...I give up. What did I forget? Jane asks.

"I'm not allowed to be in bars," says Tanaya, discouraged.

"That's okay. I can't vote. That makes us even, so tonight, we're going to have a drink." Jane says. "I can't vote either, that doesn't make it even," objects Tanaya. "I don't like it, sounds like trouble to me." Tanaya says.

"Don't worry honey, with your alabaster skin and those almond eyes, there isn"t a place in the world you couldn't walk into." Jane says with a smile. Jane pulls up to a parking space just as a car pulls out, directly across from the SOHO Lounge. She sets the parking brake and grabs her purse. With a flick of a lighter, Jane begins searching for a hair barrette.

"Turn around little girl, I am going to fix you up with a 'Gibson Girl' hair do," says Jane as she begins to comb out Tanaya's straight auburn hair. After a quick but effective hair make over, she finds a tube of red lipstick, and a tin of rouge.

"Oh my God, will you look at that, I've created another Gloria Swanson." Jane says with a smile. Tanaya smiles back, looking like she just stepped out of a fashion magazine.

"You're sure of this?" Tanaya asks. "Believe me sister, all eyes will be on us when we walk through those doors."

Inside the piano bar, 'happy Hour' is winding down. A nondescript piano piece can be heard. Jane and Tanaya continue to walk through the smoke filled lounge.

Tanaya notices that Jane is walking with exaggerated hip movements. In an instant, both are sashaying through the bar, towards an available table by the stage. As predicted by Jane, all heads turn to watch the two women walk towards the rear of the bar.

The piano player smiles broadly as the women walk past the small stage. Inspired by the classic entrance, he leads into 'My Melancholy Baby,' played in a sultry key.

"A gin martini and a glass of white wine in a chilled glass please." Jane says to the cocktail waitress.

"Before I bring your drinks, I have to ask. I mean, it doesn't make a bit of difference to me, it's the bartender, he thinks you girls are working," says the waitress, slightly embarrassed.

"Working girls', she asks," says Jane mockingly.

"He's the new bar manager, and he doesn't like 'working girls' in his bar," explains the waitress.

"Well, we worked all-day today, but we're not working now." Jane says with squinty eyes. "We have one client, he seem to like it that way," says Tanaya with wide-eyes. The waitress steps back and turns to leave without taking her eyes from them.

"Here's my business card, and another for your new bartender. This is my secretary, Tanya and I'm Jane, just like it reads on the card." After the waitress leaves, the two women huddle over the table to cast aspersions on the embarrassed waitress.

"How do you like that? My very first time in a real bar and no one has come to give me the bum's rush!" Tanaya says softly. "The only rush that's going to happen is them rushing to our table. I tell you, you should've seen their faces," Jane says.

"I dared not look...I was watching you, and trying to get that walk down," Tanaya says in a shy voice. A toast is made with make believe glasses.

"I know we're here to relax, but I've dying to ask. When Inar spoke tonight, he did explain that he witnessed Captain Smith board a lifeboat, before the Titanic went down. Was he speaking metaphorically?" Jane asks.

"I thought about what he had to say about that night. Now that you mention it, I'm wondering if I had translated it correctly," says Tanaya. She pauses to carefully choose her words, but the waitress shows at their table with drinks. Jane and Tanaya patiently wait as she sets their drinks down neatly with napkins.

"Drinks are on the bar manager, he asked me to let you know that he only second generation himself. He really appreciates the work you do for immigrants in their plight." The waitress says apologetically.

"This is for you," says Jane as she hands her a tip. Let your bar manager know that his appreciation is well taken," says Jane. The waitress leaves, and their conversation is resumed.

"In describing what he had seen really puzzled me. Our belief system has been taught by word of mouth for centuries. Uncle, may have been describing how the captain was received by the sky spirits," Tanaya says.

"Are you saying it was an apparition, and not Smith?" Jane asks. "I don't know. I was certain at the time that's what he meant, but then I became confused. I could tell by the way he began to emphatically explain the story in hand gestures. I've listened to the elders when they've told their stories. Hand gesturing and arm waving is something elders do to emphasize a point. I mean, if it had been an experience in the spiritual way, he would have been reverent. Did he appear that way to you?" Tanaya asks.

"Are you kidding, he became so animate, I became enthralled in his sincerity. My mouth dropped wide open when you gave the translation. It's still hard to believe what he described," says Jane in a puzzled voice.

"Once, during lunch hour at the Indian School, Uncle asked me a profound question. He asked what happens to white people after this life is over? Is there a place for them in the Sky World?" Jane falls silent. Slowly a crooked smile comes to face, and their eyes meet. Tanaya's eyebrows raise and laughter breaks out, which again draws attention from the bar.

"I needed a good laugh." Jane says, then adds: "Tanaya, I have to tell you something," she says with apology. I feel that Harrison is going to place Inar in a position he will not be able understand."

Tanaya takes a sip of wine and replies; "Uncle has looked into the eyes of sea animals that could have swallowed him up with one bite. He has survived a tragedy, of which most did not. While I cannot speak for him, I can tell you he remains confident in his convictions of what happened that night.

Everything he has experienced, from the day he stepped off the Carpathia, could not compare to those days and nights out on the Atlantic. If anything, he'll probably find all of this interesting, at most," says Tanaya.

"You're absolutely sure?" Jane asks. "Our people have nothing but the natural way, and truth comes from nature, it's all we have. If Uncle is asked to tell the truth, it's what he will do." Tanaya says. "He will be put upon the stand in front of a jury, a court room full of journalist and curious on lookers," warns Jane.

"All I have to tell you is this; the parka hood is lined with the Arctic Wolf which he had taken in a fight for his life. To Uncle, it was a taking of his own relation, one that was of the Earth. In his village shelter, he slept on a white bear skin. That bear was also taken in a fight for his life. He not only saved his own life, but those in the hunting party standing behind him. He won't be moved by anyone who would attempt to discredit his account of the Titanic," says Tanaya.

Jane begins to explain a court room cross examination and how, sometimes, can be unnerving. She is cut short by Tanaya. "One day at lunch, Uncle explained to me that, when he was a younger man, his hunting abilities came into question. "Honor is not without question," he said, referring to a council he had been summoned to attend. He told me that the tribal chief wanted him to explain to the council, the killing of a young man in his hunting party."

"Something he did?" Jane asks. "No, the young man was killed by a white bear. The council asked him to explain what had happened, on that day."

"Were they holding him responsible for the death?" Jane asks.

"Uncle knew that it was his hunting party and he was in charge. It was his responsibility to see that everyone safely returned and the hunt was successful. It wasn't the council that questioned his ability to lead, it was Uncle himself."

"That must have weighed heavy on his conscience." Jane says. "Uncle told me that if it were not for the council calling on him to answer for the death of a village young heart, he would have lived with it on his conscience the rest of his days. He explained to them in great detail, how he took the bear that killed the young man. The old bear had killed before, but Uncle felt that if he let him live out his life, it would die in a natural way. It was that guilt which Uncle felt, he should have sensed the old bear's presence. The bear surprised them and he could nothing to save the boy. He said that old bear was quick, and he did not look to be starving. Uncle explained that the bear just liked to kill Inuits. Anyway, I have faith in Uncle. He knows truth, and he knows how to present it in order to defend himself," says Tanaya.

"If a question is asked of him, Inar will answer 'yes' or 'no' is that right?" Correct. Unless he is asked to explain something, he will do it in detail. He will do this because he knows, no one understands the language of the Inuit unless they have lived among them or are part of the blood line." Tanaya says. She then notices that Jane has become distracted. She is looking beyond her towards the stage. The piano player has her attention, and with eye contact he is directing her attention towards the bar.

Jane takes the hint and scans the bar area. She sees a neatly dressed man at the corner of the bar. It strikes her that he is slightly out of place. She can see that most of the business men sitting at the bar are relaxed, collars unbuttoned with loosened ties.

"I have a feeling we're being watched." Jane says, trying to be inconspicuous. Another look to the piano player, she receives a slow nod.

"Who is watching us, and why?" Tanaya asks. "Don't know, but I wouldn't put it past White Star's firm to hire a private dick to keep an eye on us," explains Jane.

"What good is that going to do? It's not us who are going to tell the story to the judge. They can't get any information out of Uncle, they don't speak the language." Tanaya says.

"But you do." Jane says. "Well, you don't have to worry about this Inuit girl, she can take care of herself," says Tanaya adjusting her jacket lapels.

"Here, take this cigarette and pretend you're smoking it." Jane says. Tanaya shakes her head slightly. "If you are going to sit there looking like Fashion Review, at least appear as such. Who ever he is doesn't recognize you, tonight anyway." Jane says.

"I don't smoke cigarettes." Tanaya says, politely pushing the cigarette away.

"Oh, come on. Really? Someone may have lied to you, ever hear of Indian hemp" just hold the damned thing," says Jane.

"Jane this was your idea. Remember?" Tanya asks. "I know, and I can see where this may be confusing, first I talk you into having a drink, then let's have you look like a model. Then..." Jane says, as Tanaya interjects.

"Wait a minute, it just hit me. Followed by a private dick?" What is that supposed to mean?" Tanaya asks, eyes blinking. "Okay,

okay. I am not trying to make this seemingly little excursion difficult.

"I believe you, that thing about being followed, I had that feeling tonight, when we left Mr. Bennett's apartment." Tanaya says. "Oh, you are just full of surprises." Jane says.

"In your culture, in this time, I can see why you would not be aware of predator presence. My people call them the Watchers. They wait and they watch, and when the time is right, they take," says Tanaya. Jane nods as she looks off to one side.

"So, look towards the corner of the bar, brown hair, dark suit, and the only man wearing a hat in the bar, that one," says Jane. The two women look to one another in silence.

"It's like I said, it was that exact feeling I had before we got here. We're okay for now, if he's a Watcher, he'll approach. Jane, how much more of this sort of thing are we in for? Are we in danger because of this court case?" Tanaya asks.

"I don't know. Harrison explained to me that a certain amount of risk is not out of the question. He doesn't trust the firm that represents White Star. He said they will do anything to win a case, foul play is not beyond their practice. Harrison is a

151.

brilliant attorney. Myself, well...when I was given Inar's case, it came out of Harrison Bennett's office."

"How did he become involved" I thought it was you, who brought Mr. Bennett into the case?" Tanaya asks.

"Inadvertently, he used me as a mere instrument." Jane says as she places a closed fist slowly onto the table. "If you're talking about Mr. Bennett's viewpoint on the insurance end of it, I feel he could have brought that case without getting involved with Uncle." Tanaya says.

"By himself, Yes, it's why I am so concerned about what degree of manipulation Harrison can impose." Jane says, looking at Tanaya through a half empty martini glass.

"Jane, you would've never made it in the old days, simply put, you would've been left along side the trail," says Tanaya with a giggle.

Placing an empty martini glass down on the table, Jane nods her head as she gulps down the remainder of the drink.

"I don't know what that means, but, it sounds profound, and it was used with my name attached, so you just let me have it." Jane says, as she rests her chin in the palm of her hand.

"If you were to put Uncle to the question, this question would have to be in the terms of hunting," says Tanaya.

The cocktail waitress shows up at their table with two more drinks. Jane looks towards the far end of the bar with disdain.

"How did this happen?" Asks Jane. The waitress motions towards the piano stage.

Jane looks over to see the musician, sitting behind a 'Baby Grand' piano, he has a huge smile on his face. He is about to wrap-up his last set. Tanaya watches as the elderly piano player approaches their table.

"Excuse me ladies, but if you don't mind me saying, you are a sight for sore eyes. You don't know how uninspiring it is to play to an unresponsive crowd every night." The piano player says as he stands at their table uninvited.

Jane stands as if to confront him. "Thank you, kind sir." Jane says as she place her fingertips gently upon his chest. "The pleasure is all ours. My name is Jill and this is Tina, and you are?" asks Jane.

"Rufus, but, you may call me Roof." Rufus says, taking her hand. "That would be 'Through-the-Roof-Rufus,' replies Jane.

"As you wish." Rufus says politely. Jane makes a gesture for him to join them. Rufus declines, seeing that most of the bar patrons are looking-on. Jane smiles and takes her seat.

"If you will allow me to convey indirectly. My visit to your table, is to thank you for your generous tip. We can say the overall appearance is; I am being most gracious, and we are having pleasant conversation, says Rufus cautiously. "Young ladies, be careful tonight. Be very careful," says Rufus.

"Very careful?" Jane asks with smile and challenge.

"Yes, it's like this. I've been playing at this piano bar for over five years. I've seen them all come and go, the majority of them honest hard working folks, with an exception of a few. Now take that fellow at the end of the bar," says the musician.

"Interesting you should mention that, is he a cop or a P.I.?" Jane asks.

"Worse, he's a cleaner. Watch out for that one," warns Rufus.

"Thank you Rufus." Jane says as she slips him a five dollar bill. "What's your favorite song?" Jane asks.

"Tonight, my favorite song is, 'The Girl On The Magazine Cover' by Irving Berlin," replies Rufus.

As Rufus steps up to the piano, he smiles at the women and begins playing the tune. The bar becomes a little quieter as it is a popular tune. Jane glances toward the bar and discovers that the suspicious man has left.

"What in the world is a Cleaner?" Tanaya asks. "Why should we be afraid of someone who cleans?" She adds.

"I don't know, but the so called cleaner didn't look the type that would be pushing a Hoover around all day." Jane replies. The effects of the drinks come over Jane and Tanaya, and with a smile they toast to the song dedicated by Rufus, the piano player.

Later after leaving the night club, they brave the chill of the night air on the ride back to Jane's apartment. "Every time I feel the cold harshness of winter, I can't help but think of the hundreds that perished in the freezing water of the Atlantic that night." Jane says, as they roll along the bumpy street.

"It's like this for me," says Tanaya. "The events that took place from the time Uncle was set upon the ice drift, I can accept. I know of this life, and it is natural for the Old Ones to accept it also," says Tanaya. The tire of the vehicle catches a trolly's rail rut and causes Jane's car to swerve into oncoming traffic. The annoying squawk of a car horn interrupts the conversation.

"I'm okay, damned train tracks, streets were build for cars, not trains." Jane says apologetically. "Go on with what you were saying about your culture."

"Well, Uncle's experience on the open sea in the North Atlantic is, at best, very possible." Tanaya offers.

"Wait a minute." Jane interrupts. "Earlier tonight you were in awe of Inar's feat of survival, and now you're saying it was a mere possibility?"

"According to our people, the Old Ones never lie, you see, in order for a story to be told with the right affect, the experience has to be bent just a little bit.
If the experience is bent beyond a certain point, then it is a lie." Tanaya says.

"Are you referring to his account of Captain Smith" Jane asks, as she pulls over into a parking space on the street. "Here we are, my place. Now, please explain what you just said."

"There are certain things that the Old Ones can see, one being the ability to read a situation and know the outcome, we young people can only guess at an outcome...but the Old Ones will know the outcome with certainty. What I am telling you is that if Uncle looked into the eyes of Captain Smith, he may have seen what Smith really wanted to do that night, instead of going down with the ship."

Tanaya says. "Come on, let's go inside." Jane says as she climbs out of the vehicle.

Inside the apartment building, a ride in an Otis elevator has Jane smiling as she watches Tanaya's expression. It is her second time riding in an elevator. "This is what it must feel like, going to heaven." Tanaya says reverently.

Unlocking her apartment door, Jane motions to Tanaya with a sweeping arm. "Welcome to my humble abode." Jane says as she helps Tanaya off with her jacket.

"Some hot cocoa will top this night off and we will jump back into the trench tomorrow. Sound good to you?" Jane asks. Tanaya smiles at Jane as she walks into the living room carrying two cups on saucers.

"Now." Jane says as she seats herself onto the couch. "Early tomorrow, we are going to meet the boys down at the dock. We are going to time, by stopwatch, an incoming ship as it approaches the harbor." Jane says.

"I am glad Mr. Bennett is taking it upon himself to prove the timing of the event. While I have confidence in my uncle's experience, I sometimes feel I am only telling half of what his words really mean." Tanaya says.

"I'm with you on that one. I'm not telling you this to color your interpretation, but it's a matter of fact, that White Star had knowledge of Inar being aboard the Titanic. One of the sea men gave testimony in the British court hearing of apprehending a stowaway. The transcripts read that he and another sailor escorted the prisoner below to be jailed, near the bottom of the ship's hull. It was the night the collision occurred," Jane explains.

"I'm okay with that. It's just that, after it happened, Uncle tried so hard to tell the story, but there was no one to tell, until now.

"Please, don't get me wrong if I seem to doubt. I believe Uncle. Can you, or anyone, imagine experiencing something like that, and live to tell about it? This is a story that has to be told," explains Tanaya.

"I hear that. As you read further into the hearing transcripts, you'll find that it's a matter of record. A claim was filed against White Star Line by Cunard, the owners of Carpathia. The cost of recovery entailed the costs of survivor rescue and for transporting the survivors to New York. More than anything, it was the cost of coal burned during the trip.

"Inar was among the list of survivors. I should say, there was a description of Inar on the list of survivors. At the very least, it is proof he was at the scene of the collision," says Jane.

"Under the circumstances the cost included Inar's fare. In truth he was transported against his will, he did not want to be taken from the North Atlantic waters. Do not put yourself in a place where you'll be disappointed." Tanaya advises.

"What do you mean by that? You believe him...don't you? Jane asks.

"Remember what I said about the Old Ones. When native people get a certain age...well they begin to see things." Tanaya says.

"Things? What sort of things?" Jane asks. "The closer the Old Ones get to passing into the spirit world, they enter into an understanding with the spirit, and they begin to see other spirits. It's what I thought when he told me about Captain Smith. It's thought he went down with his ship. That's dead as it gets," says Tanaya.

"That's very interesting. I prefer Inar saw Smith in the flesh. I would be a little discouraged, but I really don't think I would be disappointed. I am an attorney, I know where our leads will come from. The British government's Board of Trade allowed faulty construction in building the Titanic, they allowed Titanic to sail with insufficient lifeboat accommodation. The government simply had not kept up with advances in marine engineering and based all lifesaving regulations on ships up to 10,000 gross registered-tons.

"The Merchant Shipping Act of 1864 was the first comprehensive set of rules and regulations governing ships that companies were required to follow. They had been updated in 1902 and 1906 but, typical of government, even to this day, they are hopelessly behind the curve.

"Instead of trying to prove Inar was there and how...we are going take it from the point he was hoisted onto Carpathia and regress back into his experience aboard the final minutes of the Titanic," Jane says with a gleam in her eye.

"The total claimed survivors was 315, but only 314 claims were settled, minus Inar. White Star would not acknowledge his being a survivor because he was not listed on the passenger list. A passenger list that went down to the bottom of the Atlantic.

"What we are going after is the all out failure of the crew to respond to an emergency at sea. The background research tells the story. Titanic was 46,329 tons. A ship designed to accommodate 3,511 passengers and crew was only required to provide lifeboat accommodation for nine hundred and sixty-two passengers. In-fact, White Star provided her with four extra collapsible boats, increasing capacity to 1,178. If Smith had been in control of his command, all these lifeboats could have been loaded to their stated capacity. The first life boat to leave, contained 12 people; its capacity was 40," explains Jane.

"If there is justice in your courtroom, then the echoes of that night will be heard through Uncle's voice." Tanaya says.

"With that, I will show you where you'll sleep tonight." As they walk into the guest room, Tanaya"s eyes light up. She walks towards a four-posted bed with a down comfort spread. She reaches out to touch its softness.

"I don't sleep well in any other bed, than my own. Thank you Jane, I'll sleep well tonight," assures Tanaya.

It is a clear spring morning, and the banks of the Hudson River are speckled with a greening of budding trees. Harrison and his associates have assembled on the dock. The cold river water pulls remnants of ice from its muddy banks as it flows to the sea. Inar is leaning over a rail, watching the waves gently break onto the cement abutment of the dock. The air is brisk, and the on shore air is cold enough to bite the skin. Tanaya stands facing the breeze and soaking in the rising sun. Jane is scanning the horizon for an approaching ship. Even though there are ships already approaching in the shipping lane, she is searching for a ship that has breached the horizon and can be seen with the naked eye.

Harrison pulls out another pair of binoculars from its case and begins to focus on the horizon. Inar quietly slips up next to him, and silently observes.

"Inar, I can feel you staring into my right ear." Harrison says without taking the glasses from his eyes.

"Uncle, ask Mr. Bennett to have a look." Tanaya says in the Inuit language.

"Please?" Inar says in English. Jane looks to Tanaya who shrugs her shoulders. Harrison gives Inar a smile of approval and hands the binoculars to him. The binoculars are placed to his face, Inar peers through the glasses momentarily, then hands them back.

"Oh...you have to adjust them to your eyes." Harrison says as he demonstrates the adjustment. Inar begins to adjust the glasses and with a hearty laugh, and starts walking with them to his face. When he finds his field of vision, an expression of surprise comes over him. "Ahhh..." Inar breathes, as he lowers the glasses from his eyes to get a true view of the clouds on the horizon.

Inar hands the binoculars to Harrison, and points to the towards the horizon. After a quick look, Harrison reaches into his coat pocket and pulls out a stop watch. "Here we go," he says excitedly. There is a sharp "click" as he looks down to take a reading from his wrist watch. Jane opens a ruck sack and takes out a thermos bottle. Harrison begins to explain the process of ship navigation.

"The approaching ship appears to be a steam cargo ship. There is no way of knowing what her speed is, at this point. The average speed in open waters is 17 to 20 knots. On the night of the sinking, it was a clear, and calm night, so it is not a matter of night or day, as long as line of sight can be established. Right Inar?" Harrison asks. Inar hears his name and nods smugly.

Harrison's intentions to find a target ship to gauge his calculations has come into sight. He points at the arriving ship and looks to Inar, who nods his head and indicates to Jane and Tanaya. Harrison records the time on a notepad, and Inar begins to assure Tanaya that on the night of the sinking, there was no sea fog or haze.

The line of sight from ship to ship was perfect with no obstructions.

"Okay, now we will record first sighting of the ship's port hole. As I understood, the 'mystery ship' was approaching the Titanic, then turned to port, exposing its starboard side," explains Harrison.

"Uncle says he is positive of the distance. He said that if he can see the round holes on the approaching ship from here, then it would almost be the same. Not exactly the same but a reasonable depiction of the ship at night," conveys Tanaya.

As the targeted ship continues to steam up the Hudson River, it follows the designated shipping course. When turning to the right, its port holes are exposed, and Inar is quick to point out that they have come into his view. Harrison looks at the stopwatch, then records the data on into his notepad.

"Are we through here, professor?" Jane asks through chattering teeth.

"This experiment, Mr. Watson, is at an end. Thank you, Inuits and attorneys. If my educated guess is right, we have what we need to continue with the case," says Harrison holding up the stop watch.

A few days later, a meeting at Jane's apartment has been arranged, Harrison and the others have gathered for a case briefing. The information that was gathered at the dock was given to a calculus instructor, and he is eager to share the findings with the others. "Thanks to one of our local community colleges, we now have a court room exhibit," says Harrison, as he hands a document to Jane.

"In holding true to his teaching ethics, Dr. Miles has included a short history of the knot, the nautical knot, as it is," says Harrison. "Dr. Miles has provided the information as a favor to me, and I feel we should all revel in the findings." Harrison adds.

"A unit of travel that is equal to the length of one nautical mile, is a calculation defined at a speed of approximately 1.151 miles per hour or 1.852 kilometers per hour. The latter is equation is preferred by the International Hydrographic Organization, a membership that includes every major seafaring nation on the earth.

In an equation rule of the I.H.O., a vessel traveling at one nautical knot along a meridian, travels one minute of geographic latitude in one hour. Very interesting, there's also a short history on the knot,"

The term "knot" derives from counting the number of knots tied along a line of rope that is unspooled as the ship sails along. The system involved a weighted anchor and an hourglass. A turn of a 30 second hourglass, and the toss of a weight attached to a rope that had a knot in it every 50 feet, gave early Sea fares nautical knot. In modern times, the symbol; M, NM or NMI, is a unit of length that is about one minute of arc of latitude along any meridian, but is mostly one minute of arc of longitude only at the equator. By international agreement, it is exactly 1,852 meters or approximately 6,076 feet," Harrison reads aloud.

"Whew! Ok-aay." Jane says with surrender. "With our expertly performed research, and this brilliant calculation, I am certain we have enough to go to trial with this case," says Harrison.

"So, when Inar first sighted the starboard lights emitted from the 'nonexistent' ship, he was on Titanic's boat deck. That being the case, the bridge may have not yet been overcome by sea water. It's possible that Captain Smith may have escaped the sinking," says Harrison. "Everyone still on board?" He asks.

"Deck chairs, anyone?" Jane asks under her breath.

CHAPTER TEN
The Right Of Way

Come the day of the court hearing, both parties have been scheduled to appear at the Hearing Room at the New York City, City Hall. The plaintiffs file into the hearing room with Harrison leading his small but confident legal team. Jane stops upon entering the hearing room, she takes a deep breath to calm her nerves.

Inside the conference room there is an Administrative Judge seated at the end of a long polished conference table. It is Judge Henry Meyer, an unbiased and respected judge. His vested suit catches Inar's attention. Unexpectedly, Inar stands and begins smiling approvingly at the judge. Jane can see that Inar's behavior is making Judge Meyer somewhat uncomfortable. Inar continues to stand facing the judge, nodding and smiling. The White Star legal team observe Inar's actions and start writing into their pads. Tanaya speaks to Inar, to see what is on his mind. Tanaya smiles at the judge.

"He likes your suit, Your Honor, he would like you to know, he has one just like it." Tanaya says.

"Well, I'm flattered. Is there some reason your client did not dress for the occasion?"

"It was at my request, Judge Meyer, that he dress in traditional tribal wear. I wanted to show that he is faithful to his native beliefs and customs." Harrison replies.

"Point taken, certainly grabbed my attention. Now, everyone please be seated, so I can call this hearing to order." Judge Meyer says with a rap of the gavel. Harrison, Jane, Tanaya and Inar, quickly take their seats. On the other side of the table, are the defense attorneys, arrogantly observing their every move, like so much prey. Meyer addresses the plaintiffs and the White Star attorneys. "For the benefit of your client, Mr. Bennett, I will explain a few ground rules. Mr. Katerpar, this is a lawful preceding, it is not a trial.

It is with full confidence that we carry on knowing that Miss Navaran will translate every word to its nearest correct meaning. Am I correct in assuming so Miss Navaran?" "Yes, Judge Meyer."

"Now, for the sake of continuity, we have provided earphones for Mr. Katerpar and yourself and you will be translating in the conference room next door. Mr. Katerpar, do you agree with this arrangement?" The Judge asks.

"Thank you Judge Meyer. My client has been apprised of this arrangement and is comfortable with it," says Tanaya, in English translation.

"A motion for Summary Judgment has been placed before me by the defendants in this case. That reason being your client, Mr. Bennett, cannot prove he was ever on the Titanic, before or after the sinking. With that, we shall move on with this hearing. Miss Navaran you are excused, the matron will escort you to your seat in the conference room next door, where you will translate Mr. Katerpar's each and every word," says Meyer.

After a short voice check on the intercom, the judge directs the defense attorney's to continue. "Attorney Scott, you're up." Judge Meyer says.

Trying to lure Inar to look into his eyes, Scott pauses, with a pencil tap in a broken tempo. Inar looks up slowly.

"Your client claims that he was on the Titanic at the time of her sinking, but we need to hear him answer, yes, or no to the allegation, Mr. Katerpar. Were you aboard the R.M.S. Titanic on the night of April 14th, leading into April 15th of 1912?"

Inar cups his hands onto the headphones. "Yes," Inar replies looking straight at Scott.

"At this time, Your Honor, and for the sake of continuity, let the record show that I will direct my questions to Attorney Bennett.

"We have passenger boarding lists, of which were taken at the time the Titanic took on her passengers at two separate ports of call, including South Hampton. Why is it your client's name does not appear on any of these lists?" Scott asks.

"My client did not pay for a ticket to board the Titanic nor was he a passenger. He was not a member of the crew, nor was he hired entertainment. Mr. Katerpar had the misfortune of being knocked onto Titanic's forward well-deck, by the force of a collision, three hours before she sank."

"Knocked onto the deck of Titanic?" According to your client's deposition, he was on the iceberg that hit the Titanic," says attorney Scott.

"No. That is not what was said. What was given in deposition was this: The Titanic struck the iceberg, on the night of April 14th. That, is what was said." Harrison says, as he hands Judge Meyer a document.

"Just a second. To be clear Mr. Bennett, your client, was on the iceberg that struck the Titanic." Judge Meyer asks.

"No, Your Honor, the Titanic..." Harrison begins. "One-half dozen or six of the other. What-in-the-world was Mr. Katerpar doing on the iceberg?" Any iceberg for that matter...?" Meyer asks with astonishment.

"Please, with due respect Judge Meyer, we feel that it would be detrimental to our case should we divulge that information at this point. I assure you we will get to that matter, once we have received documented evidentiary material that can be submitted for courtroom exhibit," says Harrison. The judge sits back in his chair. His eyes trained on Inar, who is looking back at Meyer with wide eyes.

"Hence the whole point of our motion, Your Honor. Attorney Bennett would like to have us believe that his client fell out of the night sky, and landed on the Titanic. Attorneys for White Star intend to prove that Mr. Katerpar stowed away. If on the Titanic, he was there illegally.

Now, three years later with the help of Attorney's Bennett and Reynolds, he is attempting to cash in on the tragedy. Isn't that so Mr. Katerpar?" Inar is listening to translation and begins to shake his head in denial.

"Let the record show that Mr. Katerpar has indicated it is not true" Judge Meyer says. Harrison hands a note to Jane, who takes the lead.

"This notion of a stowaway, gets more interesting every time you mention it. Tell me Attorney Scott, where would an Inuit native, whose aboriginal homeland lies within Baffin Island, have the opportunity to commit the illegal act of stowing away, on any ship. Surely, ship's personnel of Titanic would have noticed our client. He, without a doubt would have been picked out of the crowd as soon as he boarded the ship.

"South Hampton maybe?" Jane asks, preparing to answer her own question. "No. Anyone with such peculiar appearance as Mr. Katerpar would not slip by the crew so easily," upon hearing the translation, Inar crosses his arms and looks sideways at Jane.

"On the other hand, would you consider France? With clothing styles being featured in magazines around the world, I'm sure mukluks and seal skin parka's would be much in demand. Nor would the appearance of anyone in such attire, be accepted as a norm. Access to the ship would have been next to impossible for our client.

"As for Ireland, well there's not much chance at all that our client with his bizarre appearance, would have been able to enter the country, much less a boat dock." Jane says.

"Eeyah." Inar expresses disapproval as the translation comes through the earphones.

"What was that, Mr. Katerpar?" Judge Meyer asks. "It's an Inuit expression Your Honor. One-of, well...Wonder," explains Harrison, as Jane continues.

"Of those three ports of call, stops in which Titanic made on her maiden voyage, Attorney Scott. Which port is going to convince a jury that my client boarded the R.M.S. Titanic illegally?" Jane asks. The judge begins writing onto a notepad, while the White Star attorneys huddle at the table.

Attorney Fletcher for the defense, continues the argument. Pressing the unlikeliness of Inar's presence on the iceberg. "Judge Meyer, if I may, there is another point we would like to bring up," attorney Fletcher says. With the wave of a hand he motions for aids to bring in three boxes of documents.

"Interviews eighty-two witnesses at various phases of this case, including numerous field interviews involving fifty-three British subjects. Twenty-nine U.S.

citizens. Among those interviewed are two members of the International Mercantile Marine Company, Board of Directors. Seated President, J. Bruce Ramsi of Liverpool, England, and Vice President, P.A.S. Franklin of New York.

"Among the interviews, we were able to meet with four surviving ship's officers of the Titanic. We obtained statements from Second Officer, Charles H. Lightoller, of Hampshire, England. Third Officer, Herbert J. Pitman, of Somerset, England. Fourth Officer, Joseph Boxhall, of Hull, England and Fifth Officer Harold G. Lowe, of North Wales. In questioning, all thirty-four of Titanic's surviving crew and officers, we asked of each; 'to your knowledge, did you or any that you know, see Mr. Katerpar on aboard the Titanic the night of April 14th leading into April 15th of 1912? Each answered: 'No.'" They had not seen Mr. Katerpar. When asked if they had seen any person resembling Mr. Katerpar, each answered: 'No,'" Fletcher explains.

"We intend to prove that, by the statements of these witnesses, Mr. Katerpar had not been seen by anyone who survived the sinking. Your Honor, if their client cannot prove he was aboard the Titanic on the night of the fourteenth, then we shall move to a Summary Judgement," says Fletcher.

"Judge Meyer, if not for the fact that our client has identified photos of the three ship's officers and a member of Titanic's board of directors, we would not be here today. In the light that Mr. Katerpar was on aboard the Titanic the night of the sinking, a case has emerged amid the complications of the event. While it may be true that none of the survivors witnessed Mr. Katerpar on board that particular night, does not prove that our client was not aboard ship.

"White Star attorneys have produced affidavits to the contrary. It simply means that none of the surviving witnesses remember seeing Mr. Katerpar. A jury may consider the circumstances surrounding the sinking; a night filled with fear, panic, and tragedy. We needn't go into the appalling details, today. Not today. We have a case, Your Honor, and we intend to show that our client Mr. Katerpar, has a valid claim to damages," says Jane.

"Eskimo's, Icebergs...and now a convenient placement of their client in a crucial moment in history. What next? Katerpar enjoying tea and crumpets with Smith during the accident?" Fletcher taunts. The gavel comes down on the strike block.

"A jury may find it interesting that the interviews conducted by White Star attorneys, came up with zero witnesses. Moreover, the fact that the White Star interviews missed thirty-four passenger survivors. A traditionally dressed Inuit, aboard a luxury liner, may raise some eye browse in the jury box," says Jane, as a silence falls over the room. Judge Meyer contemplates the assertion.

"You can show that your client identified these witnesses?" Judge Meyer asks.

"My client can't read, write or understand English. How else is it possible for him to identify individuals that he had ever seen before? Our client was an eye witness, a witness to the tragedy. A tragedy in which the loss of lives was and still is, inconceivable," says Jane. Harrison rests on his elbow, wondering what direction she will next take her statement. Judge Meyer also sits back in his chair and scrutinizes her demeanor.

"Had these souls been lost as a direct result of the collision, it would have been an accident. For example, in an auto accident where two cars collide in a head on collision. Death resulting from that incident would be deemed accidental. In an incident where a vehicle intentionally caused death by knowingly put that vehicle on the road without brakes, then it becomes a matter if vehicular homicide. The truth is; 1,527 passengers lost their lives, not because of the iceberg. They did not freeze to death in life boats, had life boats been provided for those unfortunate souls. They died in the freezing waters of the North Atlantic, needlessly. That gentleman, places the tragedy into an act of negligent homicide on a massive scale," asserts Jane.

A small but crooked smile comes to Harrison's face, as Judge Meyer's gavel come down on the striking block.

"Miss Reynolds, I am warning you to keep your views and statements within the scope of this hearing," admonishes Meyer.

"If I may Your Honor. The assertion my associate presented, was not accusatory but, more in line with exemplification. The statements merely gave insight to added suffering, knowing many lives could have been saved. Mr. Katerpar has endured the terrible effects of the tragedy of that night in the freezing North Atlantic," says Harrison, as he turns and winks at Jane.

"Can we revisit the possibility that your client could have seen any one of the survivors on the front page of a newspaper?

"We feel this is an important point. Are we to consider that a person cannot distinguish between images? That in some cases said images have been over publicized, is plainly arguable.

"Case in point, a child who cannot read or write may be able to associate a photo of the Titanic with an iceberg, simply because of the notoriety. Moreover, if their client was allegedly on the Titanic, he was there illegally. A claim to damages is out of the question," refutes Fletcher.

"Well, Councilor, which is it, was he on board the Titanic or not?" Judge Meyer asks. The defense team for White Star show their disappointment in their colleague's performance by shunning him as he returns to his seat. Judge Meyer continues to write notes regarding the statements when Jane interjects.

"In a light of that revelation, can we at least agree that our client was not on board legally, but rather on board, against his will," asks Jane.

"Your client willfully boarded the Titanic, with full intention of defrauding the White Star Line. It was an illegal act and we intend prove it by presenting the passenger list as evidence. The story about living on the iceberg that hit the Titanic is preposterous..."

"No." Jane interjects. "The iceberg did not hit the Titanic. That is not how my client found himself on board the night of," says Jane before she is interrupted.

"Enough with who hit what, or what hit what. It is alleged Miss Reynolds, that your client was living on an iceberg. Who does that?" Meyer asks. "Yes, Judge Meyer. That is what my client claims," says Jane. "How do you intend to prove this? Your client has no evidence. Your evidence no longer exists, it has melted into the sea," says Judge Meyer.

"We will present the evidence in a courtroom when it gets to trial Your Honor. In a matter of discovery, we intend to prove the iceberg was not the only factor in the sinking of Titanic. There is evidence that will show in the law of nature, ice floes and icebergs are pushed by the ocean currents in the same direction every spring. A force of nature that has taken place since the beginning of time. Our client, and the iceberg he was aboard, had the right-of-way at the time of the collision," rebuts Harrison. Judge Meyer exhales with exasperation.

"I see. What was he doing on the iceberg, or should I ask, how did he get on the iceberg?" In translation, Tanaya conveys that Inar's answer. "The iceberg I was put upon was taking me to the Sky World, I was to be with my relatives, in time."

"You may have that opportunity, as I and everyone else in this room Mr. Katerpar. No one lives forever. With that, we are going to break for fifteen minutes. When we return Miss Reynolds, you will explain to me how your client managed to find himself on an iceberg.

"Convince me of that, and you will have your day in court." Judge Meyer implies with a strike of the gavel. "Hearing is in recess for fifteen minutes," he adds.

A small cafeteria down the hall from the conference room, is where the team meets for a briefing. They are planning their presentation to Judge Meyer. Inar takes a sip of tea and speaks to Tanaya in native tongue. She smiles. "Uncle says he didn't know white people could turn so red."

Harrison laughs. "Both Williams and Scott looked like they were going to lose their councilor wigs." Jane says.

"Now listen-up everyone. Jane, I want you to handle the photograph recognition that Inar popped up with last night. I'll walk

Meyer through the events that led up to the collision," advises Harrison.

"Not a chance. Judge Meyer will have Tanaya translate everything. Mark my words, Meyer won't allow a third party translation." Jane says.

"You're right, no one can tell the story like Inar, Meyer is going to get an ear full in about ten minutes.

"Is this the part where we get to go to trial?" Harrison asks mockingly.

"I'm hoping our opponents will have photos of the thirty-four surviving members of the crew." Jane says.

Tanaya raises her hand, and waits to be called on. "I would like to add my two cents," says Tanaya.

"You go right ahead honey, we're all ears." Harrison says.

"Well, you see, when Uncle was hired on at the Indian school I was asked to show him around the grounds. Because of his position as a janitor, he had to acquaint himself with the location of every building. His living quarters is situated in a boiler room, in Building 10 on the East side of the school grounds. When I helped him unpack, his belongings consisted of very few things. Beside the traditional clothing, he had a skinning knife, an extra bird skin undershirt, a pair of walrus tusk ice cleats, and a fur covered seal bladder." Tanaya explains. Harrison and Jane listen with interest, waiting for her point to emerge.

"When Judge Meyer pointed out that as evidence, the iceberg had melted; it struck me," explains Tanaya. "Yes?" Harrison asks. "I remembered the seal bladder. When I lifted it from his journey bundle, it felt half-full," says Tanaya.

"Good. A half-full seal bladder. Would that be water or urine?" Harrison asks mockingly.

"Water, Mr. Bennett - iceberg water," says Tanaya. There is a silence before a realization comes over them. A loud felicitous sound of laughter breaks through the marbled halls. "You are the Bee's Knees, an angel in the flesh." Jane says, hugging Tanaya then Inar.

"Jane..." Harrison begins. "I'm on it Harry. Dr. Miles and lab tests, ASAP." Jane says, finishing Harrison's sentence. A bailiff appears to let them know the hearing is about to resume.

"Thank you Tanaya, it's a brilliant piece of evidence that you provided us with." Harrison says as they make their way to the conference room.

Inside, the White Star attorneys have just been seated. Judge Meyer is waiting patiently as the plaintiffs file in.

"Miss Navaran, please instruct Mr. Katerpar to take a seat here with us at the conference table. Attorney Bennett, I would like to ask your client a few questions, and of course Miss Navaran will translate."

"I have no objection to the questioning." Harrison replies. "My first question to Mr. Katerpar is; how did he manage to be on the iceberg?" Meyer asks as Tanaya translates. Inar takes a deep breath. There is hesitation as he begins.

Inar lets Judge Meyer know that it is very difficult for him to recall the events that led up to the collision. He seems to trust Meyer, they being about the same age.

"It was not what he expected." Tanaya says. "What, was not what he expected?" Meyer asks.

"He says, he was filled with disappointment that he was not taken to the Sky World. In the Inuit way, the right of passage to this world begins at birth. Mr. Katerpar feels as though he has been denied that right, an interruption caused by the collision," Tanaya conveys.

"Okay, but if he were on the iceberg, how long does he believe he was there, on the iceberg?" Meyer asks as Tanaya begins her translation.

After a minute of thought. Inar motions for a pencil and notepad. The entire staff of lawyers are forced to wait as he draws figures onto the pad. The paper is then handed to Jane.

"It appears he was on the iceberg for twenty-three days and twenty-four nights." Tanaya says, handing the notepad to Judge Meyer. The story continues as Tanaya translates from the beginning of his journey. On the day of his departure from his village, he tells of the happy event in which the entire village bid him farewell.

"Standing at the edge of the ice floe, Inar tells of saying good-bye to everyone. To his son, a hearty hug. Pointing at a section of ice approaching, he assures his son that it is the floe that will take him to the Sky World. His son excitedly told the villagers the time has come. Inar and his son begin running alongside the floe, with the villagers running not far behind them. Cheers and good wishes are shouted as Inar jumps onto the moving ice. There is still snow pack which makes the ice not so slippery, he turns and waves good-bye. The villagers continue to run along the floe, throwing gifts and shouting farewells.

Soon the cracking and banging of the ice, would drown out the shouts of encouragement. The ice floe continues toward the Hudson Straight, Inar becomes a tiny dark speck amidst a white sea of heaving sheet ice.

Inar hands another page from the notepad. "In this depiction, it appears by the number of circles and moon segments, that he was on the ice floe for 15 days," says Tanaya, handing it to Judge Meyer.

"There is something else that Mr. Katerpar had explained," says Tanaya. "Please, continue," says Meyer.

"He stated that his journey on the ice floe was interrupted by a snap freeze that froze the sea around him. In order for him to reach open water, it was necessary for him to walk tree days over the frozen sea, that would make it a total of 18 days on the floe." Tanaya says through translation.

"Yes, I remember the winter of 1912, the coldest days on record to this date," says Judge Meyer.

"According to our calculations that would put him adrift on open waters around the middle of January 1912," adds Jane.

Inar goes on to tell of the night he was put upon the iceberg. "After days at sea, and no sign of being taken into the light of the Sky World, my deep instinct pushed me into full survival mode. I had eaten all of my food stock, and I was near dying of dehydration. My slab of ice had melted down to the size of a small boat.

"One night as I lay on my back, looking up at the stars. It was very quiet, but I knew I was amidst several icebergs, and like my ice platform, were being pushed south by the ocean current.

"The reflection of the night sky was shining bright. I could hear my heartbeat, it was becoming more fast. I could see my breath against the stars in the night sky, it was next to freezing. Suddenly and without warning, a familiar sound broke through the sounds of the calm ocean. It was the blast of air that could only come from one animal. I heard it before, but never that close, it scared me. Then I felt water on my face. "It felt like rain, but I recognized that particular whistle of a blowhole. Slowly I turned my head, I had a feeling it was Arrluk, the killer Whale. Sure enough, it was Arrluk. I was looking eye-to-eye with him, I knew he was there for me."

"You see, my people admire this killer of the sea, and the hunters fear it. It was my experience with Arrluk, that left me with memories of violent battles with him in the bay. Arrluk always ate most of our catch, we were always in competition with that animal.

"Over the years many of my hunting party would not go to sea after seeing Arrluk. In my memory, Arrluk never ate any Inuit, but he would kill the Inuit from time to time, and there he was, right next to me. I could hear him breathing. Arrluk stayed just above the surface, we just looked at each other.

"Arrluk. You have come for me?" I asked, and with one blast of air, he answered me. I am honored, the Sky World sent such a worthy opponent to make my death a good one." Inar says, through Tanaya's interpretation. The story is interrupted by one of White Star's lawyers.

"Judge Meyer, this whale tale isn't getting us anywhere, the focus of the hearing has diminished because of this rambling." Attorney Scott protests. "I will decide the progress of this hearing, and unless you can refrain from further interruption, you will find yourself on a seat in the Justice Hallway," admonishes Judge Meyer.

"Miss Navaran, please have Mr. Katerpar continue," he says.

"Thank you Judge Meyer." Tanaya says as she continues to translate, Inar's account of Arrluk, the Killer Whale. "That thin slab of ice I was on began to heave, then Arrluk slipped beneath the surface. I closes my eyes and waited for him to take me under and into the deep.

"Then it happened. A sudden uplifting had me bracing myself against the flat ice surface. I opened my eyes and saw the stars spinning in the night sky, then the ice slab fell away beneath me. It was like something was pushing me upward to the stars. I could see myself flying, my journey bundles were in the air above me.

"I was floating and slowly turning. Then I felt himself falling downwards. There was an impact and all the air left my body. I rolled on my side and I was gasping for air," says Inar.

"Mr. Katerpar states that he had the breath knocked out of him," Tanaya conveys. "It was then he found himself on the iceberg, where Arrluk had tail-tossed him," adds Tanaya.

Judge Meyer continues to write notes, as White Star attorneys confide among themselves. Inar hands Tanaya another page from the notebook. With a smile and a nod, she hands the paper to Harrison. Looking down onto the page, he can see that Inar has sketched a side view of the iceberg and a top view.

"Judge Meyer, you may find this depiction interesting, hand drawn by my client just moments ago." Harrison says.

"This I take, is Mr. Katerpar's depiction of the iceberg as he remembers it?" Meyer asks. "Yes, Your Honor, Mr. Katerpar would like for you to know, the two circular forms at the lower part of the sketch are iceberg melt ice pools. Melted glacial ice was a source of drinking water," explains Tanaya.

"If I may add, it has been documented that just hours after the tragedy, a sailor on the Steamer Bremen, photographed an iceberg thought to have sunk the Titanic." Jane advises.

"If you are suggesting that a comparison be made for the purpose of evidentiary value, I suggest that you pursue a more solid line of evidence, Miss Reynolds," says Meyer.

"Yes, I would tend to agree, but what if that particular photo went unpublished" There would be no way our client could depict an iceberg with such similarity," says Jane.

"Then you may have evidence, circumstantial as it might be, but evidence a jury could deliberate over." Meyer replies.

"Very well. I have heard both sides, and after I have reviewed the information in front of me, I will let you know of my decision tomorrow morning at nine o'clock in the morning," says Judge Meyer with a rap of the gavel.

Later at the Gateway Cafe, it is just before the dinner hour and the cafe is beginning to receive their usual customers. At a table at the far end of the dinning area is Harrison's group, they are all seated and their dinner has been served.

"I want to hear everything Dr. Miles had to say about the iceberg water, and any suggestions he may have offered," says Harrison as he pours a beer into a mug.

"When I spoke to him over the phone," he suggested a few referrals, one is a biologist to test the water. Dr. Miles explained that glacial water is a very unique fluid, almost a substance. In that, can contain pollutants, even trace elements of plant life, and numerous elements that contain micro organisms. Most unique to glacial water is a normal presence of, and get this, 'ice worms,' says Jane.

"Ice Worms," repeats Harrison in a far away voice. "The expense account can bear a Biologist. What of the other referral?" Harrison asks. "A Geologist," replies Jane.

"He also strongly suggested that expert testimony on glaciers and its melt water should be considered. These testimonies will win over a jury by educating them on how they are formed," explains Jane.

"Nix the Geologist and go with the lab tests and reports on water contaminants. After dinner, we are going to the Indian School and retrieve the seal bladder," says Harrison.

Tanaya and Jane look at one another. "I think you should know Harry, the Thomas Indian School is not right up the block, or at the other end of the city," says Jane. Tanaya agrees.

"Okay then, how about a drive to the countryside, it's spring time, it'll be a refreshing ride. Will it not?" Harrison asks. Jane and Tanaya chose silence for an answer. Inar chuckles, even though he has no idea what is being said, but finding the exchange of reactions amusing. "That sounds delightful. The Thomas Indian School is almost 400 miles away," says Jane.

"Where is the Indian School" In the middle of Lake Erie?" Harrison asks with astonishment. "No, but somewhat close to its shores. By rail it's approximately 386 miles to Arcade by way of the Arcade-Attica Railway. Once there, it is another 36 miles of dirt road to Thomas Indian School," says Tanaya.

"I thought the whole idea of Indian schools was to somehow introduce the children to white ways of life? How can that happen if one is stuck out in the boondocks?" Harrison asks.

"The Thomas Indian School," Jane says with an exhale. "Asylum, as they originally called it, was established for orphan and destitute Indian children. Back in 1855 that part of New York had the biggest population of Indians and Indian villages. The region was devastated by bloodshed which accounted for the hundreds of orphaned Indian children, orphaned by genocide. In those days Indians were hunted and killed, and their lands confiscated," recites Jane.

"I'm thinking, your natural curiosity about the Thomas Indian School would be greatly enhanced by an all-expense paid trip to beautiful Up State New York. Whadda-ya say gang?" Harrison asks.

"Sounds good to me," says Jane. "Lab research is extremely boring for me. So Tanaya, Inar and I will leave by train first thing in the morning," says Jane, smiling as Harrison writes a check.

CHAPTER ELEVEN
The Cleaner And The Ice Worms

Way across town, a fog bank has moved over a Manhattan Borough. Headlights can be seen as a Dodge Brother's Touring Car pulls up onto a sweeping circular driveway. The car parks in front of a sprawling mansion owned by R.J. Houghington. Randall Houghington invested heavily in the Titanic and as a stockholder in the International Mercantile Company. The loss of his investment has forced him to protect, at all costs, the remainder of his fortune. A covert meeting has been called to resolve issues concerning the Katerpar claim, and Harrison Bennett.

A butler greets Attorney Scott at the door, and he is led through the manor to the awaiting senior officials. The interior reflects the elegance in design that once graced the Titanic. The butler continues past a vaulted room that appears to be a replica of Titanic's First Class entrance. Scott bumps into a chair, he amazed at a sprawling ornate grand staircase complete with a hanging crystal chandelier.

They arrive at room that has tall paneled doors, the butler opens the doors and ushers Scott into a large den. The room is dimly lit, but he can see that it is lined with bookshelves. Joseph Hillcrest, and Charles Barnes, greet him upon entering.

"Thank you for your punctuality, Attorney Scott. Please, have a seat, we know you must be eager to hear our performance report on the hearing today," says Houghington.

"With all due respect sir, I was under the impression that Judge Talbot was to referee the hearing," says Scott.

"Judge Talbot died unexpectedly on Thursday. There was not enough time for us to position another one of our judges in his place. The matter was out of our hands, Meyer was appointed by the State Supreme Court," says Barnes.

"The firm's attorneys did everything we could to point out to Meyer that a case of this caliber could not possibly make sense to a jury - the Bennett client living on an iceberg, that ends up sinking the Titanic. It's laughable, we're hoping Meyer will see, and uphold our motion for a Summary," says Scott.

"We understand that Joseph gave it his best shot at the deposition, did you or any of the lead lawyers find out how much of a settlement they are willing to accept?" Houghington asks.

"The last offer made was $75,000. Bennett does not seem to be interested in a settlement, he's hell bent on taking his ridiculous fable into court," says Scott. "$75,000 was the last offer?" Houghington asks. "Pending Meyer's decision, if it goes on to court, then we offer $175,000. Be sure that Bennett is apprised of this before the settlement conference. Meyer will be contacted tonight for review of the hearing," says Barnes.

"Bennett will hold onto this claim like a bull dog. He wants his record to reflect that it was his legal team that took down the firm by getting his client into court for a judgement. I am confident HT&B will prevent that from happening," says Barnes

"Bully for you attorney. Be sure to let your fellow councilors know that we approved the performance report, you may go now." Houghington says. The butler leads Scott to the door.

As the door is closed, out of the shadows steps the man who was identified as the "Cleaner" by the piano player Rufus. Vincenzo Bravo, is a career criminal not associated with organized crime. He is known in the underworld as "Butch" short for "The Butcher" is a hired assassin now working for Houghington. Although known by the organized crime mob, his cover is that of a coffee broker or a corporate director, some would say chairman of the Board.

"We have retained your services for a specific task. So far, we have had no real need to engage a plan to use your talent, until now." Hillcrest says, handing him a large envelope.

"All the information you will need is here, put it to good use. We trust you will use utmost care in this installment. Avoid any difficulties, your only thought from here-on-out is to leave everything clean and tidy. Do we have an understanding?" Hillcrest asks. Bravo extends a hand, and a firm handshake is shared between them. The butler steps up and gestures towards the door, and he is then shown out.

The door is closed gently, Barnes turns to Houghington. "No claimant, no case, no settlement. Bennett must learn that all things do not converge under the law. We will prevail, and he will not have his day in court, not with us," says Houghington.

"That's the trouble with lawyers who have bleeding hearts, eventually they have to come to terms with how the world turns, and who makes it turn. He should've settled." Barnes says.

Later, at the Cornell University, there are lights shining through the huge double paned windows in the science wing. Inside a modern biology laboratory, a figure can be seen hunched over a microscope. Richard Miles, Professor of Biochemistry and head of the department, is a close friend of Harrison Bennett.

The professor pulls away from the microscope and places pressure with one hand onto his back. With a shaky finger, he pushes his wire rimmed bifocals back onto his nose. Miles is approaching seventy years of age, and is still sharp as a tack. The research he performed for Harrison was of great interest to him. The subject matter of 'ice worms' was unique and a welcomed excursion from the norm of college academics. It is getting close to the end of a twelve hour day for Miles. As he stretches his arms upward, his tall frame contorts until he hears his back pop. He stands and smooths his Einstein styled hair, which springs back, making him seem even taller.

Through rows of steel tables and glass test equipment, a lab assistant comes walking up to Dr. Miles. "Excuse me

Professor Miles, this message was received a few minutes ago, and it's marked urgent," says the lab aid. After a quick glance, Miles leaves his work area and walks towards his office.

Inside Harrison's apartment, a ringing telephone is heard. Harrison is seated on his living room couch, he is hesitant on picking up. Through out the day he has answered several calls with no voice at the other end. The phone continues to ring as Harrison uncaps a bottle of milk. He takes a bite of a sandwich and walks over towards his phone.

"Richard, I didn't expect you to get back to me so soon...I take it that you are interested in testing the specimen" Excellent. Are you willing to testify as an expert witness?"

Back at the university lab, the lab assistant enters the office while Dr. Richard Miles is on the phone with Harrison. A cup of tea is set down onto his desk.

"...in a nutshell?" Well, glacial water is sort of a primordial liquid soup, made up of many different carbon-based elements, that over time have dissolved to form this unique substance. The properties are very unique, including the suspension of finely ground rock and volcanic dust yes, even pollen and at times, prehistoric bacteria, which is now extinct," says Miles over the telephone.

"The bottom-line is; there is a significant amount of colloidal minerals that have an average particle size of 7,000 times smaller than a human red blood cell. If your specimen has all these properties, it will be hard to disprove that it is not glacier water, or in this case iceberg water. Just let me know when we can start on a courtroom exhibit," adds Miles.

After ending the phone call, Miles opens an evening edition.

"HEARING FOR TITANIC CLAIM DECIDED," he then dials the phone.

"Yes, operator, Rochester, New York, please. The number is Chase 2156. Thank you operator. Hello Ed, I have some lab work that you may be interested in..."

CHAPTER TWELVE
The Asylum

Morning has broken, a cab pulls up to Grand Central Rail Transfer in Manhattan. Jane pays the driver while Inar and Tanaya rush towards the turnstiles with their luggage in hand. A ticket taker observes the trio as he lifts the boarding steps from the platform.

"Wait, wait!" Jane shouts. The engine whistle blows just as the porter pulls the boarding steps from the dock. "It's a good thing you bought our tickets yesterday evening," Tanaya says breathlessly as they make their way into the passenger car.

The train begins to pull away from the station. They find their seats in 'passenger coach,' Tanaya helps Inar with his bulky journey-bundle. The bundle contains his belongings among other things, one of which is his seal skin parka. Inar and Tanaya work at pushing the bundle into the overhead rack.

"Uncle should've left his parka back at the apartment, but I'm glad he agreed to wear the Roland overcoat, it makes him look very stylish," says Jane. Inar takes a seat across from the women, not wanting to miss one bit of scenery he snuggles next to the window. As the train picks up speed, he smiles with eyes shining with amazement.

A ticket conductor has made his way through the coach where the trio is seated. Jane has all three of the railway tickets and has them out, ready to be validated.

"I see you're traveling to Arcade. There will be a transfer in the town of Arcade, then from there to Cattaraugus. Lucky for you, the Railroad Commission has suspended transfer charges, so you will not be charged the extra," says the conductor.

"Thank you, and thank the commission. Lord knows, every little bit helps," says Jane. She then pulls a thermos and three sandwiches from her bag.

"The Club Car should be serving from the breakfast menu about now, and their tables are usually taken up in no time at all," advises the conductor.

"We'll consider the option, but these tuna sandwiches are a product of my own little hands, and by golly they will be eaten," declares Jane.

"A tuna fish breakfast. Are you serving wine with that? Tanaya asks in a tone most proper.

"You are absolutely right, sister. To the Club Car! With the money we saved on transfer fees, breakfast will be on the railroad company today," says Jane.

Later, after breakfast, Jane and Tanaya return to their seats in the coach car. They find Inar bundled up and napping in his seat. It is a perfect time to share ideas on information discovered while going through interview files.

"When I spent the night at your apartment, I fell into a deep sleep. I hand't slept long before I woke up, you know how it is, tossing and turning. It wasn't until midnight that I realized there was no getting back to sleep. I made myself a sandwich and went into the living room. I gathered up some files from a box marked; Interviews - Ships Crew and Passenger Survivors. I wanted to locate written account of the events Uncle had described to me," explains Tanaya.

"Not to slight the extensive research already done by Mr. Bennett and yourself, I did so with the intent of discovery. After an hour or so, I came across some very interesting facts." She adds.

"I hope you found the statement that was given by the Marconi Operator. I read through interview after interview and couldn't find it," says Jane.

"That's because the file was mislabeled, I assume it was done intentionally, but it can't be proven. Anyway, it was marked: 'New York City Mother's Club/Relief Fund,'" explains Tanaya.

"The New York City WHAT? Did you bring the files with you?" Jane asks impatiently. Tanaya points upwards to the overhead luggage rack. Hastily, Jane retrieves a document case from the luggage rack. Opening the folder she begins to read through the information. "This is absolutely incredible," says Jane as she begins to read from the document.

"Herald S. McBride, in his account of that night stated that Captain Smith personally relieved them from their duties," she says, reading from the document. "It says here, he and the other operator continued out onto the Boat Deck, but once outside the door he said everything became so chaotic he felt I had to bail down to the deck below,'" reads Jane.

"Skip down to the middle of the next page and tell me what you think," suggests Tanaya. Jane places the page face down and goes on to the next.

"...and as I descended the stairwell, I heard music. My curiosity got the best of me as I started down to the Bridge Deck. While in the stairwell, the sound became more faint. Turning towards the direction of the music,

I caught a glimpse of what had left me dumbfounded.

"There on the Promenade Deck, I saw Titanic's band performing, and they were playing as if showcasing for another tour. There were passengers who chose to stop and listen, those women who were listening began to weep. They were comforted with spirits of brandy to keep them warm. A saloon steward, meandered through and around frantic passengers to serve drinks, it was unbelievable. I could see that the disorder was spreading from the lower decks upward, I say this because the Third Class passengers were being allowed onto First and Second Class decks. There was an Eskimo on the Promenade Deck!" Jane reads.

"My God..." says Jane astonished. She puts the document folder down and looks across the isle where Inar sitting quietly, enjoying the passing scenery. She is struck with a realization; she is in the presence of a living legend.

"In another account, Edward Wheeler, Saloon Steward, stated that he witnessed McBride"s protest to the Third Officer," says Tanaya.

"Sir, you must do something. Steerage class passengers are being allowed onto the First and Second Class decks! McBride complains.

"Damn it man! Can you not see what is going on here? The ship is sinking!" The Officer shouts.

"You can be sure that when this is over, I will see to it that Marconi International hears about this!" Jane reads. "And, that they did," says Jane with a somber expression.

"You had mentioned earlier in the research that just before being locked in the storage room, Inar witnessed mail bags floating throughout the corridor?" Jane asks.

"Yes, he remembered that incident because the bags looked like seals, floating in the water," replies Tanaya.

"I found this statement by Allen Bright, Mail Room Clerk. When asked; 'did you see any Third Class passengers your way towards the upper decks, and did he try to warn them of the impending doom," offers Tanaya.

"It says here that Bright stated: 'The only passenger that looked to be Third Class was an Eskimo, and he was being led down into the hull by two of the crew. We shouted out to them to get topside, the lower compartments are flooded out completely," reads Tanaya.

"These Marconi operators? Were they related to Titanic's owners? Who were they?" Jane asks.

"The wireless telegraph operators were not employed by the liner company. The were sort of leased through the Marconi International Marine Telegraph Company. They had one duty, and that was to operate, receive and send wireless messages. These guys were acting under a different set of rules," says Tanaya.

"I'll say, the book of 'How not to proceed,' says Jane as she begins to write notes for Harrison. "Do you think...?" Tanaya says. Jane then realizes that the Cattaraugus Indian Reservation may be the safest place that Inar can be for now. She begins to confide in Tanaya her realization, but she sees that she has fallen fast asleep. Jane puts her pencil down and the folder is laid in her lap. She finally allows herself to relax.

Looking out the window at the scenery, Jane wonders if the case goes to trial, will the evidence appear to be unsympathetic to the survivors? Will the press and the public turn on them for survivor bashing? Worse yet gold digging. There is another card they have not considered to put into play. After all the tragedy, Inar also witnessed bravery and selfless acts of heroism. In the last final hour of the Titanic, there were true accounts of gallantry told of crew and passengers.

Newspapers were flooded with such accounts, and one was of the engine room crew. The eminent threat of death by drowning did not hinder the engineers who kept the generators running. Time and again it was told how these brave men kept the ship lights burning. The main concern among the engineers was to keep the generators running so that passengers still below deck, could see their way to safety. There was a great number of the crew risked their lives by performing their jobs far beyond the call of their duty. Only one of the Marconi Operators survived the tragedy, the accounts in the hearings were headline news;

"I went through an awful mass of people to his cabin. The decks were full of scrambling men and women. I went to my cabin and dressed. Every few minutes, operator Phillips would send me to the Captain with little messages. I noticed as I came back from one trip they were putting women and children in lifeboats. I went out on deck and looked around. The water was very close up to the boat deck. I thought it was time to look about and see if there was anything detached that would float. "I remembered my life belt under my bunk. I went and got it. I saw a collapsible boat near a funnel and went over to it. Phillips ran aft, and that was the last I ever saw of him alive. I went to the place I had seen the collapsible boat on the boat deck, and to my surprise I saw the boat and the men still trying to push it off. I guess there wasn't a sailor in the crowd. They couldn't do it. I went up to them and was just lending a hand when a large wave came awash of the deck. The big wave carried the boat off. I had hold of an oarlock, and I went off with it. Smoke and sparks were rushing out of her funnel.

"There must have been an explosion, but we had heard none. We only saw the big stream of sparks. The ship was gradually turning on her nose just like a duck does that goes down for a dive. I had only one thing on my mind; to get away from the suction. I swam with all my might. I suppose I was 150 feet away when the Titanic went on her nose with her aft quarter sticking up in the air, she began to settle slowly. I was floating out in the sea with my life belt on, and the band was still on deck playing the Autumn tune. How they ever did it I cannot imagine," testified one of the operators.

It was how the Marconi Operator told his story immediately upon his arrival in New York, while still fresh in his mind, reads a side note. Jane turns her thoughts to Inar's account of his experience of the last minutes of the sinking ship will undoubtedly be called into question.

"There should be no question as to the where a-bouts of Captain Smith at the time of the sinking. The fact is, there is written testimony of Captain Smith risking his own life to save an infant from drowning in the frigid seas of the North Atlantic," the transcript reads.

Jane is confident that as far as the defense is concerned, they will present this account. Instinct tells her that every mother who reads the account will counter that an infant will succumb to extreme cold within minutes.

Jane goes over her notes, which she reads to make sure she noted everything of importance between Tanaya and herself. Edward Wheeler, Saloon Steward, serving brandy to passengers on the Promenade Deck, identified Inar dancing a jig while the band played a Rag Time tune. Earnest Arter, and William Brice, both Abel Body Sea man, identified by Inar as the sea men who took him into custody. Allen Bright, Mail Room Clerk, identified Inar being escorted down towards the hull of the ship. Harold McBride, wireless telegrapher, identified Inar as a Third Class passenger on the Promenade Deck.

The train whistle awakens Tanaya. "Are we there yet?" She asks. "We are about an hour out from Arcade transfer station," says Jane.

"How's Uncle doing?" Tanaya asks as she looks across the isle. "He's doing just fine, over there enjoying the ride." Jane says.

"Tell me what you think of this idea; what if we talked Inar into staying on the reservation until the trial date is set?" Jane asks. "You are concerned about Uncle's safety, aren't you?" Tanaya asks. Jane nods her head.

"Me too." Tanaya says. "Good, first chance I get, I'll call Harry and get an okay from him," explains Jane.

CHAPTER THIRTEEN
While The Cats Are Away

An apartment door is pushed open by a police officer's night stick. In the hallway of Jane's apartment, two uniformed police officers stand in the doorway. While peering behind the door frame, the neighbor who called, sneaks a peek into the ransacked apartment. "Just as I thought," says the neighbor.

"You reported a loud disturbance, and it looks to me like a loud disturbance it was," the officer's replies.

Upon entering, the responding policemen step over Jane's belongings, strewn across the floor. "And you reported, no hollering or screaming?" The officer asks.

"None at all, just a-bunch of slamming and banging," the neighbor replies. Having cleared Jane's bedroom of any intruders, the other officer announces a theory.

"There are no bodies, no sign of breaking and entering. Looks like vandalism to me," says the officer.

"Same here, that painting would have brought at least ten bucks on the street," says the other officer. "Aren't you going to do anything about it?" The neighbor asks.

"Do anything to who? You're the only witness, and you didn't see anyone coming in or going out of this apartment?" Asks the officer.

Just then one of the officer's turns towards the entrance door. "Who are you?"

Standing in the doorway is Harrison, shocked at the damage to Jane's apartment.

"I'm Harrison Bennett, I'm an attorney. Jane Reynolds is my associate in law, and this is her apartment. What happened here?" Harrison asks. "This is a police matter councilor. Why are you here?" The officer asks. "Miss Reynolds left me a key, we are working a case, I came by to retrieve some files," replies Harrison.

"Good luck finding anything in this mess. Looks like someone came in and went crazy. Take a look around, see if you can I.D. anything that's missing," he says.

Harrison goes to a file drawer by Jane's desk, where he finds the file drawers empty. "There are some documents missing. A case we're preparing for trial. Looks to me like burglary." Harrison says.

"Burglary he says," the officer says to his partner. "Okay, councilor, how should we enter this in our report? Paper theft? How many pieces?" The officer mocks.

"To be precise, if it were my report, I would enter the stolen items as confidential court documents...a term you will have to become familiar with, since you may have to repeat the term on the witness stand," advises Harrison. "Confidential court documents it is, councilor," agrees the officer.

As the door closes behind the officer, Harrison searches further and finds a single empty file folder under the sofa.

"Oh shoot. They made off with our entire case." Harrison sits back onto a ragged couch, resting his head in his hand.

Back on the tracks, a train whistle is heard as the train nears a road crossing. A conductor walks down the isle of the coach announcing the next stop. "Cattaraugus, Cattaraugus, next stop." Inar is awaken by a gentle tug on his shoulder. Jane's smile is the first thing he sees as his eyes open.

"Wake up Uncle, we're here," she says gleefully. Jane and Tanaya help him up and guide him into the isle. Tanaya waves out the window when she sees two of her friends waiting on the dock. "We have a ride to the school," she says with relief.

"Tanaya, thank you for arranging transportation. I checked the depot hours and they lock up everything at 10:00 p.m. and it's now a freezing 9:50 p.m," says

Jane. The early spring weather in Upstate New York is stubborn, signs of winter are still present.

After introductions, Tony, the driver and "Scooter" the mechanic, help everyone onto the Thomas Indian School bus. "Oh my, I forgot to telephone Harrison to let him know of our arrival." Jane says, just as Tanaya boards the bus. A mechanical lever is pulled and the bus doors are shut.

"I just got-off the phone with Mr. Bennett." Tanaya says as she seats herself beside Jane. "I'm sorry, but the ice is so slippery, I didn't want to have you make your way back to the station ticket room," explains Tanaya, looking down at Jane's high heels.

"What is it?" You're not telling me something Tanaya." Jane insists. "He was frantic, he was shouting over the phone, I couldn't understand what he was saying. Also, the connection was very bad and breaking up," says Tanaya reluctantly.

"Good try. Tell me some of the words you were able to understand; and take your time," pleads Jane.

"He said someone entered your apartment and smashed to bits," blurts Tanaya, not knowing how Jane will react.

"Hillcrest! That dirty son-of-a-gun, unleashed his thugs in my apartment! What else did he say?" Jane says.

"Words that concerned case files, records, and trial." Tanaya says. Jane stands to leave the bus. "The station manager has closed the doors, we will have to wait until we get to the school. You can call there," says Tanaya solemnly.

"Before I had a chance to tell Mr. Bennett that the remainder of the case files were on the Island, the phone went dead," says Tanaya.

"Harry is going crazy right now. We have to get word to him." Jane looks out the bus window and sees the train station dock lights go out. "How much longer to the school?" Jane asks. Overhearing the question, the bus driver answers in a drab voice.

"Given conditions; ice roads, slush, mud and more snow are on the way, ten miles an hour," says the driver. "Anthony, we have to reach the school before the administration office closes," explains Tanaya.

"Tanaya, there's no-way we are reaching the administration office before they shut down. It's the Easter weekend, nothing but non essential staff for at least three days."

Anthony says. Tanaya looks to Jane with a hopeless look, and shrugs her shoulders.

"Tell you what, if you hang on to your seats, we'll see how she handles at twenty miles an hour. That's the best I can do for now," says the driver.

The remainder of the road trip is bumpy and at times, they find themselves going side ways over the slippery road. Soon the lights of the school can be seen in the distance.

"I am feeling uneasy about having stored the case files at Ellis," Jane says as she confides in Tanaya.

"It seemed like a good idea at the time but, now under the circumstances, when I think of the security, and the lack of it; I feel uncomfortable," says Tanaya. "Did you hide them someplace, or are they lying on your coffee table?" Jane asks.

"The files are not in my room. Tanaya says, looking to a puzzled Jane. "I hid them in the kitchen storeroom; a locked kitchen storage room, inside a flour crock," reveals Tanaya. "Thank heaven. I hope you have the key." Jane implies.

Tanaya dangles a skeleton key. The bus slows and as it turns into a gated entrance, the Indian school comes into sight at the end of a long driveway. Jane reads aloud as the bus headlights shine upon the school entrance sign.

"The Thomas Asylum for Orphan and Destitute Indians. Hmmm, nothing like a gloomy welcome sign to brighten a person's visit." Jane says looking away.

Anthony pulls up to the Administration Building, and looking out of the school bus window, he can see that there is a single light shining in the hallway. He turns in his seat and faces Tanaya and Jane.

"Looks like you're in luck, Ronnie Black Eye is guarding the building tonight. Oh, I meant to say Sergeant Black Eye," says Anthony. Jane springs upward in her seat. Tanaya grasps her wrist and pulls her back.

"We'll go take a look if you want, but it looks to me like it's locked up." Scooter says, as they step down from the bus. Tanaya and Jane watch as he tries the door handle. Anthony bangs on the door while looking through the door panes. Jane becomes discouraged and sits back.

"I have an idea that I think will work, let me try something here...But I'll have to use your make-up bag for just a minute." Tanaya says. "Ahhh, you mean the little magic bag of tricks? You got it sweetheart," Jane says.

When Jane looks out the bus window, she sees Scooter and Anthony exchanging concerns with a uniformed guard. It seems to her that Anthony is doing all the talking as he points a finger towards the bus.

"What's he saying to the guard?" Jane asks, as she turns to Tanaya. She looks again to see her looking into a compact powder case applying red lipstick, her lips stretched into a perfect oval opening. Jane lends a hand and rubs a little rouge on Tanaya's perfectly chiseled cheek bones. Leaning back, Tanaya's reflection gives her a better look. Jane eagerly agrees.

"I don't know who he is, but the poor guy doesn't stand a chance," says Jane. Anthony boards the bus, followed by Scooter. He takes his place behind the wheel and turns to the passengers.

"Ronnie says, 'No dice', the doors are locked and they will stay..." Anthony drops his voice mid-sentence. He catches sight of Tanaya, as she gracefully stands and struts towards the door. Jane smiles, clasps her hands into her lap, watching Tanaya as she approaches the front of bus.

"Stunning, absolutely stunning," says Jane as if praising an understudy.

As Tanaya approaches the steps of the four-story red brick building, she turns slightly to see the faces of Jane, Anthony, and Inar, looking out of the frosted bus windows, towards the Administration Building.

Ronnie Black Eye stands, blocking the entrance. The door is open enough to reveal a well built frame.

"Hello, Ronnie. I'm so happy to see you," Tanaya says seductively.

"Tanaya?" The astonished building guard asks. "Yes, you silly boy." Tanaya says as she reaches out with a gloved hand and touches his chest.

Jane can see Tanaya gesturing with her hands, pleading with the guard to let her use the school telephone. "Come-on, come-on," says Jane with urgency. Then a smile comes to her face as she sees Tanaya lift her hand to signal for Jane with an outstretched arm.

"Please, Anthony, can you wait? It's just a telephone call, I promise it won't take long," pleads Jane as she steps from the bus. "Miss Reynolds, I don't know what you girls are up-to, but it looks a little sketchy to me, and I don't want to have anything to do with it," says the driver as he pulls the bus doors shut.

Looking into the interior bus mirror, Anthony can see Inar sitting quietly in a seat, looking out a foggy window. "Your are really something, Inar Katerpar getting mixed up with those two firecrackers," says Anthony. "Yeah, I hope you have enough energy to keep up with them," says Scooter with a grin. Inar can tell by their tone that they are making light of the situation. He extends an appreciative chuckle.

Inside the Administration Building, Tanaya is quietly talking with Officer Black Eye, while Jane winds up her conversation with Harrison.

"There might be a problem getting to the train station tomorrow morning...5:30 a.m., yes. We'll try our best...see you then, Harry," relates Jane as she hangs-up the receiver.

Later, after the school bus pulls away from Building 10, Inar leads the way to his sleeping quarters. The school officials have arranged makeshift sleeping quarters that lead past the boiler room, the main source of heat for the school.

"Harry was so relieved and grateful for your decision, to leave the files in a safe place. He informed me that Ellis Island burned to the ground in 1897," says Jane. "Really?" Tanaya asks quizzically. "Yup. Are you ready for this? The fire started in the facility kitchen," Jane says.

"Don't have to tell me where we're going when we get back. What are the odds of it happening again?" Tanaya asks.

"Probably one in a bazillion. Harry's odds are different, he seems to think it'll burn tomorrow," says Jane amusingly. "He strongly suggested that if possible, I return with you tomorrow, with the H2o specimen," explains Jane.

"What about Uncle?" Tanaya asks. "Harry also asked me to have you talk with Inar. He feels it would be best for Inar to stay here at the school. Do you think he would mind staying here at the school until a trial date can be set?" asks Jane.

"I think he will agree that it makes sense. The school will be the safest place for now. We have a full staff of security here that will look out for him, and the Bureau of Indian Affairs have a Police Station here at the school," says Tanaya.

"Do I hear a 'but' in there?" Jane asks.

"Well, yes. There is a little something about my job at Ellis. I'm beginning to see this case is going to consume me." Tanaya says wearily.

"Harry and I discussed that very matter a few days ago. He says he may be able to pull some strings at Ellis Island Immigration. How many times have you been absent?" Jane asks.

"I haven't been sick one day," Tanaya says. "Good, because we can work that into the case management and expenses. Are you sure that you're all right with this?" Jane asks.

"Sure thing, all I need is to be confident that Uncle remains safe. Once that is made clear, you and Mr. Bennett will have my complete cooperation," pledges Tanaya. Jane breaths a deep sigh of relief.

"Your little conversation with Ronny Black Eye? What was it you said to him that made him change his mind about unlocking the doors?" Jane asks. "There is a Spring gathering coming up on the reservation, I agreed to attend the event, as his date." Tanaya replies.

"Well done, Princess Navarra," says Jane. The sound of a raging boiler fire fills their ears as they enter the main boiler room. The watch man stands upright, as Inar and his guests pass. "Hey, Inuit. Where you been, I've missed playing cards with you." Fire Watch says in native language. The trio turns to see a hulking figure shadowed by the blinding furnace light. With a half-raised shovel, the fire watcher waits for a response. Inar looks towards the fire watch, and Jane sees his face, orange shadows dancing from left to right. With an upheld hand, an acknowledgement is given with a quick nod. The metal scraping against cement continues, but becomes less annoying as they continue to walk down a narrow stone corridor. The corridor remains lit, only by the flaming coals of the furnace.

Jane's mind is spinning. The school had arrangements to place Inar in what they called a "dungeon," but for Inar, it was simply home. Inar's life within the stone walls of the basement have been decorated with photographs and drawings from newspapers. A seal skin bundle is pulled out from beneath his bunk. Once the leather straps are untied, the contents are revealed as the skin unfolds. The seal bladder is lifted from the skin and handed to Jane. There is a sloshing sound as she holds it in her hands.

"Hear that? That is the sound of a jury returning a verdict in favor of our court case," Jane says. "Harry wants me to mail several specimen tubes to Harvard University, but we'll be back in the city before the mail gets there," Jane explains.

"We have a couple of beds reserved for us in the girls ward, we'll see you at breakfast. Good dreams Uncle," says Tanaya. Jane gives Inar a hug and a smile.

Early the next morning at a breakfast diner in Manhattan, Joseph Hillcrest raises a coffee cup to his lips, while enduring the crude sounds of Vincenzo Bravo, noisily devouring his breakfast. As he looks on, he wonders; this is the way it's done in prison, having to hurriedly eat one's food before it is snatched by another prisoner. Hillcrest's patience begins to grow thin, but Vincenzo is unaware of his annoyance. There is still food left on his plate. Hillcrest places his cup down onto the saucer with noticeable intention. Bravo drops the silverware down onto his plate and pushes it away.

"As I was saying; our clients have managed to disappear on us." Bravo says. "No Mr. Bravo, they have not disappeared on us, they have disappeared on you." Hillcrest says with a cold stare.

"With one exception, Bennett is still holed up in his apartment, my men report that he payed a visit to his associate, but as you know she was not there. We would have made a move on him then, had it not been for the cops," Bravo says.

"Our concern now is, there cannot be any incident that will tie your crew's failed apartment fiasco with Bennett. I thought we made it clear, whatever occurs, it must appear to be an unfortunate and random event," says Hillcrest poignantly.

"That is the way it was arranged. When we couldn't find the documents, we intensified our search, things got a little messy. On the other hand, we can't do a thing about Bennett, he doesn't leave his apartment. The guy doesn't visit his office and his secretary is handling the footwork for the claim," says Bravo. "It's not complicated. Find the associate, and the client, and you will find the files," says Hillcrest, as he places an envelope on the table before Bravo. Hillcrest starts for the exit, as Bravo begins pick at the breakfast leftovers on Hillcrest's plate.

CHAPTER FOURTEEN
Quasi-Immigration

Inside Harrison's apartment, a stack of testimonial files lay amid Chinese food cartons, candy wrappers, beer bottles and assorted clothing. Harrison has remained in his apartment for days. Except for the short excursion to Jane's apartment, his research into Titanic's last hours afloat, have been extensive. Throughout the night, Harrison continued to read article after news article from newspapers across the country. Hand written notes and short compositions are gathered into an overstuffed folder. Harrison is hoping he found an account in the following article from the Evening Tribune, describing how the U.S. allowed immigration without being fully processed.

TITANIC SURVIVORS QUESTIONED
April 29, 1912   Evening Tribune

With the country still reeling with news of the loss of over a thousand souls, new light has come to bear on corruption of the Immigration Service. Questions of immigrant processing have officials running for cover. The sinking of the RMS Titanic brought a number of laws and regulations under scrutiny. Insurance investigators as well as political inquiries into the tragic event of the Titanic are now subject to subpoena. In 1891, the Federal Government assumed the task of inspecting, admitting, or rejecting, and processing all immigrants seeking admission to the United States. Immigration laws go back to 1600's, but most relevant are Acts passed into law this century. In 1890, the House Committee of Immigration chose Ellis Island as the site for a new immigrant screening station, and Congress passed it into law.

On January 2, 1882 a new Federal facility opened on Ellis Island in New York Harbor. Under Immigration regulations, commanders, and officers of ocean liners were deemed responsible to place every passenger on a manifest, or list. Arriving U.S. citizens who disembarked at a U.S. Port their entry was naturally admitted. Immigration regulations read that some reasons for not being admitted were based on moral standards; for example, if an immigrant was found to have more than one spouse, he was denied entry. The fine for allowing passage of an immigrant found in violation was substantial, but affordable to the liner companies. As the onslaught of immigrants continued with some 20 ships per day disembarking passengers and immigrants onto New York City piers, those immigrants found not to be admissible became a liability to profits.

As numerous fines continued to be imposed, the liner companies began to lose profits and collateral losses began to climb. In addition, the fines, immigration would force on the company, owning the ship or ships, to provide passage for the deported immigrants back to their port of origin, at company expense. To protect their interests, ocean liner companies began processing the immigrants at ticket counters. It was required of a non-citizen to complete immigration forms before tickets were bought. The Immigration law required certain criteria to be completed in full. Basic to the forms were the person's age, sex, marital status, occupation specialty, country of origin, last permanent residence, and destination. The immigration forms then became the liner's passenger manifests. Prior to embarkation, a U.S. Confluent official then certified the documents according to the answers given on the person's immigration form. Once on U.S. soil the documents were taken into custody by the U.S. immigration authorities.

Before disembarkation at Southampton in April 1912, the ship's manifest, or passenger list, was the responsibility of the head steward of Titanic. This manifest was a detailed account of each passenger, and was to be presented by Titanic's purser to Immigration Officials upon docking at the White Star pier. The passenger list was also important to officials when performing functions of admittance and recording immigrant statistics.

Government tax accountants would also use the statistics to levy taxes based upon the ship's manifest for a 'head tax' to bill passenger lines. In the end, the documented immigrants would be placed before immigration examiners before becoming naturalized by the United States Naturalization Service who also would use the records to process legal admissions for U.S. Naturalization.

It has been three years since the tragic accident of the Titanic. There are still questions that have to be answered. The spot light will remain focused on the ship's owners and surviving ships officers.

Harrison gently closes the folder and places it on top of a stack of documents, he dials his office, where his office secretary, Martha answers the phone.

"Is this the Executive Secretary of the Bennet Law Office?" Harrison asks with admiration.

"I do hope you are enjoying your little vacation, Harry. I have received a lead to one of the many you had requested. Just a little notation Harry for your personal records. I have been here everyday and I have waylaid my days off in hopes that you will return and lead your troops. Troops who remain faithfully in the trenches," says Martha through the phone.

"I'm thinking about it, thinking...yes, I can see it now. A vision has come to me, and given me a very mysterious answer..." Harrison teases, countering Martha's taunt about his troops.

"Okay Mr. Smarty Pants, I didn't know you were moonlighting as a fortune teller. All kidding aside, it looks as though your hunch about the press being squelched is right. Get a pencil and pad," says Martha.

"First message came from Dr. Miles, he wants you to call a political science professor, at Princeton, by the name Harold

Wendell at phone number 1656," explains Martha. "You have two days to get your mother a birthday gift," she adds.

"Thank you for reminding me, once again you've save my skin. I'll give the professor a call. Sign all the checks for me, and get them in the mail, or we will be working by candle light," says Harrison.

The phone is dialed, and the operator connects a line to the professor. "Hello, Professor Wendell" Doctor Miles gave me your number, my name is Harrison Bennett." At the other end, the professor is at his desk, he places his tobacco pipe in an ash tray.

"I have some information you may appreciate. But first, I want you to know that I admire your courage. Someone has to step up and raise a voice in the name of all those lost when the Titanic went down. I will help you in any way I can," Wendell pledges.

"Now understand, the information I am about to give you has never been divulged. It is highly sensitive, and can place you into a dangerous situation. Take it and be sure, the information came straight from a reliable source," says Wendell.

"I'm willing to accept the risks professor," assures Harrison. "A few years back I was in Washington, D.C. visiting a colleague.

He shared something with me that I found disturbing and interesting at the same time. My source also found it oddly interesting, Wendell continues:

"I'm going to take you back to April 15, 1912. On that day within hours after the tragedy, a wireless message was received in the capitol.

It was from a law firm based here in the U.S., representing Titanic. The message was delivered to the Commissioner-General of the Immigration Service. Get it? Wendell asks.

"A-firm. Please go on," replies Harrison.

"While I can't recall the exact wording of the message, I can recall to a point of certainty; the attorneys were pleading with the commissioner to take a corroborative action on the tragedy. They were in deep need of assistance regarding the Third Class survivor passengers. It was explained to me that soon afterwards a communiqué was sent out as 'confidential' in nature. It strongly suggested to 'expedite transition' in each case of the survivor process. Officials took this request as a directive and acquiesced. The 'special arrangements' became an across-the-board admission into the United States," says Wendell over the phone.

"It's troubling to me that a shipping company could have that much pull with a government agency. Why do you think that communique went out? What could be gained by the Immigration Service handing out free passes to enter the country?" Harrison asks.

"This act of expedited transition, broke the law. There is a word for it, and it's called Treachery. You see, when the Immigration Service allowed, what is legally deemed as a 'migration' into the United States, they broke Federal law. As we all know, there are laws against illegal immigration. A person can be prosecuted under the 'Naturalization Act' and the 'Alien and Sedition Acts'. These poor immigrants cannot be naturalized without signed documents from the Immigration Service. They are in the country illegally, and once found, can be deported back to their country. Get it? Wendell asks.

"Good God. What better way to prevent negative testimony by immigrant survivors - deportation. They would be outside the jurisdiction of the United States, thus eliminating any and threat to the owners of Titanic," says Harrison in disgust.

"It's amazing. How the ship continues to haunt Americans with myriad of unanswered questions.

"It seems as though someone wants the public to believe that not even the government is not immune to the terrible event," adds Harrison.

"Got that. You can add the press to that immune deficiency, because right now, I'm running down a lead that may implicate the President," says Wendell.

"Taft?" Harrison asks. There is no reply.

"Republican. It was only a matter of time before members of the democratic party to elect Wilson, caught wind of the immigration scam. Senator Smith approached Taft in the Capitol, and he asked him to take decisive action against the owners of Titanic. A congressional admonishment would politically insulate the United States from the tragic event.

"This plea was ignored because a U.S. Citizen was a member of the International Mercantile Marine Company. Taft flatly declined. 'I don't want anything to do with the situation,' was the statement. In doing so, he denied any connection to his constituents," says Wendell.

"Enter, the mud slinging contest. What was the story on the inside? He asks.

"The democrats threatened to go public with a statement, saying that the President knew of the Titanic the day she went down. The major newspapers along with thousands of family members, relatives, and friends, waited without a word of the number of survivors, who they were. How do you spell complicity? With one 't' or two?" Wendell asks.

"I was thinking of another word. Impeachment," says Harrison.

"Here is something else you may be interested in; immigrant survivors could have been placed into custody by Port Officers the minute they tried to leave the dock. Port officers chose not to act. They said it was too complicated to tell who were the immigrants, and who were not. They used the nonexistent passenger list as an excuse not to process," Wendell exclaims over the phone.

"That is totally absurd. It would seem to anyone else that those survivors who could not speak English, were the immigrants," says Harrison.

"It was my understanding that many of the accounts were news worthy, but the better of the major newspapers did not bother to place them into print. There were some independent syndicates that reported the survivors were quickly whisked away before news reporters could get a story from them," says Harrison.

"Truth being, it was obvious the regulations governing immigration were set aside to accommodate what many have perceived as a huge government cover up," explains Wendell. "Is that your take or newsprint?" Harrison asks. "Believe it or not, it was a small town reporter that had the balls to write it up. It was a scolding bit of print," says Wendell. "When did it get published?" Harrison asks. "It didn't. James Wilcox a reporter for the Progress Citizen, tried to spill the beans. His boss and his boss's bosses, round-filed the piece before it reached the print editor," says Wendell.

"There is one more item that can back up the immigration issue. In an article published by the 'New York American,' a year before Titanic met her end, reporter Noah Wrinkle wrote; 'Ellis Island, Yesterday And Today.' The article traced the history and the workings of the island. Wrinkle observed and wrote;

'Once a steam passenger ship entered the navigable waters of the Hudson River, a docking procedure took place at a designated pier. Like a choreographed dance, tug boats would guide the liner into position until secured at the dock. The next step in the arrival and disembarkation process, a screening process of all passengers, First Class down to steerage. The Immigration Officials would take the lead in coordinating the process. The New York Quarantine Officials, along with doctors and nurses of Public Health Service, would take their place in the process,'" reads Wendell.

"The way it was explained to me, by an associate who works on Ellis, was that when it came to the process at Ellis Island, she placed the importance of the process on the thoroughness of the immigration screening. Now, questions are being asked by normal citizens, public officials, and newly arrived naturalized U.S. Citizens. What happened to the process?" He asks.

"Harrison, that's all of it. If I hear of any more leads, I will contact you. What you have now is the meat of it. Good luck," says Wendell, ending the call.

Harrison returns to the couch. His head is reeling from the phone conversation. Stretching out on the couch, he hopes to take a short nap.

A loud banging at the door startles Harrison awake. Jolting to an upright position, he looks at the clock. "Three thirty? Some cat nap that was," says Harrison, thinking aloud. The knocking continues. Harrison pulls a baseball bat out from under his couch. Peering through the peep hole, he can see a delivery boy with a telegram. Harrison opens the door.

"Wireless message for Mr. Harrison Bennett," says the delivery boy. After signing for the message, a tip is offered and Harrison closes the door, but not before looking up and down the hallway. There is a letter opener on his desk. He opens the envelope and reads the message; "Have some ice water. Will be back today 6:45 p.m. - Jane."

"Well, I'll be...she's got the proof," Harrison says triumphantly. The phone rings. On the other end is Harrison's secretary again.

"I just received a call from a lead on one of the immigrant survivors. The first piece of evidence to collaborate the finding was a Miss Hanna Turjia. She had been taken from the Carpathia directly to St. Vincent's Hospital. There at the hospital, she was found in good health. It is a matter of record that she spoke no English, and is a survivor of the Titanic. Turjia was 'tagged' by an Immigration Aide who just happened to be at the hospital, and put on a train. She was escorted to Ashtabula, Ohio, her destination. Except for the prior clearance, or 'free pass' at New York Harbor, she was still expecting to be processed by the Immigration Service. This bit of immigration deviance should have been splashed across headlines all over the state.

If not for a local newspaper reporter, the incident would have gone unnoticed. The reporter wrote about her arrival and the celebration of the townspeople who treated her as though she was royalty. Every major newspaper in New York sent it to print," Martha says on the other end.

"Excellent, Miss Mills. I really do appreciate the work effort while the Katerpar case progresses. I'm expecting to meet with Jane later today and we will work throughout the weekend," says Harrison, replacing the receiver.

"The London Times had no problem reporting; 'A Great Loss of Life,' on the morning of April 15Th. The New York Times reported only that Titanic sent out a C.Q.D. Message," says Harrison aloud, as he vents his frustration.

CHAPTER FIFTEEN
Propeller 401

Secretary Mills comes to mind as he recalls the last words offered to her; "If your office work is finished and there are no pressing messages, take the rest of the day off and get a head start on your weekend, but be sure to lock all the filing cabinets, before you leave the office," Harrison recalls. He begins to hope it was the right decision to leave the law office unattended. He picks up the phone and calls a security company to post a guard out side the building. Harrison then prepares to travel to Grand Central in Manhattan to meet Jane and Tanaya.

The lobby elevator door is pulled open by a bell hop and Harrison steps into the lobby. "Your messages Mr. Bennett," says the desk clerk. Harrison glances through the messages.

One of the notes grabs his attention - Call MA-4755 after 8pm. prop 401. Harrison steps toward the lobby entry doors, his eyes still focused the note.

As he looks towards the glass entrance doors, he sees two men sitting inside a parked car across the street from his apartment building. He follows his instincts which tell not to go through the doors. His thoughts turn to Jane and the incident at her apartment. Harrison stops and stands still, then back steps out of view of the men outside in the parked car.

"Something wrong, Mr. Bennett?" The desk clerk asks. "No, not at all. I just forgot, I had something to do on Madison Avenue. I'll use the rear entrance today," says Harrison.

Once out on Madison Avenue, he quickly hails down a cab. "42nd, Grand Central Terminal, please," says Harrison. He sits back and reaches into his pocket, again he looks at the note left as a message. "Prop 401," he says, wondering out loud. His recall is vague concerning the number 401. Deep down inside he feels it is significant, and he tucks the note back into his shirt pocket, thinking he will call the telephone number later. "Driver, would you happen to know what time the last ferry leaves for Ellis Island?" He asks.

"That would be 9:30, departure on this side," says the driver. "Thanks, by the way, is this a new cab?" Harrison asks. "Yeah, I had a Detroit Electric, but after 80 miles or so, she had to go to the garage for a charge. This year, I decided to go gas engine with Henry Ford. The gas is a more, but it's made up by no downtime for battery charging," says the driver.

"How was the price? Just as, or more than the electric?" Harrison asks. "Are you kidding me?" The cost of a standard electric car is $1,000 all the way up to $3,000. This Model "T" Ford cost me $500, I can't complain about that. It's the way of the future for cabbies here in the City," says the driver.

The cab driver slows the vehicle as they pull up to the Manhattan Grand Central. After paying the cab fare, Harrison makes his way through the crowded train terminal to Track 21.

Within the cavernous main terminal lobby Harrison, by chance, comes across Jane and Tanaya.

"Well, how about that? I was just coming to meet you," says Harrison. "Not your fault, some sort of train committee dealings at the transfer. How you doing Harry?" Jane asks.

"Just fine for now. Now that you're here," says Harrison with a gleeful expression. Jane looks at Tanaya. "We don't like the way you said that Harry," Jane says with apprehension.

"I'll explain on the way to your hotel," Harrison says, as he takes their bags and heads for the terminal doors. "Hotel?

Harry what's going on? I want to go to my apartment, I have to check on the damage," Jane demands as she hurries to catch up.

"Walk with me, and listen-up," says Harrison as they pass through the exit doors. "I had put you up at the 'Astor' for several days," he says while climbing into a cab.

Inside the cab, Harrison looks around nervously, thinking someone may be following him.

"Why are we going to the Astor and not my apartment, Harrison? Is there something else you're not telling me?" Jane asks.

"Well, it's like this; it's probably not as bad as it seems, but I had a lengthly conversation with a friend of a friend. Remember that proverbial can of worms? Well, it's been opened," Harrison says in a hushed tone.

"I thought we were talking about my trashed apartment, did you find out who broke into my apartment? Jane asks.

"It was ransacked with no apparent motive. That's the way the police put it," says Harrison, exposing the top of his head towards her.

"Is that your humble act? I want to go home, I want to go back to my apartment.

Please, have the cab driver take me to my apartment," insists Jane.

"Jane, maybe you should listen to what he is saying. He maybe right. It could've been worse, we could have been there." Tanaya pleads. "How bad is it?" Jane asks. "It's a mess, I don't know what was taken, if anything at all. I just wish to get you set up at the Astor, and we'll devise a plan there," says Harrison.

"Who would do such a thing" And why my place" Jane asks. "Two guesses, and the first one doesn't count," says Harrison.

"I talked with the police officers who were called to your apartment because of a disturbance. They explained me that it didn't look like a burglary. None of your valuable items had been taken, to them it looked like a classic case of vandalism, nothing more. Without evidence, they had to report the break-in as such," says Harrison.

"Seems to me that Oceanic is sending a message," offers Tanaya. "It's a terror tactic, and it's what Hillcrest does. The method seems to work, it's why no one had filed suit against them," says Harrison.

"Hotel Astor," the driver announces, as the vehicle pulls to a stop. "Jane, trust me, it's better this way," adds Harrison.

"What'll we do?" Jane asks. Harrison reaches into his overcoat and produces a copy of the Evening Times, he shows the headline which reads:
"HEARING FOR TITANIC CLAIM DECIDED."
Jane and Tanaya read through the article. An unenthusiastic boost of motivation is expressed when they read of Judge Meyer granting their right to a trial.
"We are in the spotlight now. Anything that happens from here on out, will be considered collateral risk. It's something that Hillcrest won't do - risk the firm's integrity," Harrison pleads. "He's right Jane," says Tanaya. Harrison and Tanaya silently await Jane's response to the her situation. Jane buries her head into her hands and begins an elated cry.
"It's okay, everything's going to be all right," says Harrison as Tanaya joins in. Jane regains her composure, a handkerchief is offered by Harrison. It is then they notice that she is not weeping, but laughing.
"I can't believe that through all of this, it all came down to me," she says in a broken voice. "No, no," Tanaya says in a reassuring voice.
"It came down to me, worrying about my precious jewelry box, filled with costume

245.

jewelry," says Jane with tears in her eyes. Harrison sits back and smiles, while Tanaya offers Jane a hug.

"Okay Harry. You were saying?" Jane asks gratefully. "Tomorrow we will contact the police and have them meet us at your apartment. There will be reporters and curious neighbors there at the scene of the crime..." Harrison says. "And, don't fret about your apartment. We'll have it cleaned up in no time," assures Tanaya.

"I'd like for you to get some rest. Stay here, call room service, get some hot cocoa and relax. I know you understand how important it is for us to retrieve the files from the Island. We'll be back, soon as we can," says Harrison. As they leave the hotel room, Tanaya drops a folder into Jane's lap and continues to follow Harrison towards the door.

On the ferry heading to Ellis Island, the calm and sunny mid afternoon boat ride is a welcomed one. Harrison and Tanaya have just come from a small galley on the boat, warming their hands on cups of coffee. They stand at the railing, looking up the Hudson River at the New York Harbor skyline.

"The longest name I have ever seen for a boat; The Department of Commerce and

Labor, Immigration Service why not just Ellis Island Ferry" Tanaya asks.

"Then, that would be way too simple. I wonder what Inar is doing today," asks Harrison. "There was a violent wind storm brewing when we left, he's probably sawing up the downed trees," says Tanaya.

"How is he taking all of this, will he be able to endure?" Harrison asks. "Oh, I think he might get a little bored from time to time, sitting in the court room day after day.

He expressed to me that when this trial is over, he would like to go back to his village in the Baffin. At the same time, he's afraid some of his relatives may drop dead at the sight of him," says Tanaya.

"That's right," says Harrison in agreement. "Once on the old ice floe, you don't come back," adds Harrison.

"Well, if things go as planned, he should be there at the end of summer," says Harrison. "He'll be glad to hear that," Tanaya replies. "What about yourself" Are you in?" Harrison asks.

"You can count on it, this whole experience has taught me that things certainly work in strange ways," says Tanaya.

"How's that" Harrison asks. "Well, a few years back, I had applied for a secretarial position at Jane's office. On the way back from Indian School she assured me that if this case jeopardized my job at Ellis Island, I could work for her. I couldn't ask for more, being a secretary to Jane," says Tanaya.

"Would it help if I put a word in for you" The Superintendent at Ellis is the father of my college room mate," suggests Harrison.

"Thank you Mr. Bennett, but I don't think I will have any problem with my days off," says Tanaya. "Now that's exactly what I wanted to hear. After we retrieve the files, we can head back to the Astor and get back to work," says Harrison.

Later, after Harrison has dropped Tanaya at the Astor Hotel, he returns to his apartment on Park Avenue and Madison. Feeling confident that the men who were watching his apartment have left, he has the cab driver pull the vehicle to the front of the building. At a view point from across the street, a man watches Harrison as he leaves the cab and enters his apartment building. The man can be seen running across the avenue towards the apartment building.

Inside the lobby, the man sees Harrison standing at the elevator and he approaches.

"Mr. Bennett, can I have a minute?" The man asks. Harrison turns to see a man dressed in a tweed suit and newsboy hat.

"How can I help you?" Harrison asks.

"Did you get my message? The one left at the front desk?" Asks the man.

"The cryptic note; Prop 401?" Harrison asks.

"Yes, I hope you don't mind me dropping in like this, but when you didn't call...you see I left the note two days ago."

"I was going to make it a point to call tonight, but then I've been away for a few days. What can I help you with, Mr...." Harrison asks.

"Ira Brown. I wonder if we could talk in private, it's about your case against White Star," says Ira.

"There's a small coffee shop down the block," offers Harrison.

"Begging your pardon sir, I don't think that would be a good idea," he says. Harrison becomes wary and looks toward the front desk clerk. "Tell me why that is," says Harrison.

"I was sitting on a park bench waiting for you to show. It was then I noticed a couple of men in a parked car. They were keeping an eye on your apartment building, then they left, driving south on Park Avenue," explains Ira.

"They weren't there when I returned from running my errands," says Harrison.

"I don't know if they caught sight of you, but just as you entered the building, they returned," says Ira. There is a sense of urgency in Ira's voice, and Harrison does something he rarely does. "We can go up to my apartment, and talk there," says Harrison.

Inside Harrison's apartment, the sound of a door being unlocked, then the two men enter. Harrison cautiously steps into his living room. The incident at Jane's has him wondering if he will be next.

"You will have to pardon the mess, I've been doing case research for the last couple of days, I'll put on some coffee," says Harrison as he reaches for a can of coffee.

"I have to say, your note that was left at the desk, really peaked my interest. I have been wondering about it all day, 'Prop 401' and what it means," says Harrison.

"Really, Mr. Bennett, you don't have a clue?" Fisk asks. "Not a clue," Harrison acknowledges. "Your accent tells me you must be Irish. Is that right?" Harrison asks.

"That'd be correct sir. Belfast, Ireland," replies Ira.

"Why are you interested in the lawsuit against White Star?" Harrison asks, placing a cup of coffee before Ira.

"Three years ago my brother was killed, in what was termed an 'industrial accident' by an insurance company. It is for reasons yet to be made known, that I hold them responsible. I want them to suffer the consequences," he replies.

"Your brother died in 1912? His place of death wouldn't have been in the North Atlantic? On the Titanic?" Harrison asks. Brown nods his head, in agreement.

"I want to testify against the bloody bastards," he says. Harrison suddenly becomes very attentive. "Another cup I have some Irish Whiskey that goes great with coffee, how about it?" asks Harrison.

"And-how. I wouldn't say no to a drink or two," he says. "Tell me as best as you can, what kind of evidence can you take to the stand?" Harrison asks, pouring drinks.

"My brother Jeremiah was a ship builder, just as I, and our father before us. We worked on the RMS Titanic, from the laying of the keel, to the finish of the grand staircase. The RMS Olympic was another Harland and Wolff ship that we worked.

"Prop 401 is a designated number, stands for the four-hundred and first ship built by Harland and Wolff at a shipyard in Belfast,

Ireland. Number 401, was stamped onto the propeller that was machined for the Titanic," explains Brown.

"Is there a connection? If there is, I don't see it," he says.

"There is a connection. You see in 1911, after the Olympic was so badly damaged in the wreck with the battleship Hawke, Titanic's propeller shaft was fitted into the Olympic. Then later in February of 1912, Titanic's center propeller 401, was also fitted onto the Olympic.

"When that happened, she effectively became the Titanic," says Brown. Harrison puts his coffee cup down. He looks into Ira's eyes, and ponders the allegation. He reaches for a pen and begins to take notes.

"State to me, everything that happened, leading up to the disaster," says Harrison. Brown stands slowly, and becomes agitated. Harrison goes to the kitchen and returns with a glass of water. After drinking half the glass, Brown begins;

"On the 20Th of September 1911, we were working on the Titanic at Shipyard 401. Jerry and I usually worked together in most aspects of ship building. That year Titanic was being fitted out, and there were a couple of weeks in September, Jerry and I were split up. I was fitting emergency exit ladders in the boiler rooms, along with some of the internal piping in the hull. Jerry was topside fitting out her boat davits.

"At the days end, my brother had told me that he was pulled off the davit fitting and was put on a job to paint over all the four-foot lettering on the nameplates of Titanic. The explanation given was, that the letters T-I-T-A-N, were not linear to the eye and had to be taken off and refitted.

"It was the same day, the 20Th, the news of the collision between the Olympic and the HMS Hawke was spread throughout the shipyard. In October of that year, we were pulled off the Titanic for six weeks of repair work on the Olympic," says Brown. Harrison pulls out a newspaper article dated September 22, 1911, and floats it onto the coffee table in front of Ira. Harrison hands Ira a newspaper clipping.

"This is what came out state side, when Captain Smith was found at fault for the wreck," says Harrison. Ira reads the clipping, and floats it back onto the table.

"That was the way of it. They played it different over there, hardly anything at all. Other than seeing her damage first hand, this is one of the few photos I've seen of the damaged Olympic," says Brown.

"You said the props were switched out?" Harrison asks. "That's right, Jerry and I were on the crew that pulled a graveyard shift to fit Titanic's four-blade prop onto the Olympic. It was a small crew of eight, the job wasn't a hard one. The damaged propeller shaft had already been removed by another crew, then replaced by yet another. Everything seemed to secretive. We moved propeller 401 from a barge located by Slipway No. 3, it was there because it hadn't yet been fitted onto the Titanic. It was then moved it to the stern, then fitted onto Olympic's propeller shaft. It was done before the morning crew came on shift," says Ira, as Harrison continues to write as fast as he can. Wishing he had taken short hand while in college.

"The Olympic should have been scrapped after the wreck," says Ira. "As in scrap metal?" Harrison asks.

"Sure. From what I saw of her, the collision left her with an unbalanced propeller shaft. When that happens, you can be sure there is damage to the superstructure. With such powerful engines, the vibration from the unbalanced shaft will shake a ship apart in less than a year. To make matters even worse, word around the shipyard had it that the keel wasn't straight as it should be," explains Ira.

"That 1912 news article from the Chicago American, described it perfectly. When they reported that the Olympic will be made duplicate to the Britannic. They left out the part explaining the Britannic was made to match the Titanic, in almost every way," says Brown.

"Your decision to testify against Oceanic and White Star, is based upon your brother's death on the Titanic. What happened that made you want to seek vengeance?" Harrison asks.

"My brother Jerry should not have been on the maiden voyage, he should have been home in Belfast on the night of April 14th 1912.

I should have never let him get on that coffin liner," says Brown tearfully. "Coffin liner?" Harrison asks.

"Yes, Ship builders like myself know certain things about sea worthy construction. First, and most important, a ship the size of Titanic with single hull construction is nothing but a floating coffin," says Ira.

"It's been rumored that the original design of Titanic was approved as a double hulled construction. Did you hear anything like that around the shipyard?" Harrison asks.

"The day we began to lay Titanic's keel, one of the crew leaders brought it to the foreman's attention. He was fired that day, and of course, word of it spread like a wild fire through out the ship yard. Not another word was said about Titanic, and her phantom double hull," says Ira.

How was it that your brother happened to be on the Titanic?" Harrison asks.

"We were placed on assignment by the shipyard foreman..." begins Ira. "I'm sorry, you said we. Do you mean that you were supposed to be on the Titanic with your brother?" Harrison asks.

"Yes sir, my wife was due to have our son during that time, there was no way I could go. I can't help but think, if I had been there with Jerry, maybe I could've found a way out," Ira says tearfully.

"I want to help you bring those who are responsible to justice, Ira. You being here today, is a Start. We can work together on this," says Harrison. Ira holds out his hand. There is a firm handshake and he continues. "I started to put it together when I realized, most everyone on the crew that fitted the props on the Olympic, were given engineer positions on the Titanic. In September of 1911, the shipyard foreman told us that owners were cutting back on positions. That if we wanted, there would be other positions to be had, one would be as ship's engineer. My lord, our wages were 2 pounds a week. What were we to do? There was a coal strike looming on the rise, the shipyard and ships is all we knew," says Ira.

"As it turned out, all of my former crew were lured with positions as Assistant Junior Engineers. Jerry and I were promised positions as Boatswain Assistants. With that dangling carrot, there was nothing to keep my brother off the Titanic. We had no idea why we, as a crew, were chosen. It really puzzled me until I remembered the shift boss making the suggestion one day. He suggested that the propeller fitting on the Olympic went so well, they may consider keeping us as a specialized crew," says Ira. Harrison places his note pad on the coffee table.

"I have to say, the information just given to me is mind boggling, and the implications are staggering. Where can we reach you if we decide to put you on the stand?" Harrison asks. "Decide to put me on the stand?" What else do you need from me for Pete sakes. I've just given to you, all that you need to prove your case," scolds Brown.

"Ira, now listen. I didn't mean to slight your statements. It's just that the information you gave to me belongs in a criminal court. We are going to trial in a civil matter, an insurance settlement," explains Harrison.

"You have to believe what I tell you. Everything about the sinking is so twisted with undertow. Try to find an article printed in the London Times. They interview a Mrs. Carson, who stated that she heard gun shots and witnessed ships officers wrestling each other for a velveteen purse or bag that fell to the deck. The officers were scrambling for the jewels that fell out of the bag. Why didn't anyone follow up on that? Could it have been contents of Titanic's safe?" Ira asks.

"We won't know that unless the Titanic is raised and we look into the purser's safe," says Harrison.

"My point is, if that was over looked, then I take it, that you can't use my account of what was done to the Olympic? Ira says.

"Ira, you have to understand, it is not the proper venue to present your claim," begins Harrison.

"Isn't that a fine how-do-you-do. I brought my family to America, just to find someone who could help me with the whole mess.

"I know you're a top notch lawyer, if you can't bring them to justice, who will?" Ira pleads.

"It will happen, just not in this court of venue. The judge won't allow your testimony, Ira. If you can hold on until this trial is over, I will get in touch with you. We can start over, you'll have your day in court. I intend to file criminal charges against Titanic's owners, and everyone involved," says Harrison.

CHAPTER SIXTEEN
Hurley The Sea Dog

Back at the Astor, Jane and Tanaya have ordered room service and are enjoying a dinner with wine and candles. The friendship between them has grown to a point of total trust. Earlier, a call to the school was made to let Inar know that they made it safely and will be in touch soon.

Two crystal wine glasses chime as a toast is made to their victory in the court decision, and friendship.

"What do you think? Let's call a cab and go pick up my car and go for a spin? Jane asks. "I think we ought to stay right here and relax. You know what Mr. Bennett said, there are some big meanies out there," says Tanaya.

"Yeah? They're going to think mean when I get a hold of them. In life there are three things that you don't do. You don't step on Cesar's cape. You don't piss into the wind, and you don't mess around with my stuff," says Jane, followed by an un-lady like burp.

"Holy cow. Must be the wine talking," she adds. "What was all that cryptic language Mr. Bennett was talking about in the cab, the proverbial can of worms? What was that?

"I don't know, see for yourself, it's in a manilla envelope inside my briefcase," says Jane, with non-interest. Tanaya gets up from the dinner, retrieves the briefcase and returns to the table.

"Are you sure that you want to do this right now?" Jane asks. "You just relax and let me do the work, my curiosity has the best of me," says Tanaya as she opens the envelope and pulls out some documents.

"There is an attached note, and about two pages of court transcripts," says Tanaya.

"What's in the note?" Jane asks.

"It's cryptic. You may understand what it means," says Tanaya. Jane takes the note;

"Re: The U.S. Senate Hearing. Binns testimony. Last Paragraph:

"As nearly as I can remember, this double cellular side construction which I have described was a condition precedent to the granting of a subsidy by the British Government to these ships."

Meaning: That Titanic and Olympic were both single hull construction. In order for them to win the government subsidy, Harland and Wolff would have had to submit the ships' architectural construction that specified a double hull. An absolute act of defrauding the British government of money, a serious offense. Both ships were thought to be in compliance with government specifications, (double hulled) until the Olympic collided with the HMS Hawke, news photos clearly show the Olympic having a single hull. The damage so great, it made her structurally unsound. Do further research and see what you can come up with. P.S.

Someone in the British Board of Trade dropped the ball and approved the fraudulent plans or onsite government inspectors were paid off, maybe both. Good Luck.

"Research? How can we do anything on the level of credible research? Harry has all the documentation, Inar is at the school," says Jane as her interest suddenly become revitalized.

"Research is in the eye of the beholder. Take for example, this note on the Binns testimony. I found that reading between the lines posed some interesting questions. Like the first question for me would be; Who was responsible?" Tanaya suggests.

"You're kidding. Right? Because only 99.999% think an iceberg was responsible, the other 1/1000TH percent is you, me and Harry. That big mystery is solved. Next," says Jane, jovially.

"Well, okay learned scholar; the second question I see here is: Who allowed it? Who set the tragic event in motion?

"Egads, the Jesuits...I don't know," cries Jane mockingly.

"Jane, you are quite the little lush, a couple of bottles of wine and you're ready to take on the world," says Tanaya.

"Are you ready for the third question?" Tanaya asks. Jane holds up her wine glass as an acknowledgement.

"Okay, the third, and final question. Who had more to lose? The ship builders? The investors? Maybe corrupt British officials who allowed themselves to be bribed? Tanaya asks nonchalantly.

"Off with their heads," answers Jane.

"I take that answer to be the British government?" Tanaya asks. Jane comes to a sobering realization, she leans forward, elbows on the table, and finger to her lips.

"The powers that be. A scandal like that would've shook the political foundations of the British government," says Jane with astonished restraint.

"Right now, I'm wondering, is there a chance we may find an actual cost comparison of a single hull construction to a double hull? Tanaya asks.

"What's the professor's name that calculated the distance of iceberg travel?

Let's find out some readily available dimensions of the Titanic and contact the professor," says Jane.

"I think it's time to call Mr. Bennett," says Tanaya. "Let's not. Let's you and I conduct this part of the investigation and surprise Harry, what do you say?" Jane asks. A smile comes to Tanaya's face. "Where do we start first?" she asks.

"I know why you're so testy. You miss 'Hurley the Dog.' Who did you leave him with? Tanaya asks.

"'Hurley the Dog' is at the 'Barking Dog Hotel.' And I do miss the little pot licker," says Jane forlornly.

"I'm sure they're taking good care of him. What time are visiting hours? Tanaya asks.

"Let's go get my car and break him out," says Jane. "Then what? This is the Astor, a mouse can't even get in," says Tanaya. "Yeah, I guess you're right. Today is Saturday, we'll go get him first thing Monday morning," says Jane. "Uncle sure likes Hurley," says Tanaya.

"Hurley likes Inar, I couldn't believe how he just jumped up into his lap, curled up and went right to sleep," says Jane.

"That day when we were at your apartment? When you were at your desk doing some work, Uncle and I were at the kitchen table talking. The incident when he

264.

left the storage room that the two sea men put him? Well, after he escaped and was making his way up to the upper decks, he said that a little dog was following him around. The way he described the dog, it sounded to me like a Pomeranian breed, he'd never seen such a small dog. The dog would not come to him, so he couldn't catch it, he wanted to take it up with him to the top decks.

"After the ship sank and he was drifting on top of the debris, he heard the whimpering of a dog. His eyes had adjusted to the dark and he could see a small dog trying to climb aboard his raft. It was so cold and weak, the little dog was about to give up when Uncle reached down pulled it up by the nap of it's neck.

"The little dog was tucked into Uncle's parka, and that is where it stayed until he was picked up by the rescue ship. It didn't occur to me at the time, that the dog was a significant part of his experience," explains Tanaya. "Why is that?" Jane asks, with a quizzical look.

"I realized that when a pet is saved from a very tragic event. It is always newsworthy, the owner of that pet would remember Uncle. It turned out that when aboard the Carpathia, the dog would not leave his parka. The dog would start growling when he reached in to pull him out. It wasn't until a crew member saw Uncle feeding the dog while still tucked into his parka, that it became a spectacle.

"The little dog drew so much attention, word spread throughout the survivor deck. Then Uncle heard this woman crying out a name, he said it was pronounced, 'Feefee' she started bawling when she saw her pet. When the little dog allowed her to reach into Uncle's parka and pull her out, he knew that she was the owner," says Tanaya.

"Wow, that is a great pet story," says Jane close to tears. "You have to tell me, why the significance?" she asks. "The owner of the dog became a 'potential witnesses' the moment she claimed to be its owner.

Uncle can now be placed on the survivor deck of the rescue ship," says Tanaya.

"Outstanding evaluation. It is significant, we can use in court.

The woman who owned the dog, was a passenger, more than likely a First Class passenger. There were some documents found floating with the debris, one of the documents outlined an event that was to take place on April 15th, there was to be a dog show on the Promenade Deck. The names of the contestants and the breed of the dog were listed on the document. If we cold find her, she would be an excellent witness. She could place the dog on the ship at the time of the sinking, corroborating Inar's account," says Jane.

Across the state in wintery upper New York, exhaust vapor from a tailpipe can be seen coming from a car parked just outside the gates of the Thomas Indian school.

"Welcome to the Thomas Indian School," reads Vincenzo Bravo, sipping on a thermos cup filled with coffee. After driving all night, they have reached the Indian school. Their mission is to kidnap Inar Katerpar and take him back to the city, where he will be found in the Hudson River. Vincenzo sits in wait with a henchman named Roscoe Leone.

"Why don't we just go in there, snag the hairy little bastard and get out of here?" Roscoe asks.

"Because you dimwit. I have a plan and we're going to stick to it. We're not in New York, we are on an Indian reservation. Out here, they can still scalp people and get away with it, and you know why? Because they're freaking Indians that's why," scolds Vincenzo.

Roscoe takes his Fedora off and runs his hand over his hair, as if making sure his scalp is still there.

"You know what they did to Custer? Vincenzo asks. Roscoe's eyes grow wide. "The stuck bone prongs in his ears," says Vincenzo, making Roscoe more uncomfortable.

"Yeah. They did that because he wouldn't listen. That's what I'm going to let them do to you if you don't listen to me and follow the plan," scolds Vincenzo.

"Okay, okay. We follow the plan," says Roscoe, as he pulls out of his pocket, two identification wallets.

"These things have badges. How'd you swing that?" Roscoe asks.

"Never mind, just show them the badge and don't say a word, let me do the talking," says Vincenzo.

Inside the Administration Building on the Indian School grounds, most of the staff and teachers have taken the holiday off, leaving a crew to maintain the grounds.

Officer Ronald Black Eye, has command of the B.I.A. Security Force on the school grounds, and is standing inside the Administration Building entrance doors. Through the frosted window pane, Ronnie can see two figures walking up the steps. Before the Vincenzo and his 'associate' can reach for the door handle, the entrance door swings open.

Standing in the open door way, Vincenzo is taken aback by a tall, muscular, uniformed officer.

Without saying a word, Ronnie motions them into the arrival lobby. Upon entering, Vincenzo and Roscoe size up Ronnie as they walk past.

"What can I do for you, gentlemen?" asks Ronnie as he scrutinizes the two thugs standing before him.

"We are with the Immigration Service, out of the Commissioner-General's Office, Washington, D.C.," says Vincenzo, holding up an I.D. Wallet.

"Where are your I.D. Photo's?" asks Ronnie.

"We're undercover agents," says Bravo in ad lib. Ronnie nods his head with raised eyebrows.

"We would like a word with the Superintendent of this school," he says. Ronnie looks at Vincenzo suspiciously.

"The Superintendent is away for the holiday. Is there anyone else you would be interested in seeing?" Ronnie asks as Tony, the bus driver enters the lobby. Tony is acknowledged by Ronnie with a glance.

"I'll be honest with you, officer. We're here to apprehend Inar Katerpar, he is in the country illegally, we have been given orders to take him back to Washington, D.C.," says Vincenzo.

"Well, did you hear that Inar?" Ronnie says, looking at Tony, which catches him with total surprised.

Bravo and Roscoe look at Tony, who is standing motionless, is wearing a parka with a hood. Having never seen Inar in person, they accept Tony as their fugitive. Ronnie places a finger to his lips, and Tony acknowledges with a slight nod.

"Mr. Katerpar, you are under arrest for illegal entry into the United States. Please place your hands out in front of you," says Vincenzo. As he places handcuffs on Tony's wrists, two more B.I.A. Officers enter the lobby.

"Thank you for your cooperation in apprehending this fugitive, if you don't mind skipping the formalities, we'll be getting back Washington," says Vincenzo. Ronnie steps between them and the doorway. The other officers step up.

"You're not going anywhere with this man. There's paperwork," says Ronnie.

"Paper work? We're Immigration Service, this is our prisoner and we have the right to apprehend him, paper work or not," says Vincenzo, stumbling over his words.

"You are on a Federal Indian Reservation and Katerpar is a member of an indigenous tribe of North America. In order for you to leave with him, you will have to produce an arrest warrant," says one of the other BIA Security Officers.

"Our arrest warrant is the order we received out of Washington, you can argue the issue with the government," says Vincenzo as he pulls Tony towards the doorway. Ronnie steps closer into their path, while the other officers close in.

"After you acquire the warrant," says Ronnie adamantly.

"While you're at it, pay a little visit to the F.B.I. Because other than the Bureau of Indian Affairs Police, they are the only law enforcement that can arrest a native on an Indian Reservation. You have no jurisdiction here," advises Tony. Vincenzo looks at Roscoe.

"Say, what is this? This isn't Katerpar, what are you trying to pull here?" asks Roscoe dumbfounded.

Ronnie points to a bulge where Vincenzo's pistol is holstered. "No, the question is, what are you trying to pull? Ronnie asks, pointing to his chest.

"Since when are agents of Immigration, allowed to carry guns asks Ronnie. "If that's who you are," he adds.

"What? I'm supposed be lectured on Federal law by a security guard? I know people. I can have all of your jobs with just one call," threatens Vincenzo.

"I suggest you get to calling, the telephone is right in there," says Ronnie pointing to the lobby desk.

Suddenly and without warning, Vincenzo and Roscoe reach for their weapons. Ronnie leaps towards Vincenzo and Tony reacts by grabbing Roscoe's wrist. The other officers pile onto the impostors and a scuffle ensues. The thugs are disarmed, and are held to the floor.

"Call the Cattaraugus Sheriff's Office, have them send out a deputy," commands Ronnie, while holding Vincenzo.

"On what offense," asks one of the Officers. "Trespassing onto Federal land with intent to kidnap, impersonating a Federal Officer, bringing weapons onto private school grounds," says Ronnie.

Much later, Vincenzo and Roscoe are being led down the steps of the Administration Building by Sheriff's deputies. Ronnie continues to give an account of what took place during the incident.

"I gathered the other officers when it was reported that a suspicious looking car was parked outside the gates. I had established a lookout with binoculars and it was confirmed that it was not normal," says

Ronnie. "I think we have all that we need for now. Good work Officer Black Eye, we'll be in touch."

The New York City skyline can be seen through the upper levels of a high rise building. Joseph Hillcrest has invited Judge Meyer to his penthouse for a discussion. Hillcrest has decided to appeal to Meyer's better side of legal sense, citing the consequences of a failed attempt to avoid a civil trial between Katerpar and White Star. It is the last of a series of high pressure meetings that Hillcrest had initiated, to halt the proceedings with a legal move. Judge Meyer has agreed to schedule a settlement conference between the defense and Katerpar attorneys.

"It's in the better interest of the court and its venue, public opinion is already stirred up, no one wants to bring up the memory of Titanic. Harrison Bennett can only guess what consequences would arise out of such a bizarre civil trial," says Hillcrest.

"I'm sorry you see it that way Joseph. I, on the other hand, still have a mind that tells me different. At the same time, I feel that if the trial were allowed to go on, the papers will have picked it apart like the scavengers they are. In the end the trial would emerge a disaster - on both sides of the bar," says Meyer.

"We are prepared to meet almost any amount in settlement, that will be necessary to put his case behind us. Under the circumstances, there are certain concessions that we must attend that will also prove costly to our clients. I hope you can appreciate our position in the matter, Judge Meyer," suggests Hillcrest.

"Yes, but we need not mention the sensitive issues regarding those matters. How do you propose to deal with the undying questions still being asked about the tragedy? Meyer asks.

"As far as I know, there are no new questions being asked, short of Captain Smith being discovered in some island country, there is nothing new about tragedy. We are going to meet any challenge with the straight facts. The Titanic struck an iceberg and sank. It was an accident," says Hillcrest confidently.

"I have no problem with the accident claims and issues, the way I see it Mr. Katerpar and I have something in common. Retirement will soon come upon us both. Albeit, in the 'Sky World' for him and a resort for me," says Meyer with a smile.

"Harrison Bennett is our only concern, as far as his associate, we have no reservations about her. We have prepared a number of alternatives, none that will leave a trail, there will be no residual effect that will concern you," says Hillcrest.

"I believe that I am insulated, I have sat in judgement of the most vile and horrendous acts of violence anyone could possibly perceive. Because of the Titanic tragedy, most of them have been forgotten. The Titanic is now a sad memory, an enigma," says Meyer.

"Please spare me the postscript. I have gone over the facts a million times. I am convinced the collision was an accident. There was no premeditation, no secret plot to sink her, it was an accident," insist's Hillcrest.

"I know who Bennett is, and I know what he can do. I am not going to trial on this case out of my choosing. Left up to me, I would continue, just to see you squirm in your seat as he presents his case," says Meyer poignantly. "Yes, but I can assure you, the pleasure of your presence will be deeply missed," says Hillcrest.

Judge Meyer stands, his eyes do not move from Hillcrest. He place's a drink glass firmly down upon cherry wood table, and turns to walk to the door. When he reaches the door, he places his hand on the doorknob, then turns.

"I think you know this already, but I'll repeat it just in case. The memory of

Titanic, will never go away. You and your firm cannot hide the fact that 1,503 souls perished in the pitch black Atlantic that night, there will always be questions. Those who choose to answer in truth, will also be remembered. Good day, Joseph," says Judge Meyer.

The elevator ride down is a long one for Judge Meyer. The Elevator Operator stands attentively, and remains quiet as the elevator descends. The meeting with Hillcrest is brought to mind as Judge Meyer recalls the comment about Captain Smith. A recollection of the hearing, has Meyer wondering if the comment my be connected to Harrison's statement regarding Inar's recollection of certain officers on the Titanic. An objection by defense halted a photo recognition demonstration that Harrison had suggested. Oddly, as he was trying to present his evidence, Jane had place a photo of Captain Smith on the table directly in front of Harrison, and in view of Meyer. The thought holds his attention, then shaking his head, Meyer rejects the notion.

"Operator, how many feet per second does this elevator cover in a second," asks Meyer. "We were told the distance is four feet on descent, and three feet per second

going up," says the operator. Judge Meyer
begins to wonder how long it took for the
Titanic to reach the sea floor of the
Atlantic.

CHAPTER SEVENTEEN
A Settlement of Secrets

At the country estate of Judge Meyer on Staten Island, Harrison Bennett has been invited to have a breakfast meeting and to discuss the settlement with White Star. Looking out over a patio railing, Harrison and Judge Meyer are enjoying a quite moment, watching the shadows cast by the clouds as the sun appears. Harrison is reminiscing about the earlier days when he was a child. A smile comes to his face as the warm sunshine warms his skin. It's the spring grass growing to the edges of the long winding gravel driveway, reminds Harrison of his days on the family farm.

"Beautiful day," says Harrison, looking out over the sprawling estate. I was raised on a farm that had a sweeping buggy road just like the one I'm looking at now," he adds.

"It's exactly why I bought this place, I love this view," says Meyer.

"As a kid, I'd walk that buggy road every morning. The field where we Elsa, our milk cow, was fenced off just before our farmhouse. Every morning, there I'd be, walking Elsa to the barn for a good milking," says Harrison.

"This was a farm before I bought it, the barn still has all the equipment, and spacious hay loft. Now, the only animals that walk the grounds are a couple of dogs and my wife's cat," says Meyer, as he fills Harrison's coffee cup.

"How is Mr. Katerpar? I hope he's well and ready for what is in store for him," says Meyer. Harrison looks at Meyer inquisitively.

"If you don't mind me saying so Judge; that seemed an awful lot like a bated question. Actually, one I don't mind answering," says Harrison.

"I didn't mean it to be, but I am truly interested in his plight. It isn't everyday you run across such an astoundingly interesting human being," Meyer says with a smile.

"Miss Reynolds and I are of the same mind on that matter. Things have worked out in a way that he will be the least affected by rigors of the court trial," says Harrison.

A housekeeper wheels in a breakfast cart and begins to serve. Harrison patiently waits for the plate to be served. The Housekeeper continues to serve in silence while the two men hold one another's stare, a slight smile comes to Harrison as the serving cart is pushed from the patio.

"Harrison, I was appointed to my first Judges position when you started your practice in Brooklyn. In law circles, you were known as 'The young Turk', young, courageous and fearless, now, you're just fearless. It is to be hoped, that common sense will not be effected by the bravado," suggests Meyer.

With a fork full of scrambled eggs and toast, Harrison manages to get in a few words before washing it down with a sip of coffee.

"Really? Harrison says, clearing his throat. "I thought the bravado was the best part," he adds.

"Have you given any serious thought about settling the law suit out of court?" Meyer asks, as he meticulously spreads preserves on a slice of toast.

"Oh come now, we doing so well, enjoying a beautiful morning, having breakfast, in a perfect setting. I was hoping to finish my eggs before we discussed settlement procedure," says Harrison, placing a napkin to his lips.

"I didn't mean to interrupt your breakfast, but I thought we both agreed to a working breakfast?" Meyer recalls.

"Those who know me well, never get between me and breakfast," quips Harrison. Meyer finds the remark very amusing.

"Then you have thought about it? Since my ruling of a trial? Have you discussed it with Katerpar and Reynolds?" Meyer asks.

"Let me be honest with you Judge Meyer. My joining this suit had nothing to do with a damage claim. There are some extraordinary circumstances that surround the claim. They are so appealing to me, as a criminal trial lawyer, that I wish this simple claim would just go away. There are factors in the case that have lead me to a more deeper facet of the Titanic, they are sinister and criminal," says Harrison.

"Understood. It's no secret as to why you joined Miss Reynolds in this suit. Hillcrest, what little hair he had left is now gone, thanks to you. White Star attorney's, like their superiors, have also been pulling out their hair trying to find a way to discourage litigation. From where I sit, their next move will be a dire and desperate attempt to neutralize your efforts. Nothing will stop them from keeping you out of the courtroom," explains Meyer.

"And you, Judge Meyer. What is going to be your take on the matter if I succeed? Harrison asks.

"What I will have to say about won't matter. I'll be retired by the time they have their day in court. If you really want my take on it...it won't be soon enough for me to see that happen," says Meyer.

"Level with me Judge Meyer. There's a small circle of respected scholars and people who are professionally involved in politics who believe that the Titanic was sent to the bottom of the Atlantic, through no accident. How do you feel about that? Harrison asks.

Meyer does not respond, he sits back in his chair and studies Harrison, who sits patiently, waiting for a reply.

"If I answered your question, and I answered it favorably, do you think it will change anything? The Titanic sits at the bottom of the sea, nothing will change that. You should know this; there are forces at work that are far beyond reach of the law. These people are like ghosts, there is no single one, yet there is only one, you can't win against them Harrison," warns Meyer, as he lights a cigar.

"You know this for sure? Harrison asks.

"It is only an assumption, an educated guess, you might say, but then again, if asked of you, this meeting between you and me, never took place," says Meyer solemnly.

"Who are these people?" Harrison asks as Meyer remains silent.

"Who gave the order to sink the Titanic?" Harrison repeats. Meyer shakes his head, then looks up. Harrison sees a sadness in his eyes.

"My whole life, all I wanted was to serve judicially, in the most honorable way that I could. When the Titanic went down, and all those souls were lost at sea, like the rest of the nation, I too felt a need to pursue the cause of the tragedy. I can tell you this; take whatever evidence you have uncovered, safeguard it with your life. There will be those who will take every advantage to see that you do not succeed in presenting the evidence in a courtroom. Remember, exposure is the worst thing that can happen to dark societies that are in our midst, exposure it is light, and light always prevails over darkness," says Meyer.

"You are not going to give me anything that will help me along with my endeavor, are you? Harrison asks.

"I would only be guessing at what really happened, who the actual string pullers are, I cannot say. The answers lie in a riddle, and riddles as you may know, start with questions. A devils advocate might point out; the validity of your source, can it be trusted," says Meyer, with a convicting stare.

"Copies of the original Senate hearing can be easily verified," replies Harrison.

"Type written? On parchment? Meyer asks.

"The court transcripts are authentic, Judge Meyer," says Harrison.

"Tell me what you know, and I'll see how your research comes together with the clues I have come up with," says Meyer.

"Okay, let's start with the hearing. When we tried to introduce the photo recognition demonstration? You looked at the photo of Captain Smith that was placed on the conference table," implies Harrison.

"Yes, and I halted your attempt before you made a fool of everyone. You of all should know, you do not show your hand to your opposition. Even in a legal preceding," offers Meyer. Fink agrees with a head nod.

"I've not read the court transcripts, but I know you must have something like that in your possession," says Meyer.

"There were four accounts of Captain Smith on the 15th of April, the most significant account is that he was seen inside...," says Harrison, as Meyer cuts him off.

"The wheel house," says Meyer. I personally thought that selfless heroic act, was a bit too dramatic in my view of reality. My thoughts were confirmed when I read a newspaper article about the good Captain struggling in the freezing water with a baby in his arms," Meyer says with a half smile.

A breath of relief is taken by Harrison, just knowing a man of Judge Meyer's stature would cast a doubtful eye on the tragedy.

"The other sightings involved testimony from Third Class passenger who stated he saw and heard Captain Smith, shouting out orders to the crew members while in the water. Yet, another came from one of the officer's, testifying that he saw Captain Smith jump from the roof of the officer's quarters into the sea on the port side of the ship," explains Harrison.

"Then there is the account of Inar Katerpar. What did he see that deviated from the other accounts?" Meyer asks.

Harrison folds his arms and becomes silent, he wonders how Meyer is going react at what he has to say next.

"Katerpar recalled seeing Smith, climb into a tar-black lifeboat, rowed by two other sailors," explains Harrison. There is a quiet moment that becomes awkward to Harrison. Judge Meyer burst out with a hardy laugh.

"Please. Harrison, don't get me wrong, but I just caught a vision juror's fainting dead away, while White Star attorneys sit in shock with piss running down their legs," Meyer manages to say with laughter.

"Are you aware that testimony was given by several witnesses, stating that there was a ship that steamed in close to the Titanic. They testified that the ship was close enough that they could see the starboard port holes. All this while she was slipping beneath the waves," says Harrison as Meyer's laugh dwindles to silence.

"Katerpar saw Smith being rowed away from the Titanic as she went down, he said this to you? Meyer asks.

"Well, not exactly like that, he first picked Smith's photograph from a stack of Titanic's officer staff. He has a nickname for Captain Smith; the 'White Walrus' thats what he calls him, with no disrespect," says Harrison.

"I have to say this. No one will ever will ever find Captain Smith. Even if he did escape, There could not be left to chance that he survived the wreck. If in fact he was rescued, that alone sealed his fate," explains Meyer.

"I suppose you're right, there could be no way that he would be allowed to reach land. No doubt he's at the bottom, just not at the wreck site," agrees Harrison.

"Another thing. I met with a shipbuilder who worked on the Titanic from keel to fitting. He gave this to me," says Harrison handing Meyer a folded and worn document. Judge Meyer begins to read it's content.

"This is a ships record of insured cargo, and there it is, the real reason all the survivors were allowed to forego Immigration Service procedures," says Meyer. "I don't get the connection," says Harrison.

"Young man, I think you had better start reading the more current newspapers instead of news clippings from 1912. Damages in loss claims against Titanic's insurers amount in hundreds of thousands of dollars. In personal items alone, jewelry, precious stones and uncut diamonds, sent the amount in claims sky high," says Meyer.

"I see what you're saying; eliminate the Immigration procedures, and there is no search for contraband," says Harrison, his voice trailing off.

287.

"It's what I've been trying to explain. Who has the resources to manage an operation like that?" Meyer asks.

"People with money and power," replies Harrison.

"If I were on your legal team, I would strongly suggest that when the time comes to file a criminal complaint against Titanic's owners, you strike with force, and you strike quickly," advises Meyer.

Judge Meyer's indirect suggestions, place Harrison in a precarious situation. He begins to realize the enormity of the case, yet to be brought, and his intentions to pursue the allegations against the owners of the Titanic.

"I see," says Harrison, slightly disheartened. "To me, it would seem, that the power of the law would be sufficient for an indictment. As for money to back such a lawsuit, my prospective clients have been apprised that I will serve under contract of pro bono. The evidence will be undeniable, once presented. I doubt if the District Attorney for the People of the State of New York, would refuse such a trial," reasons Harrison.

"I admire your courage. In my younger days, I would have taken up the cause," says Meyer admiringly. "Again, let me suppose, your lead research assistant is steeped in the U.S. Senate hearing that Senator Smith had brought in 1912," suggests Meyer.

"That's a fact, we haven't stopped the research since the day I acquired the transcripts," says Harrison.

"Word of the British Inquiry into the Titanic, continues to filter into the States from Britain. The inquiry, from what I gather, is very different from the U.S. Hearing," says Meyer.

"Interesting you should say that. Miss Reynolds, my lead attorney, has a different view on the British Inquiry. The news clippings from the London Times gave her the impression. I'm in agreement, the inquiry was not as thorough as it should have been," says Harrison.

"On the contrary. The British Inquiry put the survivor crew through the wringer. Look into the transcripts, they have been published in-part by British newspapers," says Meyer.

"After all's been said and done, and at the end of the day, people will see that the British Board of Inquiry investigated itself."

"Isn't that something? It's the fox in the henhouse. The part of the testimony I love the most is the testimonies that came from the officers in the wheel house. At the time of the collision, the implication was that the ship made no evasive maneuver, but rather steered into the path of the berg," says Meyer.

"Believe if or not, Katerpar was on the bridge directly after the collision, better still, he witnessed the Titanic sailing straight at him while he was on the iceberg," offers Harrison.

"Incredible, absolutely incredible. The British Inquiry brought out similar testimonial about Titanic's heading. That is, from unwilling and at times hostile crew members. There were huge contradictions that derailed the Inquiry, but still left an impression to the public that the collision should have been avoided," says Meyer.

"All this by 'word from overseas'? Harrison asks. Judge Meyer does not answer the question, he sits back and gazes at Harrison with a knowing look.

"English tabloids followed the stories of those crew members that chose not to go on the maiden voyage. Look into a story published by the Daily Tribune, it's a tabloid, but sometimes they are the best source of information. A story that made its way to America revealed that when the men who worked on Titanic were ordered to follow her to a deep water dock to be fitted out with cabins and staircases, they refused. The workers stated to the tabloids that the Titanic was not what it appeared to be, that everything else had been made to look like her, except the steam engine boilers. They stated the boilers looked to have been used for at least a year prior to the fitting process. I'll be darned, Titanic's boilers were supposed to be brand new," explains Harrison.

"The research you have conducted would prove to be the biggest threat to White Star. There is no doubt that your potential to win over a jury has White Star scrambling for an out of court settlement. Tell me this, how is Miss Reynolds going to react when you explain that her client's lawsuit has been set for a settlement conference?" Meyer asks.

"I'm not sure, she may be relieved. I'm hoping she will be relieved, she carries a gun," says Harrison.

Judge Meyer laughs. "Well, if anything, assure her that it is the best avenue available for her at this point. It'll be an honorable way to bow out of a sticky situation," says Meyer.

"Jane is a courageous lawyer, the notoriety that will arise from this case will be good for her profit margin," he says.

Both gentlemen stand to bid each other farewell. "I wish you all the luck in the world Harrison. I'll see you at the Settlement Hearing," says Meyer with a firm handshake.

At the Astor on Central Park West, Harrison is in the elevator taking him to Jane's fifth floor room. Ascending with only the elevator operator, Harrison is mentally rehearsing some carefully chosen words he will use to explain the settlement.

Inside Jane's hotel room, Jane and Tanaya are hard at work calculating Titanic's hull construction. There is a knock at the door, Tanaya jumps to her feet and starts for the door. Looking through the peephole she see's a smiling face.

"It's Mr. Bennett," says Tanaya excitedly. The door is flung open and a bouquet of roses pops into view.

"For your hotel room to brighten your day," says Harrison. Tanaya hurries to place them in a vase.

"Have we got a surprise for you," says Jane. "Yes, you are going to be so amazed at what we came up with," says Tanaya placing the roses into a vase.

"Surprises, I love surprises. Can I guess? Is it a new car? A mail order bride? Harrison says jokingly.

"We have figured out how much it cost to construct on side of Titanic's hull. You see there were over three and a half million rivets used on the hull, so we figured out how many holes were in one sheet of steel and," Jane is interrupted by Harrison.

"Jane before you go any further, I need to tell you something that directly effects your calculations, arduous as they may have been," explains Harrison.

Jane becomes disheartened, not being able to divulge her assessment of the construction costs. Tanaya places the last rose and sits down next to Jane.

"I need for you to remain open minded while I explain what went down today. I had a meeting with Judge Meyer, he explained to me that under no certain terms would he allow you case to go to trial," says Harrison.

"How can that be? He already ruled to allow us to continue to trial. Why would he change his mind, just like that? Jane asks.

"Anytime between now and the trial, a settlement conference can be placed on the table," says Harrison.

Jane folds her arms and sits back onto the couch, her demeanor is slowly transformed by a pouty face.

"I thought about it long and hard, and everything Judge Meyer presented to me, made sense. White Star has made an offer for settlement that is the highest out of court offer yet. It is a win-win situation for us, if we turn it down we will be sure to lose. We might come out ahead on the judgement amount, but public opinion will bury us. White Star was on the verge of bankruptcy when the Olympic collided with that war ship. If we go after them in court, it will surely bankrupt them, and we will end up without a dime," explains Harrison.

"How many ships does White Star own? Jane asks with challenge in her tone. "Please, Jane. Consider this, your client's interest would not fare well in a venture bound for failure. Also, if you are entertaining the thought of managing your client's financial affairs, just give up your practice, and prepare to manage a fleet of obsolete ships. Now, I'm not saying you couldn't manage it, I'm just saying that it would be a big mistake to take on such a venture," says Harrison.

"How much?" Jane asks.

"The offer mentioned to Judge Meyer by Hillcrest was...175,000," Harrison replies. There is a long silence as Jane and Tanaya look to one another, trying to absorb the information.

"I'm not quite sure I understand," Jane begins to say. "You want me to drop the entire case work-up?" Jane asks.

"This is your case. If I have overstepped my position as an associate in this matter, I'm sorry, but," Harrison is interrupted.

"You're right. I don't remember giving you authority to act in my behalf, but let me get this one little thing straight with you...one hundred and seventy-five, thousand. As in dollars?" Jane asks with a smile, that suddenly turns into a hoop and a holler.

"It might be more if we make them sweat," says Harrison over the celebration.

"It might be more!" Jane and Tanaya shout simultaneously, as they jump up and down, holding onto each other. Harrison dials up room service and orders a bottle of champagne.

The spontaneous celebration has calmed to excited chatter between Tanaya and Jane. They startle as the champagne cork bounces off of the ceiling.

"We should have Inar here a day before the conference," advises Harrison. "I can call the school and have him on a train tonight," says Tanaya.

A toast is made by Jane; "Here's to them and here's to us. If we should ever disagree, screw them and here's to us,"

295.

laughs Jane. Glasses are raised to the victory.

"Harrison, I would like to introduce you to my new executive secretary, Tanaya Navaran," says Jane, joyfully.

"You must be honored, Tanaya. Not only are you the first executive secretary, I believe you are the first secretary, period," says Harrison. "Make sure there are paid vacations," Harrison adds, under his breath.

CHAPTER EIGHTEEN
The Journey Of Sleepless Nights

It is April 1916, with the settlement conference a year behind them, Harrison and Jane have gone their separate ways. Although they remain friends, Harrison and his secretary continue to gather evidence in his ongoing effort to bring Titanic's owners to justice.

The Law Office of Jane Reynolds has taken on more clients because of the publicity of the Katerpar settlement. Even though the settlement amount will never be disclosed, public opinion was favorable. When the Katerpar case was thrust into the public eye, the public wanted the case to succeed over the Transatlantic Liner giant, White Star. Inar became their mascot, of sorts, as the Titanic issues went unheeded, the public grew more insensitive towards the matter. As time wore on, there continued to be no compromises to the tragedy. The ship struck an iceberg. End of story.

When frustration set in, the issue consequently went beyond the sinking, and emerged as an oblique effort to keep her memory alive.

The iceberg became issue to the sinking, the public demand for the government to launch an effective investigation grew stronger as proponents dug deeper into the tragedy.

For now, a journey had been in the making for weeks. Jane cleared her calendar in order to take Inar back to his Baffin Island village. After the settlement disbursement, Jane and Harrison received their attorney fee's and expenses were paid. A balance of $110,000 remained in Inar's account. With the help of Jane and Tanaya, Inar established a scholarship foundation for Indian children.

Money from returns on his financial investments set up by Jane, Inar has bought gifts and supplies for the three villages that are situated in his homeland area by the bay. With no other means of access to Baffin Island, a route has been chosen by Jane and Tanaya, to sail out of the Hudson Bay by way of a steamship. They are scheduled to board a icebreaker and supply ship out of the Hudson Bay in springtime.

The many settlements in the northern outposts rely on the ship for much needed supplies to endure the harsh winter months inside the arctic circle. The icebreaker will sail out of the bay and through to the Hudson Strait, breaking a path through to the Arctic Sea. The route has over 20 planned stops at villages, settlements, and research stations. It's not the fastest, but it is the only way to reach Baffin Island.

Having left New York almost a week ago, Jane has arranged to travel in First Class compartments by railway, and they are now in the fifth-day of the journey. They have traveled from Manhattan to Toronto, from there they transferred and traveled to Winnipeg. The final transfer is to take place at the township of Gillam, then onward by way of the Hudson Bay Railway. This is to be the last-leg of the journey, and even though it is springtime, the weather continues in its severity. The railway was constructed on the spongy Muskeg of the northern plains of the Canadian wilderness. Traveling this route makes for hazardous conditions causing the train to slow to 25 miles-per-hour in some places, continuing for miles at a time.

The tiny port of Churchill, a budding settlement in the Provence of Northern Manitoba, Canada, is where their land journey will end. Jane discovered that the settlement of Churchill is an area where the white bear gather every year. Inar came to mind when she read this bit of information, she thought; 'what a great gift to the people, a Polar Bear hide,' but there was no time for a hunt on this journey. Jane decides to keep the bear region a secret, and return Inar to his village without distractions. The information may be shared with Inar once they are well on their way, breaking through the ice on the Hudson Bay. In any event, she plans to have Churchill in her hind sight at the same time, looking forward to the rest of the journey.

Packed into cargo boxes, the village supplies that Inar bought have been sent ahead, and hoisted aboard the ship in preparation for the voyage. The cargo weighs in at over 5200 pounds, and once landed at it's destination, the shipment will have to be packed into the village by sled.

Now on the train, inside their compartment, Jane is seated at the window sipping on a cup of hot tea and looking out at the frozen scenery. She is wondering if the clothing she has packed will be sufficient.

"I know it looks bitter-cold out there, but don't let it run you off, your ancestors and mine survived in conditions like this for thousands of years," assures Tanaya.

"That's just it. My few days of survival will probably be a record in the 'Family Tree Hall of Shame.' With my thin skin and boney frame, I'll probably turn to ice the moment we step off the train," says Jane.

"Tell me again about this pack train company we hired to haul the cargo boxes to the village," says Tanaya.

"The owner wasn't sure what he would have available, but he explained it will be caribou," explains Jane.

"Caribou? I love caribou sleds, they're a lot more comfortable than a frozen saddle," says Tanaya.

"Yeah, I think he said caribou, either way it's going to cost Inar a pretty penny after the cargo is unloaded," says Jane.

"Uncle is napping right now, but when he wakes, we'll discuss how far the village is from the boat landing," says Tanaya.

"What is the summer season like around here? Jane asks.

"More better than this. Unless you've lived up here, you won't appreciate the spring weather. The blowing wind hampers travel on most days, but blowing snow, and blizzards are still normal for this time of year," explains Tanaya.

"Oh lord, help me," prays Jane.

"The conductor said it's about three degrees below zero out there right now, tonight it will drop down to about twenty-one degrees below. Technically, it's day time," says Tanaya.

"Day time? How can you tell? It's been twilight for the past three days," says Jane.

"Inar's village is right on the edge of the Arctic boundary. Twilight of the sun occurs there most of the year. Two-thirds of Baffin Island lies within the Arctic Circle. It's a kind of zone where 24-hours of daylight occur, this happens around June and July. Then another 24-hours of twilight happens between July and November, followed by 24-hours of darkness when December and January, roll around," explains Tanaya.

"Twilight I can take, but count me out on the darkness. I'm a-scaredy cat when it comes to the dark," says Jane in a little girl voice. "When I spoke to the ticket agent at Hudson Bay Company who owns the ship, she explained that the bay freezes over at night, and we'll probably be breaking ice all the way to Baffin Island," says Tanaya.

"Now, that may sound scary but it will be a journey you'll remember for the rest of your life," says Tanaya, assuringly.

"It's almost the lunch hour. Uncle should be well rested by now, I'll go wake him for lunch. Will you join us?" Tanaya asks.

"Count me in," she says in agreement. Tanaya acknowledges her as she slides the door shut. While making her way towards Inar's berth, she sees a coach attendant at Inar's door with a tray and water pitcher.

"Porter, this is my uncle's cabin, can I help you with something? Tanaya asks.

"Yes, there is miss," says the porter as he places the tray down and looks at the passenger list. Earlier, when Mr. Katerpar was in the Club Car, we managed to figure out all he wanted was a glass of water. He must have been thirsty because he drank three glasses in a row. So I brought him more water, just in case he wanted more," says the porter.

Tanaya becomes concerned, she knocks on the door lightly at first and calls out his name, there is no response. The door handle is tried and she finds his berth is unlocked.

"Uncle? Tanaya says in a soft voice. Inar's name is called again, and again no response. Tanaya reaches for his arm to give him a good shake when she hears

Inar's deep snore. Tanaya takes a deep breath of relief.

"Uncle? Are you all right? Tanaya says in Inuit. Inar rolls over and begins to apologize, but Tanaya stops him.

"It's okay. I just came to ask if you would like to have lunch with us? Tanaya replies. Inar relates that he has no appetite and that he will join them for supper. Tanaya becomes concerned, she let's him know the porter has brought him a pitcher of water.

The door is quietly closed and she goes to join Jane. In the Club Car, Jane is seated at a table and is reading a menu. Tanaya takes a seat at the table and waits for Jane to put her menu down.

"I think I will order some hot soup and a sandwich, how about you?" Jane asks.

"I'm worried about Uncle," says Tanaya.

"It's the train ride. We've been rolling on these tracks for three and a-half days, he just needs some fresh air and a good stroll. He'll be okay," assures Jane.

"You may be right about that, but he said to me that he didn't get any sleep last night. He said something about his friends keeping him awake, trying to talk to him all night," says Tanaya.

"A bad dream?"

"Not exactly. The way he explained it, well, it was more prophetic, in a way. He was concerned that every one of men at the end of his bed, had all passed-on," says Tanaya.

The waiter shows to take their order. Without hesitation, Tanaya orders what Jane is having.

"I'm not really hungry, I'll have some soup and save my sandwich for Uncle," says Tanaya. "He's not coming to lunch?

"I think he's afraid that he won't make it to the village. He said he never felt so far away, for being so close," explains Tanaya.

Throughout his life, Inar was a confidant in his village. If one of the young men had a question, that question would be asked to Inar. In tribal affairs, the leaders would always confide in him before taking action. It was in this form of communication that Inar came to believe in certain after life that elders were able to hear and see signs that let them know their time was near. It is believed that those seen before the final passing, are those who will greet you on the other side. That evening, Inar did not show for dinner.

The next morning, Tanaya discovered that Inar was not inside compartment. She hurried back to her compartment to talk with Jane, who was also gone. Upon entering the Club Car, Tanaya sees Inar and Jane sitting at a table.

"Well, there you are," says Tanaya walking up to the table.

"We were wondering where you were. I spoke to the conductor, he said we'll be arriving at 10 a.m., and, as of the last stop, it's a freezing minus two degrees at Churchill," says Jane.

The train whistle blows as the locomotive reaches a railroad crossing. "Another crossing, that's the second whistle within an hour. We must be getting closer to civilization," says Jane. A conversation between Inar and Tanaya begins as the waiter brings their breakfast plates.

"You're going to wither-up and blow away if you don't start eating more nutritious meals," says Jane, looking at an English muffin on Tanaya's plate.

"Yes, but then I would have the pleasure of not having to buy another size wardrobe," says Tanaya looking at Jane's plate of ham and eggs, fried potatoes and buttered toast.

"You might have get used to eating salmon for breakfast. Uncle says that he knows of a couple of men in his village that may like to meet you," says Tanaya.

"Tell him thank you, but I am already married," says Jane with a pause. "To my job," she adds.

Tanaya translates to Inar, who gives a hardy laugh. He then another suggestion to Tanaya. "You might change your mind, for there are some cold nights to come in the Baffin," says Tanaya. "We shall see, what we shall see," says Jane prophetically. "If they are anything like Inar, staying warm will not be a problem," says Jane, in a joking manner. A conductor walks through the car announcing; 'Churchill, one hour.'

Inar has finished his breakfast, and explains to Tanaya that he will be in his compartment preparing his journey bundle. Tanaya politely waits until Jane finishes her breakfast.

"Uncle had a good point when he mentioned he has not seen you with a man friend. Pray tell, why is that? Friend of mine."

"Well, if you must know. It's girl to girl, all right? Jane asks.

"Cross my heart and hope to die," Tanaya says melodically.

"It's complicated, but I'm not the old spinster I appear to be now...I meant that as a joke. Anyway, my senior year in college I fell hard for a Third year medical student at New York University School of Medicine. I wanted to believe he felt the same, but by the time I had graduated from

307.

Cornell, my career became my main focus," says Jane.

"A law degree. A woman with a law degree, that is absolutely outstanding. I could never do something like that," says Tanaya.

"I think you could," says Jane.

"What happened? Tanaya asks.

"We made a pact, he would continue at the medical school and I would begin my career. It was a simple plan, we both thought it would work. It didn't, he got married soon after he graduated."

"You hide it well, I wouldn't have guessed that you were carrying that around all this time," says Tanaya.

"Thank God for Inar's case and you. It has been one thing after another for the past year. Who has time to nurse a heart ache anyway? Jane says with a smile.

"Well, I think you are a prize, and whoever you meet and marry will be one lucky so-and-so," says Tanaya.

"I'm enjoying my life right now, a relationship would only get in the way. When my time comes, you'll know it by the glow about me," says Jane confidently.

CHAPTER NINETEEN
Icebergs And Sea Sickness

The tiny port at the Churchill settlement seems deserted as the locomotive pulls into the station. With just a few business establishments in the settlement, the arrival of the Hudson Bay Railway engine is always an event. Arriving with the train is the mail, as well as building and store supplies. This year, the settlement is planning a Spring Festival. A stage and dance floor is to be built entirely of cedar planks, which have just arrived.

Inside Inar's compartment, the engine steam obscures the station dock. Inar catches a glimpse of an old Malamute sled dog. He tries to push the window down to get a better look, but the Malamute trots behind an out building. Tanaya opens the compartment door and let's Inar know that they have reached their destination.

"We are closer to home, even from here. I can feel my people and their excitement at the coming of spring," Inar says to Tanaya.

"We are closer than when we were in New York. When we get to the boat, I will find out how many days we will travel before we reach the Baffin," says Tanaya. Inar gives her a smile of approval and shoulders his journey bundle. As they step down from the train, Inar immediately feels the stinging frigid air on his face. The warm air from his lungs can be seen as he exhales an appreciative expression. "Good," he says, relieved.

At the station loading dock, Jane is talking with a man dressed in a car coat, hat and goggles. "This is our driver, the port agency has provided us transportation to the dock," says Jane to Tanaya. "I hope we're not late," Jane adds.

"No matter Miss, the Nascopie will be at the dock in a few more hours, the captain's coal supply was held up by the storm last night, and they are loading her now. You say you're headed for the Baffin?" The driver asks, pulling out a smoking pipe.

"Yes," she replies. "I have been told the Hudson Bay freezes over during the night. Will we be seeing ice all the way to our destination?" Tanaya asks.

"Pretty much, that is until you get to Hudson Straight, then there's nothing but icebergs and sheet ice," says the driver in a matter of fact tone. Tanaya looks at Jane. "Let's pretend we didn't hear that," says Jane in a low voice.

"Yep, it's been said that the berg that sank the Titanic, was calved right up in the Hudson straight. Then it drifted into the Grand Banks of Newfoundland by way of the Arctic current until it was struck by the Titanic," insists the driver.

"You don't say," Jane says in feigned wonderment. "Is there a cafe or restaurant in the colony? Tanaya asks. "Everything you need can be found at the trading post. There are few tables and chairs inside if you'd like a bite to eat," says the driver.

"I was thinking about somewhere we could pass the time while the boat takes on the coal supply," replies Jane.

"It would be best for you to get settled onto the breaker before you make any plans for the rest of the day. The captain is running late, and probably won't tolerate tardiness," says the driver, as he pulls the vehicle close to the loading dock.

While climbing from the vehicle, Jane, Tanaya, and Inar get their first look at the Nascopie. The ship is mored to a long, wooden loading dock, her engines are being stoked as the coal is loaded into the bins. There are two horse drawn cargo wagons waiting to be unloaded. Jane can see the ship is in remarkable condition, considering the constant exposure to the extreme weather.

"I did some research on the ship, at the New York City Library, and discovered she had been launched just five years ago, and there she is, all 2500 tons of her," offers Tanaya.

"E-yep. She comes out at 285 feet in length, enough room for you to stroll the deck, when you get tied of watching the paint peel," says the driver. "Thank you. I'll be sure to write that down on my 'things to do' list," says Jane.

"You should know that she's a real icebreaker," he says. "Who's an icebreaker? Jane asks.

"I beg your pardon Miss, not who, it is she; the Nascopie, she's not just a ship, she's an icebreaker," he explains.

"Now, don't I feel like the classic landlubber. Thank you for being patient with me, I'm completely out of my environment here," says Jane.

"Also, from here, it will take at least six to seven days to reach the Baffin," he explains, as he tamps a pinch of tobacco into his smoking pipe.

Jane can see that Tanaya has averted her attention. She turns to see the Captain of Nascopie walking towards the vehicle, wearing an officers hat and P-coat over his uniform. Tall in stature, and a greying beard, giving an appearance of a much older gentleman.

"Miss Reynolds, I presume," says the Captain, extending a hand. "I am Captain Darby. I hope Willie hasn't given you too much macabre information about the frozen bay," says Darby.

"Not so much macabre, as useful. Hello, I'm Jane Reynolds and these are your other two passengers, Tanaya Navaran and Inar Katerpar," says Jane.

"We will be pulling out in an hour, until then I'll have one of my men show you to your quarters. There is hot coffee in the galley, and heater vents in each berth to keep you warm. If you will excuse me, I have to be on the bridge right now," says Darby, as he tips his hat to leave. A ship's sea man shows up to escort them aboard, but first the luggage.

Once aboard, the trio is shown to their sleeping quarters, the women in one berth and Inar with the crew. When shown his sleeping quarters, Inar takes a look at the hammock and scoffs.

"It would be easier to sleep under it, than on top of it," says Inar in his native language. The sea man, confused at Inar's reaction, gives in to his choice.

"As you wish, sir," he says as he leaves. Inar decides to sleep on the steel floor, under the hammock.

In the sleeping quarters for Jane and Tanaya, giggling can be heard by a sea man who has arrived. The sea man lets them know of a safety briefing before the cast off.

"You'll have to excuse us if we seem silly, but we have never slept in a hammock. After I help Tanaya into her hammock, I may have to sleep standing up," says Jane to the sea man.

"Oh, you ladies will get the hang of it, here let me show you," says the sea man.

"First, you approach the hammock and make friends with it," he says, petting the ropes. The women laugh at his amusing instruction.

"Then, place your pillow inside like this, I like to use two pillows, that way I can sleep on my side. Then you straddle it like this, steady yourself then ease into it," he says as confidently lowers himself onto the hammock.

Jane and Tanaya look to each other doubtfully. "Whose beds are those?" Tanaya asks, pointing to a set of bunked beds.

"Please forgive me for not mentioning this before. Those are your beds, ladies," the sea man says as he heads for the door. "Safety briefing in ten minutes," he adds.

"She who laughs last, laughs longest," says Jane. "He'll get his," she adds with a villainous grin.

The Mess Room, a dining area aboard ship, is the makeshift conference room for the safety briefing. Inar, Jane, and Tanaya, among other passengers, have gathered for the captain's briefing. Jane leads Inar and Tanaya towards the back of the dining area. She is concerned that Tanaya's translating may be distractive to the other passengers, which number ten in all.

"Good morning ladies and gentlemen, I am Captain Darby and on behalf of the crew of the Nascopie, we welcome you aboard. This briefing is for your safety, the crew will be at your disposal always, during your journey. We are within the northern reaches of the Arctic Circle, which means we will come across miles of sheet ice, and at times, icebergs. If the ship comes under any trouble, you should know what to do in case of emergency," explains the captain.

"While aboard the Nascopie, and until your destination is reached, always keep in mind that we are all in the same boat, no pun intended. As you may well know, Germany is in a declared state of war, and has been since July of 1914. If you see a German warship, or any ship for that matter, within distance of the Nascopie, please report it immediately," Captain Darby instructively announces.

"The Nascopie is also a supply ship, it being early spring, the settlements and outposts are in need of being resupplied. We will be making many stops during this voyage, but there will be no overnight port on the itinerary. This, of course, will be depending upon severe weather. The Nascopie will steam through to the Baffin Island, her last supply delivery."

"We are near our capacity in cargo tonnage. Right now the crew is topping off the coal bunker, to accommodate the two tons of coal we will burn per day," explains Captain Darby.

"While the Ship is sound and sea worthy, she is light at 2,520 tons, and she tends to roll with the sea. While cutting through sheet ice, she is always a bit noisy, so before you decide to drift off to dreamland, it would be a good idea to plug your ears," advises the captain.

The safety briefing continues for a half-hour, all through which, Tanaya is translating to Inar.

"One question here," says Tanaya, to which she is acknowledged. "My uncle would like to know; are there enough lifeboats?" Tanaya asks. "A good question, Miss Navaran," acknowledges the captain. "Yes, I assure each of you, there are enough lifeboats," says the captain. The galley has prepared snacks for those of you who would like to partake, we'll be under way in ten minutes," says the captain, ending the briefing.

It isn't long before the ship is precariously maneuvering away from the loading dock, of which is situated at the mouth of Churchill River. The wind begins to blow as the Nascopie steams towards channel that leads to the ice covered Hudson Bay. With the cargo hold full and decks stacked with mixed cargo, she is steaming through the river chunk ice without the expected rolling motion. When the Captain mentioned the roll of the ship, Jane became concerned about sea sickness.

Inar has already prepared for the voyage, he has donned his traditional clothing. Under his parka, he is wearing a bird skin under shirt, and over that is an arctic fox jacket, on his feet are his mukluks. Inar has found a nook at the bow of the ship and is looking down over the railing. The reinforced hull cutting through the ice, has Inar amazed. As the ship churns toward the bay inlet, Tanaya joins Inar.

"Until I floated off on that ice floe, I payed no attention to the beauty our frozen land holds. I was trying to gain journey to a Sky World that could very well be right here on earth," says Inar in his native language.

"Last year, you said the Sky World was taken from you by the sea accident. Are you still of the same mind?" Tanaya asks.

"The Sky World is ever present. The sea accident gave me life, amid so much death. So many I saw, floating through the deep. So many going under, their arm stretched upward. It was as if waiting to be pulled up into the fold. I saw their spirits being released, like blue ice melting upward towards the stars. "No, my mind is as it always was, loyal to spirit of all our relations. The feeling of being part of all of this is more stronger than ever," explains Inar in his native language.

"I have learned so much from you, Uncle. Had you have slipped away that night in the ocean, it would be I who would have been cheated," says Tanaya. Inar becomes shy, he smiles and acknowledges.

Nearing the river inlet, the ship's fog horn blares out a warning to any ship approaching the inlet.

"You will need to know, once we get to the village, the women will take you both to an isolated shelter, until they can see that you are safe to be let out in the village," says Inar.

"Does sea sickness count? Because we're both healthy," says Tanaya. "I know that, they will have to see for themselves. A sickness called the flu was brought to the village several years back. This sickness took many of our children and old folks, so now it is understood that anyone coming into the village will be under watchful eyes," explains Inar. "I am going back to check on Jane, I'll explain it to her, I know she will understand. You know she's not feeling well, but it's just sea sickness," says Tanaya as she walks away. "Don't forget, shrimp cocktail for dinner tonight," she turns to say. Inar waves to her, and continues to look over the railing as the river ice turns to sheet ice. The Nascopie has entered the Hudson Bay.

During the next three days, the weather seemed to worsen. Inar found that he was able to help the crew, with the captain's permission. Gale force winds hampered the ship's ability to steady herself on the icy bay. In the morning, after the storm Inar would help clear ice from the deck. When not on the deck, he spent spare time in the mess room. It wasn't long before he was helping in the galley.

Jane was affected by the rolling of the ship, and developed sea sickness, her dreaded fear. Tanaya spent a great deal of her time looking after Jane. The numerous stops gave Jane a short break from the ailment. When the ship was anchored to unload cargo, she stopped rolling. The less cargo meant the ship was getting lighter, and when the ship began to get lighter, Jane became more green around the gills. Tanaya became very popular with the ship's crew. Her cheerful disposition made the trip not so stressful.

On the fourth day, the weather died down. Jane is able to eat a sandwich and sip on a cup of soup. The sea sickness has left her weak. Just knowing that the last stop is a day away, gives her the strength to carry on with her endeavor to get Inar back to his village. While in the mess room, Captain Darby finds Jane and Tanaya talking with one of the galley cooks.

"It's good to see that you're feeling better Miss Reynolds. I must apologize for the Nascopie, she's not very kind to first timers," says the Captain.

"Apology accepted," Jane says, feigning her last breath. "Have you received the weather forecast for tomorrow?" she asks.

"Calm with high visibility, and that is for the next three days," replies the Captain.

"Along with the weather report, we received a message out of Churchill. Apparently, a reporter and his photographer showed up in the village, asking questions about you and Mr. Katerpar," explains the Captain.

"Photographer? Are they still in Churchill?" Tanaya asks. The captain give her a nod. "Thank God. I must look like warmed over death. Absolutely, no photographs, please," says Jane, grabbing her purse and begins applying lipstick.

"The dispatcher reported that they are on your trail, she got the idea they were going to wait for your return," he says.

"Is it possible they might find another ship to get them to Baffin Island?" Tanaya asks.

"It's not possible. The other supply ships that sail the bay usually show after the spring thaw," assures Darby.

"Correct me if I am wrong, but as I understand it, Mr. Katerpar is quite the celebrity," suggests Darby.

"Yes, that he is. Now, may I apologize to you Captain?" Jane asks beseechingly.

"What on earth for?" Darby asks.

"My intention, was to let you know of Mr. Katerpar's notoriety, that is, before I was stricken with the dreaded sea plague. I was concerned about your crew having a jinx aboard," says Jane.

"On the contrary. Although, some sea men can be somewhat superstitious, my men seem to be very logical about things like that. It is a fact, that other than a German torpedo, it would have taken an iceberg to sink a ship the size of Titanic. That's the way of it with my crew," says the Captain.

"That's good to know. In the U.S., there were rumors going around that Mr. Katerpar jinxed the Titanic. I didn't want your crew to feel uncomfortable about him being on board, that's all," says Jane.

"Nonsense. They're out there right now trying to get some resemblance of a personalized autograph from Mr. Katerpar," says the Captain. An embarrassed Tanaya covers her smile out of respect for the captain.

"Here's a bit of information. The Inuit have their own alphabet," says Tanaya, taking a pencil in hand. Mr. Katerpar's name looks like this, when put in the Inuit way of writing," says Tanaya, as she writes Inar's full name and place of origin on a writing tablet. "Well, I'll be. I know now that the men will want to wait for the photographer, to get pictures as well. It was suggested the moment they found that a celebrity was aboard," explains Darby.

"What are the chances that the press will find another ship to take them to Baffin Island?" Jane asks.

"Right now, the chances of you seeing any news reporters before you leave the Baffin are very narrow. You see, the bay freezes over at night. The only way a ship could get out of Churchill and across the bay this time of year, is to sail out after the Nascopie," says Darby.

"When will you return to Churchill?" Jane asks. "After unloading the Katerpar cargo, we will sail to Greenland, take on supplies at Nuuk. On our return trip to Baffin we'll be fully loaded, and the Nascopie will be sailing steady, something you will want to know, Miss Reynolds," advises the Captain. Jane's half smile is followed by a scoff.

"Miss Navaran and myself will board as passengers. When you return from Greenland in five days," says Jane. "Yes, then back to Churchill, and deliver you into the hands of the newspaper reporters," says Darby with a smile. "Oh that won't be so bad. After all, Inar Katerpar will be back in his village, out of the public eye, and away from the prying press," says Jane. "If you are not feeling up to it and change your mind about greeting the press, we could have you and Miss Navaran disembark with the crew. "Thank you Captain Darby, I'll keep that in mind," says Jane, twirling her hair with one finger.

Outside, on the deck of the Nascopie, there are several crew members standing at the bow of the ship. They have Inar encircled, and are in awe of the living legend. The crew have no knowledge of the Inuit language, yet they seem gratified to be in his presence.

CHAPTER TWENTY
Out Of The Hudson, Into The Straight

The next day of the journey, Nascopie can be seen from a sea hawk's view, high above the Arctic Ocean. A path of churning chunk lies in her wake, as she cuts her way towards the Tarr Bay inlet. The weather is calm, and the sun can be seen as a glowing orb, through a hazy, cloud covered sky. Inar and Tanaya stand at the bow, looking on as the area becomes more familiar. Inar has never hunted this far out at sea, this experience is a first.

The journey through the Hudson Straight was uneventful. Although the Nascopie came within a few hundred meters of the slow moving icebergs, Captain Darby navigated her safely through miles of sea ice. While passing through the ice fields, Inar pointed to a particular iceberg and explained to Tanaya he recognized a resemblance. Tanaya translated to a few of the sea men who are on the bow.

"That one there, is about the size of the iceberg I was placed on. It's a little smaller, but I could live on it. If I had to do it again, I think I could, but wouldn't want to," says Tanaya through translation. The crew men burst out in laughter, Inar smiles as he sees that he made someone laugh.

On the bridge, the Captain has ordered a 35 degree turn to port, heading into the long Baffin Island sea arm. The sea loch leading to a bay is where Inar's homeland is situated. The ship churns through the sea ice to reach the inlet and the sea current. They are now on a dead ahead course to Nunavut, a small peninsula where they will unload the cargo. Jane has been invited to the bridge where she watches the Captain command the ship through the ice floe congested inlet.

"The islands on the port side are Resolution Island and Edgell Island. The main navigational objective, is to head the ship into a course that will follow the current into the bay. In order to do so, we first we have to fight a torrent of cross currents to get to the North east shore line.

It will be rough for the next hour or so, but I've not come across any potential risk to be concerned about," explains the Captain.

"This is the last leg of the journey during of which we will navigate a few narrow passages to reach our destination," adds the Captain.

"Is this another straight, like the Hudson? Jane asks.

"No, technically this large body of water is a bay. You can't see its end from here, but it is bordered by land on three sides. We will travel about 160 miles into this body of water, known as a sea arm, until we reach the end of the bay where we can unload our cargo," explains Darby.

"Is this a usual stop on your supply route?" Jane asks.

"Not usually. The Inuit call the bay community, Niagunngut. Arctic sailors call it December Bay. At one point, there was a Canadian research station located on the shores of the bay. The station has been abandoned for about five years, it's been as long that I've been to this location," says Darby.

"How many Inuit villages are situated on the bay," Jane asks.

"My guess, about three separate villages, two are more inland. I think Mr. Katerpar's family is situated above the bay. You'll be lucky if his village is Iqaluit, if that is the case, your cargo will be transported about two miles from where we will drop anchor," says Darby.

"I'm praying the teamster we hired will be there to load the supplies," says Jane.

"There is a caretaker at the research station, Russell Brandt, he will be the one to arrange the cargo transport to the village. I'm sure of that because he is also the radio operator, maintenance manager, and ambassador for the natives of Iqaluit to the outside," says Darby.

"I'll stop my fretting. Where else would he be when we reach the bay. We communicated by wireless transmission, and he explained that a team of caribou or horses would be arranged to haul the cargo," says Jane.

"Mr. Brandt will more than likely subcontract the transport to a villager. The Inuit are nomadic tribes, reindeer herds are kept by the tribes to haul their belongings from camp to camp, taking them to where the arctic game are located," explains Darby.

The sea current begins to heave the ship up and down. Jane, effected by the motion, excuses herself to go back to her berth.

"Actually, Miss Reynolds the bridge is the most stable place to be on a rolling sea. Have a seat, the door to the head is just to your right, if you feel the need," offers Captain Darby. Jane takes a seat and settles in for a rough boat ride.

Far up ahead of the Nascopie, the Nunavut Weather Research Station is slowly becoming visible under an overcast sky.

Only five miles from Inar's village, the caretaker stands just outside the entrance gates. Russell Brandt is discussing the transport arrangements with a local tribal leader, who goes by the name of; Nanuv.

"It is my understanding that fifty-two hundred pounds of supplies are due to arrive tomorrow, by way of the Nascopie. They are destined for your village, explains Brandt.

"Are you sure? Because, as far as I know, the government rations are not supposed to arrive until sea ice melts," says Nanuv.

"No matter. It's probably from some aid organization sending a half-ton of pencil erasers and shoe strings," says Brandt.

"Not funny Russell, we still have a few boxes of shoe hooks we don't know what to do with," says Nanuv.

"I will transmit a message to the Nascopie later this evening. Shall I confirm the cargo transport is in order?" Brandt asks.

"Right on that. I will be here in the morning with three teams of deer, three sleds, and including myself, three helpers. I figure it's going to come to $200.00," suggests Nanuv.

"One-hundred and fifty sounds right to me," says Brandt.

"One-hundred and seventy-five feels better," says Nanuv.

Russell Brandt settles into deep thought. The haggling is ended when a hand is extended by Brandt.

"One seventy-five it is. Be here first thing tomorrow morning," says Brandt as he walks towards the entrance gate to the research station. Nanuv holds his hand up to bid farewell, then walks toward his staked down sled and awaiting sled dogs. The sled dogs immediately respond to his command to 'getup', and he is on his way towards his village. Nanuv is a close cousin to Inar and he was there when Inar received his sendoff to the Sky World. He does not know of Inar being aboard the supply ship. No one from his village has heard or seen Inar for almost two years. The entire village believes that Inar is with all of his relations and loved ones in the Sky World.

When the Titanic went down, the news that had reached the Baffin, was taken with the understanding that a big boat was sent to the bottom of the Grand Banks. To the native people, the tragedy was felt in the loss of life. A loss felt by Inuit families who also had relatives taken by the Great Provider - the Sea. Inar's part had no bearing on the native peoples of Baffin Island.

CHAPTER TWENTY-ONE
Homecoming For A Ghost

With the weather research station in clear view, the Nascopie has broken the ice near as possible to the research station. The First Officer orders her anchor dropped. At the moment of release, the huge chain travels through a serpentine path. The unrelenting sound of metal against metal continues until the Nascopie's anchor plummets to the bottom of the bay. It is a noise, and it is intrusive, but it be heard cutting through the crystal arctic air five miles away. A distant and distinct sound that alerts Nanuv, the Nascopie has arrived. With no time to waste, he sends one of his sons to awaken the helpers. A reindeer herd will be gathered and brought to a staging area. The helpers will drape the animals in harnesses and feed them oat grain to ready them for a days work.

The ship has arrived at 5:00 a.m., and the crew is given a briefing to pass onto the next shift of crew members. The Captain has been called to his post on the bridge. He immediately issues orders to the crew, instructing them on the precarious and dangerous task of off loading the cargo.

Later in the dining area, a briefing is under way, led by the Captain. "The Second Officer will call the passengers for breakfast in one hour. During the breakfast meal, an informal briefing will be conducted for the benefit of our passengers, who will be returning to Churchill in four days," Captain Darby explains.

"If you haven't unloaded cargo in December Bay, you should know that it will not be business as usual. The bay has a unique feature, and the ice is known to give way for no apparent reason. Stay alert at all times during the cargo unloading. The purser will carry out the duties for disembarkation, guided by the rules and guidelines. As your captain, I will require your utmost attention to detail. This will be expected of the crew on this morning's off loading of supplies," adds the Captain.

Below deck, Inar is dressed and waiting with his journey bundle on his lap. The anticipation of arriving back in his home land has left him anxious and wresting with feelings of disappointment. Inar's survival, in an act of sacred surrender for the good of a people, may not sit well with the village medicine people. As he reflects on the events that has brought him full circle, Inar's emotions are mixed. While feeling fortunate about being able to return, he is not sure. Did he have the right? Is the question that rings throughout his head. What should he do when being questioned of his presence in a world that he had been departed from?

Inar is faced with the inevitability of the village leaders and medicine people requiring a journey story of his account while away. The journey story is a taxing expectation, as he does not believe it to be viable. In his own thoughts, the journey could not have reviled an experience in which he killed a white bear. An account, even he could not believe when it happened. The killing had nothing to do with brevity or his prowess as a hunter - it was luck. Deep down, he knows that a knowledge brought by memories of the past can yield many feelings. Yet, in his heart, he knows his guilt will be sensed by his inquisitors.

Inar, as an elder stood in witness while others of his village were questioned on supernatural occurrences. He now finds himself doubting if an account of his experiences will be sufficient to answer question of his ability to produce proof of his own life.

On deck Inar stands motionless, clutching the journey bundle to his chest. Through a morning mist, Inar can see the geographical surroundings of his village. The diminutive snow covered foothills stand in the foreground of a towering mountain range. With a bowed head, he cover his eyes with his fur mitts to keep his tears from freezing his eyes shut. Silently Inar begins to weep as Tanaya walks up behind him. Tanaya places a hand on his shoulder.

"That is the place of your birth Uncle. Your tears are being welcomed by all of your relatives," comforts Tanaya.

"In the distance, I heard a faint sound of jingling bells, to me it can only mean one thing; reindeer. I can tell by the timing of the bells, the deer are at a trot. Those deer belong to my cousin, Nanuv, and they are headed this way," says Inar.

"How can you be so sure?" Tanaya asks. "He's the only one with a herd of that size," replies Inar.

Through strained eyes, he tries to determine a direction of the bells. Inar's mitt clad hands clutch the starboard railing of the ship. Images of distant black dots appear against the snow covered landscape a few miles away.

"There they are, if three sleds come over that ridge, it is my cousin Nanuv," explains Inar.

"Looks to me, you're going to have a great home coming, family and everything," assures Tanaya.

"No one will remember me, I was gone to them two years ago. In the Inuit way of life, it may be double," says Inar.

The deck begins to come alive with crew men preparing to unload the last of the cargo from the hold of the Nascopie. The gang plank is set onto the ice as the Captain comes onto the deck. "Mr. Katerpar, I hope you've had a good journey," says Captain Darby.

Tanaya translates the Captain's comment. "He thanks you, and he is happy to be home," says Tanaya.

"Let Mr. Katerpar know he is welcome, and we will miss him on the return trip," says the Captain.

"I presume the teams of reindeer coming over the rise are the cargo transport arranged by Miss Reynolds," says Darby.

"Right you be Captain. There may be an unexpected family reunion happening within the next hour or so," says Tanaya in jest. Captain Darby excuses himself as Inar begins to explain the Katerpar family tree to Tanaya.

Later, when Jane shows on the starboard deck, Inar points to the approaching transport sleds.

"I didn't see either of you at breakfast. Omelets made to order, fresh cut fried potatoes, toast and jam, and of course, the boring disembarkation briefing," says Jane.

"It's good to see your appetite has retuned," says Tanaya. Jane pauses, then without warning, a loud burp surprises Jane. Excusing herself, she goes to the deck rail.

"I think it's more like the food has returned," says Jane, hugging the deck railing.

"They've put the gang plank down, let's get off the boat and go out to meet our cargo transport," says Jane.

"Good idea. Transport's on the way, when they get here, we can meet Uncle's relatives," says Tanaya.

"Relatives with a cargo company? Inar has connections, that I like," says Jane. The Captain is notified of the crewmen assisting the passengers off of the ship. Darby agrees, mostly for Jane's sake.

Once on the frozen surface of the harbor, a farewell wave is given to the Captain and crew. It is a good-bye for now as they are expected to meet the Nascopie on the return trip. The first of the supply boxes are unloaded by the cargo crew. Passenger luggage is delivered to Tanaya and Jane, where they await the transport sleds to arrive. With luggage by their sides, Inar, Jane, and Tanaya watch as the transport sleds appear out of a white misty fog.

The sound of jingling bells and pounding hoofs make the ice tremble beneath their feet. The reindeer teams are maneuvered into a staging position to load the cargo. While busy directing the other sled drivers into a queue position, Nanuv does not see Inar walking up, his unsuspecting cousin continues to maneuver his crew into place. Inar waits patiently, not wanting to interrupt a man at his work, preferring to use the element of surprise. It looks as if Nanuv is about to finish placing his sleds. Inar cannot wait to greet him with a bear hug. Jane and Tanaya watch with curiosity, waiting to see the kind of reaction that may come from the impromptu reunion.

"Nanuv! Inar shouts happily. Nanuv turns to see Inar, arms extended and walking towards him. Nanuv's eyes grow wide, with a few blinks, his eyes roll back into his head, and he faints. Inar's smiling face turns to an expression of disappointment, his arms fall down to his side. With hunched shoulders, and a perplexed look on his face, he stands over his unconscious cousin, sprawled onto the ice.

Jane and Tanaya go to Inar. They are joined by the other team drivers, asking each other what happened to their boss. Inar faces them, and they stop in their tracks. Slowly approaching him, reaching out and touching his parka. When the teamsters realize it is Inar, they are surprised but not shocked. Their excited chatter is short lived as Jane directs Tanaya to have Inar stand on the other end of the sled and out of sight.

Tanaya calls out to him softly. "Nanuv, can you hear me? Are you all right?" Tanaya asks in her native language.

Nanuv's eyes spring open. The small crowd encircling him, fall silent as he gains consciousness. Looking from side to side, he sits up and shakes his head.

"I saw the dead, and it was calling my name," says Nanuv. He is helped to his feet by his chuckling teamsters.

"You saw Inar Katerpar and he is with us here, he is not dead," explains Tanaya.

"That was Inar? He went on the ice floe, no one comes back from the ice floe," says Nanuv. Inar slowly steps out from the rear of the cargo sled, he steps into full view and stands before his cousin.

"I am here cousin, I have come back to my village, to my relatives and friends," says Inar, as he pulls Nanuv into a hug.

"Everyone thought you had passed-on. Where have you been?" Nanuv asks.

"My journey has been long, and it has been challenging. I have seen things and been to places not known by the Inuit," he says. "You men, begin loading the sleds with cargo," says Nanuv, as he and Inar begin to walk towards the weather station. Jane and Tanaya watch as Inar becomes excited telling the incredible story of his journey. Jane becomes fascinated with the reindeer, she goes to her pack where she pulls out a paper bag. The galley cook was generous enough to pack a lunch for her and Tanaya. An apple is pulled from the lunch bag and is quartered by Tanaya. The deer are being fed the tasty bits of apple when a driver climbs onto the bench seat.

"Come on, let's load our luggage and climb into Nanuv's sled," says Tanaya. With the help of the driver, their luggage is placed on board. Tanaya and Jane climb into the sled driver seat, and they quickly make themselves comfortable. There are numerous skins that have been placed on the bench seat to soften the ride. Tanaya and Jane are soon settled into the seat, bundled in Arctic fox furs and seal pelts.

As the last of the cargo is loaded into Nanuv's sled, the Nascopie is maneuvered out into the open water of the bay. The

Captain set the course and they begin to steam their way towards their next destination - Greenland.

Later, with the Nascopie now in the distance, Nanuv and Inar climb onto the cargo sled. Jane and Tanaya are almost buried in furs in the second bench seat, low and to the rear of the drivers seat. Although barely visible, their eyes and rosy cheeks can be seen by Inar and Nanuv, who do not acknowledge their silent presence. Like two children hiding from grown-ups, Jane and Tanaya listen to the laughter and conversation as the sled is turned northward in the direction of the village.

Further up the sled path, the jingling sound of halter bells and the soft pounding of reindeer hoofs reminds Jane of her childhood.

"I love it, feels like Christmas," says Jane. "It could be just that, we are on our way to a village bearing gifts," says Tanaya.

Nanuv has sent one of the cargo sleds far up ahead to prepare the village for the surprise in the way of gifts and supplies. Now, from a distance of two miles out, Inar can see the village. A low beholden sigh emanates from his chest, a sound of relief and thankfulness is offered by Inar. Nanuv shares his thoughts and nods his head in a quiet agreement.

"Are we there yet?" Jane asks in a little voice. Nanuv hears the question.

"You girls behave yourselves back there," Nanuv playfully scolds. There is some giggling beneath the bundle of furs.

"I have to pee," says Jane with a giggle.

"We are almost there, can you wait?" Nanuv asks.

The cargo sled is pulled to a stop. The reindeer are eager to reach the village. Sensing it is near, they start calling to the other reindeer teams far ahead.

Jane takes care of her business behind the sled and is joined by Tanaya. "Not a bad idea," she says.

"We're not far from the village, I saw smoke from the village just over the rise," says Tanaya.

When they climb back into the sled, the furs and pelts are pulled back on top, laughing all the while. Nanuv glances back at the gigglers and shakes his head.

"Your friends are having fun. I'm glad, they will be welcomed at the village," says Nanuv to Inar.

"They are very courages women. I know they will understand our fear of sickness, once the women in the village clear them for good health, they will be well liked," says Inar.

"I took another wife last year," says Nanuv. "What is that, seven now?" Inar asks.

"Five, I cannot handle anymore than that," says Nanuv. Tanaya is translating the conversation, and muffled laughter can be heard from the rear sled seat.

"I keep forgetting, that one girl knows the language," Nanuv says, as he continues in an older dialect unknown to Tanaya.

"How about you? Do you think you will ever take another wife, now that you are back?" Nanuv asks.

"No. There are other things I must to do before I consider another bride," says Inar.

The men fall silent as Inar begins to reminisce fondly about his late wife, who passed on two years before his journey. Nanuv begins to urge the reindeer on as they begin to climb a slight hill on the sled path. "You two in the back, come out from that fur cave and look upon our village," says Nanuv.

As the cargo sled nears the top of the hill, Tanaya and Jane strain to see over the shoulders of Inar and Nanuv who are sitting in front of them. The halter bells jingle at a faster pace as the sled starts downhill. The vantage point gives an excellent view of the sprawling village situated on the shore of the frozen bay.

Appearing through a thin layer of lingering smoke, are hundreds of ice shelters.

Sparsely spread throughout the village are modern wooden structures, left standing by various research groups.

As the ice path levels out, Jane and Tanaya watch as a kind of commotion begins to swell throughout the ice shelters. Word of Inar's return has spread rapidly through the village. Teams of dog sleds join Nanuv's sled as it nears the village. Once inside, Jane can see women and children are running towards their shelters, screaming with fear. She can hear some cheering from men who hunted with Inar and knew him well. Jane and Tanaya witness a bazar reaction to Inar's presence among the People, most who thought he was in the spirit world.

The reindeer are pulled to a slow walk, Nanuv places the reins in one hand and with the other he pats Inar on his shoulder. He is pulled close to Nanuv, to show others he is still a friend. Inar in turn places an arm around Nanuv, it is how they enter the village.

The sled slowly comes to a halt. Nanuv stands with Inar to speak. "Inar Katerpar has returned to his people and he has brought food, supplies to carry us through the season.

There are many here among you who thought him in another place, he is not, he is here among us again. For now, we should welcome him back on this day. There are gifts for everyone, we should celebrate," proclaims Nanuv. An acceptance of his return is shown by a cheers from the men and women who remember Inar. Slowly, they begin to gather around the sled touching him, women openly weep with joy and men grasp at his hand. Inar's son, Enovar makes his way through the crowd to greet his father. The reunion sets off cheers from the crowd. Inar stands proudly with his two year old grandson in his arms.

Nanuv calls upon five village women to escort Jane and Tanaya to an isolated ice shelter. The village women are very pleased that Tanaya can speak the language. Inar watches from the cargo sled as they are led away. He can see that the village women are happy with their guests. The sled is moved to the center of the village. Inar remains on the sled, reacquainting himself with his friends and relatives, the cargo boxes are ordered off of the sled and lined up in row.

Nanuv begins handing out gifts to the children. The children's gifts took Inar months to gather, stuffed animals, dolls and stuffed warriors were all outfitted with specially made garments of toy clothing to make them look like Inuit people and animals owned by the Inuit.

A second cargo box is opened, and it is full of Hudson Bay blankets. Other boxes are opened and they are found to contain pots and pans, cups, bowls, carving knives, ladles and cauldron spoons. There are enough cups to supply every family member in each village. An overwhelming feeling gratitude fills the village, as many of the gifts are utensils they have owned for the first time. A drum is heard and then another. The women begin preparing food and a celebration is underway.

The plan to ship supplies to the villages was in the making a year before the return journey. With the help of an economics professors at the local college, Jane was able to come up with figures that would apply to every household in the villages. With more than enough, the surplus would be put into a cooperative trading post for barter and trade. With Tanaya's help the plan blossomed into a small business venture.

Inside the isolation shelter, Jane and Tanaya are made comfortable, sitting on white bear rugs and drinking mountain berry tea. The women laugh as Tanaya tells of the sea sickness suffered by Jane, a sickness unknown to the Inuit. The drums are getting louder as more village drummers join in. It is a sign to some of the women, who were placed within the isolation shelter, to help the others with the preparation.

"How long will it be before we are able to walk among the people?" Tanaya asks in native language.

"We have summoned a Pipe Woman from another village. Her journey will take a half-day by sled," says the shelter keeper.

"Well, I guess that answers that question," says Jane. "What is in this tea?" she asks.

"Just herbs as far as I know, but now that you mentioned it, I feel kinda light headed," says Tanaya.

"Oh yippie, let's have some more," says Jane as she holds her cup to the shelter keeper. "I don't think it's a such a good idea, but since we're here for another several hours; what the heck," says Tanaya.

A fire has been lit and the celebration for Inar's return is slowly getting underway.

Inside long ice shelter, not far from the celebration, a council of leaders has been called. Inar is inside the long shelter, sitting in the circle of men. Just as before, Inar must prove to the council that he is innocent of any wrong doing concerning his return.

The circumstance surrounding Inar's return has been deemed unordinary and may not be natural. When some of the leaders were told of his presence, there was a cry for the them to question Inar's right to return to the his village. Inar once considered not returning at all, as he knew the circumstances of he surviving the ice floe, would not be accepted. Even though his generous offering was well received, Inar now will have to convince his leaders that he is not a threat to anyone or anything existing in their realm of existence.

Novinuk, a large, slightly bearded Inuit, is the first to speak. Without standing he begins in a soft diplomatic tone.

"Understand, Inar Katerpar, that you are still believed to be one of the us. In the past your well earned respect, shine on your courageous acts that proved your loyalty to the People. Stories of your selfless acts continue in legend to this day. I myself spoke of you in the days past," says Novinuk.

"I too have spoke of his merits. I remember Inar, he saved my son from death. Now, because of your bravery, my grand children live to carry on, for that, I stand with you Katerpar," says Manirak. of Imnek Village.

"On the day of the ice floe, we watched from a distance, it was a great act of selflessness, and yes we still talk of that day. The generous supplies will see us through another season with store left over. Inar Katerpar, is a true man, a hunter, a provider for the People. You are a courageous warrior, who lived a life that we all wish we could live up-to.

"But now, we as leaders have been placed in a path where we must choose, before today, there was but one path, one which was always familiar with us. Your return will make us to look at other forces, powers we should not be concerned with. Nothing has ever happened this way before. You should know this - no one comes back from the ice floe," another says with regret.

Inar sits in silence, bowing his head in a slow manner.

Looking up, he makes it a point to look into the eyes of each leader sitting in the council. Inar's eyes are kind and reassuring, his peers accept the silent understanding.

"When I was a boy, the great hunter Chukchi was mauled by a white bear. My father was very sad that it happened, he

like the rest of the village, mourned for
Chukchi in his passing. He was placed in
the ice shelter for three days. It was the
day before the death ceremony, he came
crawling out, he propped himself up on his
knees and asked for help. Some thought he
was ghost, but in the long run, he lived
three more seasons in the village.
Everyone accepted his return.

"I understand, as do you, that the supplies
provided for the people will not last. I
deeply understand that my presence may
bring bad luck for seasons to come, not
only for this village, but for others as well.

"My loyalty to the survival of the People
has not changed. The blood of my
ancestors runs through this village and
others. That is my responsibility to the
future of the People. I am home and I am
happy and I see my people are happy.

"Now, about that ice floe. I do not know
why I was not taken. These questions were
asked of myself. Worthiness was one of the
questions. The strength in my beliefs was
another. Yet another was doubt of the Sky
World. Did it exist? If it does exist, why
was I not taken? I am a good man. Still, all
of these questions remain right in front of
me. There is a confidence that lingers, the
confidence of the Sky World, will give me
the right to answer those questions.

"My being is here, among my people is the only thing that matters now. At first, my thoughts on returning did not occur to me, I did not belong in a place I was no longer a part of, but the longing in my heart told me different. To you I say this; there was a journey, an unbelievable truth, a story untold in this village, in this world." Inar says.

The leaders in the council sit motionless, their empathy for Inar and his plight is shown in their eyes, some with tears.

"I will not be here long. As before, and as now, I am still old. Still trying to find my place, a place where my inner peace will see me through to a pathway that leads from here, into the Sky World," says Inar.

The leaders in the council speak softly among themselves, nodding their heads in agreement. In their native ways, they know what a struggle it is for men to gain the inner peace that Inar speaks of.

"Through my journey, I found that the place that I was set to seek, does not have to be here in my homeland. It can be anywhere in this world, I have seen this peace," says Inar.

Excited discussion starts suddenly among the leaders in the council. They now realize that Inar, in his return, can mean the opposite of bad. The return can also mean good luck in the coming seasons.

"There is only one thing to do now, we have supplies, we have food and we have happiness. Let us celebrate," says Inar with enthusiasm.

Much later when the celebration is at its fullest, the drums are pounding in beat with the round dancers. Inar is sitting with his son and grandchildren on one side and the council of leaders on the other. Standing in a long line, are friends, village elders, parents and their children, they are waiting to be received by Inar.

There are piles of traditional gift items that have been placed all around him, they are gifts of appreciation. Even though Inar's needs are very little at this point in his life, he will not turn down a gift offered in an honor of his presence.

"Will you look at that. Leave him alone for a few hours and he becomes chief of the tribe," Jane says in jest. Inar recognizes the voice, he turns to see Jane and Tanaya standing behind him, both in native Inuit dress.

"How did you get out of the shelter so soon?" Inar asks in native tongue.

"We don't know, the Pipe Woman took our hands into hers, then stood back and looked at us real hard, and that was all there was to it," explains Tanaya.

"She was always good at that. Look at all my gifts," says Inar, motioning on each side of him.

"Says to me your homecoming is a successful one," says Tanaya.

In an instant, Jane and Tanaya are pulled out onto the circle dance by two little village girls. With polite objection Jane explains her inability to dance.

"It's easy, just do what I do. Remember, it will be a very cultural experience,"
says Tanaya. Inar smiles as he watches the two women laughing with the children and dancing with the village elders.

CHAPTER TWENTY-TWO
Ice Floe To The Sky World

It is the second morning of the celebration, and most in the village are still sleeping off the effects of the night before. Outside his ice shelter Novinuk watches as a dog sled approaches the village from the direction of the bay. A neighbor comes out of his shelter holding a hot cup of coffee.

"Did you get one of these cups from the cargo box?" he asks. "Yes, I like them, for some reason my tea stays warm longer. Inar said they are metal cups, covered with something called porcelain," explains Novinuk.

"That is Taroq's dog team coming in, he must have a message from the research station," says the neighbor.

Cups in hand Novinuk and the neighbor go to the entrance to the greet messenger.

"It's a wireless message received from the Nascopie a little while ago. It says that she will be pulling into the bay at mid day tomorrow. The Nascopie's return passengers should be there to meet them," says the messenger.

"This message should be given to the Navaran girl and her friend. I will have it taken to them," says Novinuk.

Later, inside their ice shelter, Jane and Tanaya are awakened by an elder. She places a wood tray down between them. On it are two cups of hot coffee, cookies, and the message from Captain Darby of the Nascopie.

"Did you find out what they put in the tea?" Jane asks.

"Herbs." Tanaya says with a yawn.

"Funny thing, I don't remember being tired at all. Fact is, I don't remember too much of what happened last night," says Jane.

"Consider yourself lucky, it's true that everyone has trouble with sleep at first. I mean, going to sleep while it is still light out. I know I did," says Tanaya.

"Tonight, let's pretend we just got off the midnight shift. That'll do it, that and plenty of tea," says Jane, picking up the message envelope from the tray.

"We've received a message from the Captain. Looks like tomorrow, we'll be pulling out around noon. That is after the crew unload supplies for the weather station," says Jane.

"Well, guess what, today is a special day, and I'm excited. The women want us to sit with them, we are going to see how they make Inuit clothing," says Tanaya.

"Now that I remember, I love the way Inuit women dress, it is so fashionable: elegant furs, and all that intricate ornate stitching. Very high-class, you know," touts Jane. The elder returns with an Inuit breakfast of poached salmon and scrambled bird eggs. Tanaya has a brief conversation with the Elder then leaves.

"Grandma said she will be back after breakfast, she wants to be here in case we need help getting into our clothing," says Tanaya.

"They are such generous people, these jackets must have taken many hours to make," says Jane.

"It's the Inuit way to show their gratitude and friendship, it's what they do. You will have to believe me when I say you look beautiful dressed as an Inuit woman," says Tanaya.

"I want to see what I look like in this leather skirt and knee high mukluks, but there are no full length mirrors," says Jane.

"Let's hope Captain Darby has a photographer aboard when they sail in tomorrow," says Jane.

Breakfast is finished just as the Inuit elders enter. The ice shelter is quickly filled with chatter and laughter. Tanaya and

Jane are helped as they don their newly acquired Inuit clothing.

Outside, near the women's ice shelter, Novinuk is trying to find Inar. The village leaders have called for another council, and would like Inar to be present. Manirak walks up, he too has been looking for Inar. Manirak is low level leader, and one day he will take his place in the council. Although younger than the other leaders he is often asked his opinion on matters.

"I Just came from his son's shelter, he and his family are not there, and no one knows where they are," says Manirak.

"I don't know what to do, the council will convene in a short while. They have made a decision to welcome Inar as a village member. It's important that he be there," insists Novinuk.

Jane and Tanaya emerge from their ice shelter, followed by the village elders. They are both dressed elegantly and playfully model their new clothing. Novinuk walks up to Tanaya and smiles with approval.

"I see you have adapted to Inuit life well," he says. The elder women agree proudly, knowing their talents for adornment are great improvement over the Edwardian style dresses they were wearing when they arrived.

"Have you talked with Inar this morning?" Novinuk asks. Both women shake their head and shrug their shoulders.

"We haven't seen Uncle since last night at the celebration," says Tanaya.

"If you see him before I do, let him know to meet me at the long shelter for a council," advises Novinuk.

"Inar left the village early this morning, he had all of his family in Nanuv's sled," says one of the elderly women.

"Did he say where they were headed?" Manirak asks.

"Nanuv only said that they will be back by mid day. It was then Inar gave me a big hug, a kiss on the forehead, and said: "Good-bye grandma, remember me always," she says.

"What's going on?" Tanaya asks.

"I'm afraid we all misunderstood Inar's real reason for coming home," says Novinuk.

"Uncle came home to see his people, to see you, everyone," pleads Tanaya.

"When he spoke to the council leaders on the day of his return he told us not to worry, that he would not be here long. We thought he may be returning with you, but now that I think back on it he may have meant another thing," explains Novinuk.

"What's happening, I can tell somethings wrong," says Jane.

"Inar came back to complete what was not finished," says Novinuk. "Oh no, that can't be! Tanaya cries.

"Tanaya, tell me what is going on," insists Jane. Just then Tanaya sees Taroq and his dog team, and she runs to catch him before he is able to get out of the village.

"Have you seen Nanuv's sled?" she cries frantically. "Nanuv was driving his reindeer toward the West side of the bay when I came out this morning," says Taroq.

"Can you take me there?" Tanaya asks. He nods yes. Jane comes running up to Tanaya.

"Tanaya, for the last time, tell me what's going on," she cries. Tanaya turns to Jane, her eyes welled with tears.

"Uncle came back to..." says Tanaya, unable to finish. Jane grabs her arms and forces her to look at her.

"Uncle came back to continue his journey to the Sky World. He is going to place himself on another ice floe," cries Tanaya.

"Oh my! What can we do?" Jane asks.

Tanaya climbs into the sled and turns to Novinuk. "Please, find another sled and bring Jane. Meet us out at the West side of the bay," she says in native language.

"The sled cannot hold us, Novinuk will find a way to take you there," she pleads.

With a command shout the sled dogs are off and running. Tanaya looks back to see Jane weeping as she rides off. Novinuk hurries to harness his sled dogs. Tanaya covers her eyes from the freezing air as they move along the sled path. The sound of the sled sliding across the frozen snow drowns out Tanaya's cries. She quietly pleads to Inar not to go through with what he has planned.

As they reach the top of the rise Tanaya looks back to see five other sled teams racing to catch up.

The sled picks up momentum as the dogs race down the sloped path. At that point on the slope Tanaya sees Nanuv's cargo sled. Through her frozen tears she can make out a small group of people standing by the edge of the bay near the ice floe. She pleads to the driver to go faster as he shouts to urge the dogs on.

What was first seen as small black dots against the icy white bay now become larger. Tanaya can see they are all huddled together, but cannot tell if Inar is among them. She turns to see the other sled team racing down the slope. Taroq's sled team pulls up to Nanuv's cargo sled and comes to a halt. Tanaya leaps from the sled and runs to Nanuv and Inar's family. They turn to her, but their eyes tell her that Inar is not there. She pushes her way through the group only to see the ice floe carrying Inar away.

From the ice floe Inar sees Tanaya, she is screaming his name. Above the crashing ice he can still hear her anguished cry. Inar begins to wave her off. Nanuv and his family go to Tanaya and try to comfort her, but she breaks away from them. She runs stumbling along side the ice floe toward Inar.

Inar drops to his knees and puts his head down onto the ice. As he looks up, he can see his entire family running, trying to catch Tanaya.

In frustration she stops and collapses onto the ice. Inar watches as the other sled teams pull up. He can see his friends standing in silence, watching him float farther away. Slowly they raise their arms, waving a final good-bye.

In the years that followed, Tanaya came to terms with her thoughts on what happened that day on Baffin Island. It was with the help of Jane she came to understand that, in his own way, Inar died on the Titanic that terrible morning. In a strange turn of events he came back, or was sent back, to help others in their grief, a grief that became his as well. One thing was very clear, he did come back to say good-bye. Inar was never heard from again.

Jane became partners with Tanaya, and they shared a successful law practice. Tanaya married Ronald Black Eye and lived in New York, but she never forgot Inar. The weather station received wireless messages to be delivered to her friends at Inar's village. She never went back to that village, and will forever carry Inar's experience of the Titanic in those early morning hours of April 15, 1912.

Somewhere in a the quietness of an arctic village, a story is being told. In the eyes of children, wonderment can be seen as they conjure up visions of a legend. The story teller becomes animated as he tells those in the circle, of the killer whale and the aged Inuit grandfather. "Arrluk came to visit Inar Katerpar on the very last day in this world. Again, coming face to face, the old man welcomed the great animal. Arrluk's return meant only one thing to him, and he was honored.

"Inar held his hand out to Arrluk, and he took it, pulling him off of the ice slab. Down into the sea, Arrluk took him deeper, and deeper. Inar could see the darkness of at the bottom as the sunlight faded, the freezing water numbed him to the bone.

Then all of a sudden, Arrluk let go, letting Inar float further into the deep. Things became calm, and he became warm and happy.

"Floating downward, he came upon the mighty ship Titanic, resting silently at the bottom of the sea. It was his last look at the majestic vessel before he was received.

Made in the USA
Charleston, SC
25 October 2012